Into the Heart of the Reich

kirsten Dickson

Published by kirsten Dickson, 2024.

Table of Contents

Introduction

Into the Heart of the Reich is a tribute to the bravery, resilience, and unwavering camaraderie of the soldiers who fought during one of the most pivotal conflicts in history: World War II. This story follows a platoon of American soldiers as they journey from the D-Day beaches of Normandy to the heart of Berlin, capturing not only the brutal realities of war but also the enduring bonds of brotherhood forged in the face of adversity.

Through relentless battles, devastating losses, and moments of quiet reflection, these men endure hardship, find hope, and face the ultimate test of courage. While they fight for freedom and survival, they also fight for each other—uniting under a shared purpose and a loyalty that would last a lifetime. This book is not just a war story; it's a journey into the human spirit, an exploration of friendship, sacrifice, and the resilience that defines true heroism.

The characters and events, while fictionalized, are deeply inspired by the countless veterans whose stories serve as a testament to the strength and sacrifice of an entire generation. Each chapter honors their memory, aiming to bring readers as close as possible to the experience of those who answered the call and changed the course of history.

May this story remind us of the price paid for freedom, of the courage found in unity, and of the legacy left by those who walked *into the heart of the Reich* and came home changed forever.

Chapter 1: The Invasion Begins - D-Day

———

The air in the dimly lit bunker felt thick, weighed down by a silence that was neither calm nor reassuring. Each man stood at attention, lined up in neat, rigid rows as Captain Harris paced before them, his face set like stone. The flickering yellow lights cast long shadows across the walls, and somewhere outside, the wind whistled through the open slit of the barracks, as though the very night itself were whispering secrets of what lay ahead.

Private Tom Harlan stood toward the back, his rifle slung over his shoulder. He glanced around, taking in the familiar faces of his platoon. They were men he'd come to know better than his own family in the months since they'd shipped off together. There was Charlie, always quick with a joke, his eyes now fixed on the ground, mouth drawn tight. To his left was "Red" — Private Tanner — known for the fiery shock of hair poking out from beneath his helmet. Tonight, even Red looked subdued, the familiar glint in his eyes replaced by something darker, something Tom recognized as the same anxiety gnawing away at his own insides.

Captain Harris's voice broke the silence, snapping them all to attention. "Men," he began, his voice steady, echoing off the bunker walls, "tomorrow we begin an operation that will be written into the pages of history. We're making landfall on Omaha Beach, and our objective is simple but deadly: secure the beachhead and push inland. This will be the largest amphibious assault the world has ever seen."

A murmur passed through the platoon, barely audible, but enough to heighten the pulse in Tom's temples. He swallowed hard, his mouth dry. This was no ordinary mission; they all knew that. Omaha Beach wasn't just a location on a map—it was a death trap, fortified with German pillboxes, bunkers, and machine-gun nests, all waiting for them to arrive.

Captain Harris continued, "You'll be moving in at first light. The Germans know we're coming, and they've dug in. Expect heavy resistance. Artillery, mines, machine guns—they'll throw everything they have at you. But remember this: you're not alone. Thousands of us will be hitting those beaches together. The British, the Canadians, the Free French—all of us, together, to take back what's been stolen."

Tom felt a wave of something like pride, though it was tangled with fear, surging up his chest. He could feel the shift in the air around him, as if the words themselves held a strange kind of gravity. Men stood a little straighter, shoulders squared, eyes forward. They were soldiers, yes, but tonight, they were more than that. They were the vanguard of something monumental.

"Remember your training," Harris went on, "stick to your team, keep your heads down, and move fast. We don't have the luxury of time out there. The longer we're on that sand, the worse it's going to get. This mission will test every ounce of courage you have. But if we succeed, we pave the way for freedom. Not just for ourselves, but for the whole damn continent."

Tom clenched his fists, his knuckles white. He could hear his heart pounding in his ears, loud as a drum, as he thought about the weight of those words—freedom. It was easy to talk about, easy to throw around in speeches back home, but here, in this dim, cold bunker, with the faces of his brothers around him, it felt different. It felt like a vow, something carved into his bones.

Captain Harris looked out over the platoon, his eyes softened, his voice dropping to a lower, almost solemn tone. "I won't lie to you, boys. Some of us won't be coming back from this. But know this: we're fighting for each other, for the man next to you, and for everyone waiting for us back home. Remember that when you're out there."

The silence that followed was deafening. No one dared speak, as if voicing the fear would somehow make it more real. They all felt it—the same gnawing dread, the uncertainty, the unspoken question hanging heavy in the room: *Will I make it through this?*

A voice finally broke the silence. It was Charlie, usually the joker, but tonight his voice was steady, almost reverent. "We'll get through it, Cap. We've made it this far."

Captain Harris nodded, a slight, almost imperceptible smile tugging at the corner of his mouth. "Damn right we will."

As the briefing ended, the men dispersed, each heading back to their quarters for the last night's sleep before the dawn of something unimaginable. Tom found his bunk, lay down, and stared at the ceiling, though he knew sleep wouldn't come easy. Around him, the others lay down too, some silent, some whispering prayers, others, like Red, clutching letters from home, reading over them one last time as if the ink itself could bring them luck.

Tom closed his eyes, trying to block out the swirling thoughts, the images of what awaited them, but it was no use. He kept seeing flashes—sand, gunfire, blood. And then, his mind settled on a memory, a voice from back home, his mother telling him, *Stay safe, Tommy.* He clenched his jaw, willing himself to stay strong, to be the soldier he'd trained to be.

Outside, the sky began to lighten, a faint gray creeping into the edges of the horizon. The invasion was about to begin.

The dawn light was barely breaking over the horizon, casting a pale, eerie glow over the endless sea of gray-green waves as Tom and the rest of the platoon made their way toward the landing craft. The air was thick with the smell of salt and diesel, and every man's face was pale and set, jaws clenched as they moved with the stiff, automatic movements of soldiers driven by sheer instinct and training.

Tom's hands were shaking as he clutched his rifle, his knuckles white. Around him, the voices of officers and crew were sharp and quick, barking orders, directing men to their assigned boats. The shouts melded with the sound of engines roaring to life, the metallic clatter of gear, the nervous breathing of men braced for what they knew was coming but couldn't fully imagine.

Charlie was just ahead, glancing back at Tom with a wry smile that was half-hearted at best. "Looks like we're really doing this, huh?" he muttered, though the words were almost lost in the noise.

"Yeah," Tom replied, swallowing hard. His mouth was dry, and his stomach felt like it was made of lead. He forced himself to give a weak smile, but it didn't feel like his own.

One by one, they climbed into the cramped landing craft, pressing close together, shoulder to shoulder. Tom took his place in the middle, surrounded by familiar faces, though no one looked at each other directly. The men kept their eyes down or straight ahead, each lost in their own thoughts, each wondering if these might be the last moments they shared.

The boat's engine sputtered to life, and the vessel jerked forward, rocking on the waves as they pushed away from the safety of the larger ships. As they picked up speed, the noise grew louder, the engines drowning out everything else. The spray from the sea hit them in cold, stinging bursts, adding to the discomfort, but Tom barely noticed. His eyes were fixed ahead, trying to see through the fog and haze that hung over the water.

As the shore began to materialize on the horizon, so did the first signs of hell.

Explosions tore through the air, deep rumbles shaking the sea as German artillery found its mark. The boats ahead of them were engulfed in fire, fragments of metal and bodies flung high into the air before vanishing into the dark, churning water. Each blast sent shockwaves through Tom's chest, rattling his bones, filling his mouth with the bitter taste of fear.

"Stay low!" Captain Harris shouted over the din, his voice barely audible above the engine and the shellfire. Tom crouched lower, gripping his rifle like it was a lifeline. Around him, the others did the same, some mouthing silent prayers, others just staring ahead with wide, hollow eyes.

A shell exploded in the water to their left, sending a towering wave over the landing craft, drenching them in cold seawater. Tom coughed and wiped the salt from his eyes, his heart hammering as the boat rocked and then steadied.

He glanced over at Red, who was muttering something under his breath, eyes wide and unblinking.

"Just get us there," Tom heard himself whisper, though he wasn't sure if he was talking to the captain, the boat's engine, or some higher power he barely believed in.

They were close enough now that he could make out the faint outline of the beach ahead, a narrow strip of sand littered with metal obstacles, stakes, and coils of barbed wire. Machine guns opened up, the staccato rattle of gunfire merging with the deeper booms of the artillery. Bullets tore through the air, pinging off the metal sides of the landing craft, sending men ducking lower, hands covering helmets as they tried to make themselves as small as possible.

"Hold steady!" Captain Harris's voice again, a command that felt like it was meant to defy the very laws of fear.

Tom's breathing was shallow and quick, his chest tight, but he forced himself to look up, to keep his eyes on the shore. The beach was almost within reach now, a few hundred yards that felt like an eternity. But with every inch they closed, the gunfire intensified, the water around them churning with bullets and debris.

Then, in a terrifying, surreal moment, the boat ahead of them took a direct hit. The explosion tore it in half, sending pieces of metal and flesh flying in all directions. Tom's eyes widened, his mind struggling to process the horrific sight. The screams of men echoed across the water, cut short almost as soon as they started.

He felt a hand grip his shoulder—Charlie's—and he turned, seeing the same fear mirrored in his friend's eyes. "We're gonna make it, Tom," Charlie said, though his voice trembled.

Tom nodded, but the words felt hollow, almost absurd in the face of the chaos around them. The boat lurched forward again, closing the distance to the shore, and he felt his muscles tense, his body bracing for what would come next. Every second felt like a lifetime, every roar of gunfire like a countdown to something unimaginable.

"Thirty seconds!" the coxswain shouted from the front, his voice hoarse and strained.

Tom's heartbeat pounded in his ears, a rapid, relentless drumbeat that drowned out everything else. He checked his rifle one last time, feeling the weight of it in his hands, trying to ground himself in its cold, solid form. He forced himself to breathe, to focus on the shore, on the mission, on anything but the fear clawing at his insides.

"Ten seconds!"

They were almost there. He felt the boat slow as it prepared to drop the ramp, his legs tense and ready to move, his mind a blur of orders, training, and instinct.

Then the ramp dropped.

For a brief, blinding moment, Tom froze, staring out at the beach, the walls of bullets, the flashes of gunfire. He saw men fall around him, their bodies hitting the water, some struggling to stand, others lying still. Shouts, screams, and the roar of gunfire filled the air, a cacophony of noise that drowned out everything else.

And then he was moving, his feet hitting the water, his body carrying him forward through sheer will. He didn't think, didn't feel—just ran, head down, keeping low as bullets whizzed by, as the chaos of Omaha Beach unfolded around him.

The water was freezing, biting through Tom's uniform as he waded forward, waves slapping against his chest, his boots sinking into the sand beneath. He gritted his teeth, the metallic tang of saltwater mixing with the taste of fear in his mouth. Around him, the world had dissolved into a relentless, deafening chaos, every sense overwhelmed by the hell unfolding on Omaha Beach.

Machine-gun fire tore through the air, bullets slicing past him, snapping the water into sprays of mist and blood. Men all around him stumbled and fell, their bodies splashing into the surf, some fighting to stand again, others going still. Tom forced himself to keep moving, his legs pumping against the weight of the water and the sand, his eyes fixed on the narrow strip of beach that stretched ahead, littered with obstacles and craters from the artillery.

He could see Captain Harris up ahead, waving his arm, shouting something, though the words were lost in the roar of explosions and the screams of men. Tom staggered forward, his breath coming in gasps, his heart pounding as he glanced over his shoulder. Charlie was behind him, his face streaked with mud and fear, his wide eyes locked on the shore. Red was there too, a few feet away, his helmet crooked, his mouth moving in what looked like a silent prayer.

Another explosion erupted to Tom's left, a massive shell that sent a wave of sand, water, and body parts raining down around him. He ducked, instinct taking over, feeling the shockwave rattle through his bones. When he looked up, he saw a crater where seconds before a group of men had been charging forward. His stomach twisted, but there was no time to think, no time to grieve. He pushed on, forcing himself up the beach, his boots slipping in the wet sand.

"Go! Go! Keep moving!" Captain Harris's voice finally reached him, rough and strained, cutting through the chaos. Tom nodded, though the captain's eyes were fixed forward, his focus unbreakable. The man was like a force of nature, moving up the beach as though he were invincible, and Tom found himself clinging to that image, drawing strength from it.

The platoon pressed forward, inch by brutal inch, bodies hitting the ground around them, some men dropping to their knees only to be pulled up by a brother, some lying still and silent. Every step felt like a gamble, each movement a defiance of the bullets and shrapnel that tore through the air like deadly hail. Tom's ears rang from the constant barrage, his body numb as he trudged on, fighting to stay low, to stay moving.

He saw Charlie go down beside him, his body crumpling forward with a strangled cry. Tom felt a jolt of horror seize him, instinct driving him to his friend's side. He dropped to his knees, reaching for Charlie, his hands slick with blood as he grabbed hold of his shoulder, pulling him up.

"Come on, Charlie," he grunted, his voice barely a whisper against the roar. "We're getting out of this."

Charlie's face was pale, his eyes glazed with shock, but he gave a weak nod, his fingers gripping Tom's arm with surprising strength. Together, they stumbled forward, Tom half-dragging, half-carrying his friend as they made for the nearest cover—a rusted metal barrier jutting from the sand. They collapsed behind it, gasping for breath, and Tom took a moment to check Charlie's wounds.

The bullet had hit his side, just beneath the ribs, blood seeping through his uniform, staining the sand beneath them. Charlie gritted his teeth, his face twisted with pain, but he waved Tom off, his voice rough and determined. "I'm... I'm fine. Just get me off this damn beach."

Tom nodded, gripping his rifle as he peered over the edge of the barrier. The beach ahead was still a storm of gunfire and explosions, German pillboxes raining down fire from the cliffs above. He could see other landing craft struggling to unload, men spilling out only to be cut down before they'd even hit the sand. His heart sank as he realized how far they still had to go.

Red reached their cover, dropping down beside them with a harsh gasp, his face pale as he looked at Charlie's wound. "Jesus, Charlie," he muttered, his voice shaking. "We gotta get you off this beach."

"Then help me up," Charlie growled, though his voice wavered with pain. "We're not dying here."

Red nodded, his jaw set, and together they helped Charlie to his feet, bracing him between them. They moved forward, pushing toward the seawall, a low ridge that offered the faintest bit of shelter from the withering fire. They could see other soldiers gathering there, crouched low, huddled together, faces marked with blood and fear as they awaited orders.

They were almost there, just a few more yards, when another round of machine-gun fire tore through the air. Red staggered, his eyes widening as he looked down, clutching at his chest where blood was already blooming beneath his fingers. Tom felt a shout rip from his throat, grabbing Red by the arm, but Red shook his head, a sad, resigned look in his eyes.

"Go," he gasped, his voice barely a whisper. "Get... Charlie... out of here."

Tom's heart twisted, every instinct screaming to stay, but he felt Charlie tugging at him, urging him forward. With one last look at Red, Tom turned, half-carrying, half-dragging Charlie the last few feet to the seawall. They collapsed behind it, both of them gasping for breath, their bodies heavy with exhaustion and grief.

Captain Harris was there, pulling men into a rough line, his face grim as he assessed the damage. He glanced at Tom and Charlie, his gaze lingering on the blood that soaked through Charlie's uniform, then nodded, his voice steely.

"We're moving up," he shouted, rallying the survivors. "Stay close, stick to the cover where you can, and keep pushing! We're taking this beach if it's the last thing we do!"

Tom swallowed hard, his body aching, his mind reeling, but he nodded, gripping his rifle with renewed determination. Around him, the men rallied, wounded and weary but unbroken, their faces hard with resolve. This was the moment they'd trained for, the mission they'd come for, and despite the horror, despite the blood and death that surrounded them, they would not give up.

With a deep breath, Tom rose from the seawall, leading the charge with the others as they surged up the beach, each step a battle, each breath a victory. The gunfire and explosions became a backdrop, a distant roar against the singular focus that drove them forward. They were soldiers, brothers, and together they would storm Omaha Beach—no matter the cost.

The roar of battle began to fade as Tom crouched behind a shattered chunk of concrete, his breaths coming in gasps, each one tasting of smoke, salt, and blood. The survivors had pushed forward, inch by bloody inch, up the narrow strip of beach. Now they huddled in small groups behind whatever cover they could find, battered but alive, their bodies pressed against the cold, hard earth as the last vestiges of German fire rained down from the cliffs.

Tom could barely believe they had made it this far. His muscles ached, his skin was raw from the grit and the salt, and his uniform was stained with blood—some of it his own, some of it from comrades who hadn't made it. He glanced around, taking in the scene with a numb sort of shock. Bodies lay scattered across the sand, motionless in the morning light, their once-familiar faces now frozen in grim, silent expressions. Craters pocked the beach, filled with twisted metal, remnants of gear, and splintered obstacles that once stood as barriers against their advance.

Captain Harris was nearby, his face smeared with grime, his helmet slightly askew. He was barking orders, his voice hoarse but unwavering as he directed the men to regroup, to get the wounded to safer ground. The captain's steady presence was a beacon, something that kept them grounded in this hellish chaos.

Tom caught his breath, then crawled over to Charlie, who was leaning against a pile of sandbags, his face pale and streaked with sweat. The bullet wound in his side was hastily bandaged, blood still seeping through the fabric. Tom knelt beside him, checking the bandage and tightening it as best he could. Charlie winced but managed a grim smile.

"Guess we made it," he murmured, his voice a raspy whisper. "Thought I'd be fish food back there."

Tom forced a grin, though it felt hollow. "You're not getting off that easy," he said, trying to keep his tone light. "You still owe me a round back in London."

Charlie chuckled weakly, his eyes darting over the beach, the reality of their surroundings settling in. He looked up at Tom, a flicker of worry crossing his face. "Think we're gonna make it out of here?"

Tom didn't answer right away. He turned, taking in the beach, the men around him, the faint figures of medics tending to the wounded, their hands moving quickly as they bound wounds, gave water, whispered words of encouragement. He felt the weight of the task before them pressing down like a stone in his chest. They'd taken the beach, but the battle was far from over.

"Yeah," he finally said, his voice steady. "We're gonna make it. We just have to keep pushing."

A shout came from further down the line, and Tom turned to see a group of soldiers struggling to lift a wounded man out of the sand. He didn't recognize the soldier, but he recognized the look in his eyes—the same mix of fear and pain that he'd seen too many times today. Without a second thought, Tom scrambled over, grabbing the man's arm and helping to pull him toward a makeshift shelter that had been set up against the seawall. Together, they lowered him down, and Tom knelt, wiping sweat and blood from his own brow before looking around for a medic.

The medic arrived within seconds, his face drawn but focused, his hands moving with practiced efficiency as he tended to the wounded soldier. Tom watched, feeling an odd sense of helplessness. He wanted to do more, to somehow fix the nightmare they were trapped in, but there was only so much any one of them could do.

Captain Harris made his way over, crouching down beside Tom. His voice was low, but it held that familiar strength, that sense of command that had carried them this far.

"Listen up," he said, addressing the men who had gathered, huddled behind what little cover the beach offered. "We've got a foothold here, but the real fight's just beginning. Our objective now is to push up those cliffs, clear out the enemy positions, and secure this beachhead for the rest of our boys coming in. We've got to hold this ground, no matter what."

Tom felt a ripple of tension pass through the group. The cliffs ahead loomed like a wall, dotted with German bunkers and fortified positions that overlooked the entire beach. The enemy had the high ground, and they weren't going to give it up easily. It was a daunting task, and as Tom looked into the faces of his comrades, he saw the same grim determination mixed with exhaustion in each one of them.

A burst of gunfire rattled from above, and the men instinctively ducked, pressing closer to the ground. The German positions still had clear sightlines on parts of the beach, and the danger was far from over. But the fire seemed sporadic now, less coordinated, as if the enemy was finally feeling the strain of the relentless Allied assault.

"We'll go in waves," Captain Harris continued. "Half of you will hold here and cover the wounded. The rest of us will push forward, one position at a time. We take this beach, and we keep it. Understood?"

A murmur of agreement rippled through the men, each one steeling himself for the next step in this impossible battle. Tom looked over at Charlie, who gave him a nod, his hand clenching into a fist despite the pain.

"We got this, Tommy," Charlie said, his voice low but filled with that spark of stubborn resolve that had seen them through so much already. "We're not going down here."

Tom nodded, feeling a surge of courage, a flicker of hope in the face of the overwhelming odds. They'd lost friends, they'd seen horrors, but they were still here, still breathing, still fighting. Together, they could do this.

With a final look at the men around him, Tom adjusted his rifle, gripping it tight, his knuckles white against the wood and metal. Captain Harris gave the signal, and they rose, one by one, moving up the beach in a coordinated line, their bodies tense and ready. The weight of the task before them loomed large, but they faced it together, a unified force in the face of the impossible.

They had taken the beach, but now, as they pushed forward, they knew that this was just the beginning. The cliffs awaited, and beyond them, the fight to liberate Europe from tyranny. And as Tom moved forward, his boots sinking into the sand, his mind fixed on the faces of those he'd lost, he knew that they would honor them by seeing this through to the end.

This was their task, their duty, and they would see it through—together.

The sky had shifted from a dull gray to a pale blue, the early morning light casting a strange stillness over Omaha Beach. The sounds of battle had moved further inland, but the scars of the assault lingered heavily across the sand, marking the beach with the remnants of what had been a brutal, merciless fight. Tom and the other survivors were huddled together, some leaning against craters blown into the earth, others crouched low, weapons still in hand, their faces drawn and haunted.

They had a moment to breathe now, a rare respite in the eye of the storm. Tom's muscles were heavy with exhaustion, his body aching, yet he couldn't bring himself to fully relax. His mind was still racing, each heartbeat a reminder of how close he had come to not being here at all.

He looked around, his gaze drifting over the faces of the men beside him—faces etched with fatigue and grief, faces that looked far older than they had just hours before. In the chaos of the landing, time had felt like a blur, each second stretched thin by adrenaline and survival. But now, with the silence settling around them, it was impossible to ignore the toll the assault had taken.

Charlie sat beside him, his back pressed against a jagged piece of shrapnel embedded in the sand, his breathing shallow but steady. His wound was still bleeding, though he had managed to grin and wave off the medics, insisting he'd seen worse. Tom knew better; he could see the pain in his friend's eyes, though Charlie masked it with the same forced humor that had gotten them through so many nights before.

"Hell of a beach party, huh, Tommy?" Charlie murmured, his voice a faint echo of his usual sarcasm. His hands shook slightly as he spoke, his gaze distant, fixed on something only he could see.

Tom forced a smile, though it felt hollow. "Not exactly the summer vacation I was hoping for," he replied, his voice thick with the weight of what they'd endured.

The two fell silent, each lost in his own thoughts, each replaying the images that would haunt them for years to come. Tom's mind drifted to Red, remembering the look on his face just before he'd fallen, that strange, resigned smile as if he had somehow known he wouldn't make it. Red had been with them from the beginning, his jokes and wild stories lighting up their darkest days, his presence as much a part of their group as the rifles they carried. And now he was gone, another name to add to the long list of men they'd lost.

Captain Harris walked over, his steps slow and deliberate, his face drawn but composed. He gave each of them a nod, a silent acknowledgment of their shared grief, the unspoken bond they all carried now. He crouched beside them, his gaze drifting over the beach, his voice low and steady.

"We did good today, boys," he said, his tone softened in a way that felt almost like reverence. "We took this beach. We gave our brothers a foothold to get in. They won't have died for nothing."

Tom nodded, feeling a lump in his throat as he glanced back down the beach, the sand marked with the shadows of those who had fallen. He thought of the men he'd trained with, the friendships forged in the fires of battle, each one a brother in arms. Some of them lay still now, faces turned to the sky, forever frozen in that final, terrible moment.

A sudden breeze blew across the beach, stirring the sand, brushing against his face. It felt like a whisper, a gentle reminder of all they'd fought for, of all they'd sacrificed. In that moment, Tom felt a strange, profound sense of peace settle over him, as if the souls of the fallen had passed through, leaving behind a part of themselves, a reminder that their fight had meaning.

He thought of Red, of the countless others who hadn't made it, and he made a silent promise, one he'd carry with him through every battle yet to come: *I'll remember you. I'll carry your memory forward.*

Charlie, catching the faraway look in Tom's eyes, gave his shoulder a gentle shove. "Don't go getting all sentimental on me, Tommy. We're not done yet."

Tom chuckled, though it came out more like a choked laugh. "Yeah, I know. We've got plenty of hell to go through still."

Captain Harris cleared his throat, pulling them back to the present. "Rest while you can, boys. We've got orders to push forward soon, and we'll need every ounce of strength we've got left. But you did good today. Every one of you."

They sat in silence a little longer, each of them taking the moment to breathe, to let the weight of the day sink in. Around them, the survivors tended to the wounded, shared flasks of water, muttered prayers, and quiet words of comfort. They were battered, bruised, and bloodied, but they had done what they'd come to do.

As they sat there, Tom's thoughts drifted to home, to the faces of those who waited for him. He could almost hear his mother's voice, could see his father's proud, stoic expression, could feel the warmth of the life he'd left behind. He wondered how he would tell them about this day, how he would find the words to explain the horror, the loss, and the strange, terrible beauty of what they'd achieved.

But that was for later. For now, all he could do was carry on, keep pushing forward, honor the fallen by seeing this fight through to the end. He took a deep breath, letting the salty air fill his lungs, and glanced over at Charlie, who gave him a nod, the same determined look that had gotten them through so much.

"Ready when you are, Tommy," Charlie said, his voice quiet but strong.

Tom nodded, feeling a surge of strength in his chest. "Then let's do this," he replied, gripping his rifle, preparing himself for whatever lay ahead.

As the orders came down the line, and the men began to rise, gathering their gear, steeling themselves for the next push, Tom cast one last glance back at the beach, at the place where so many had fallen. He felt the weight of their sacrifice in every step, in every heartbeat, and he knew that he would carry that weight with him forever.

They were soldiers, brothers bound by the blood they'd spilled together, and no matter what awaited them on the road ahead, they would face it side by side, carrying the memory of those they'd lost in every step forward.

Omaha Beach was behind them now, but its shadow would stay with them. And as they began to move inland, Tom knew that, come what may, they would honor the fallen by fighting with everything they had left.

In the stillness that followed, he felt a strange, quiet resolve settle over him. This was just the beginning—but they would see it through, together.

Chapter 2: The Push Inland - Securing Normandy

The morning mist clung to the fields like a shroud as Tom and the rest of the platoon moved cautiously through the narrow, uneven paths that wound between hedgerows and low stone walls. The air was thick with the scent of damp earth and smoke, and the muffled sounds of distant gunfire drifted over the horizon. Omaha Beach was behind them now, but the memory of the assault still weighed heavily on their minds, each man carrying the haunting echoes of that brutal morning.

Their orders were clear: push inland, scout the surrounding area, and report any signs of German resistance. It was a task that sounded simple on paper but held an unspoken weight. Recon meant venturing into unknown territory, away from the relative safety of the main line, and facing whatever the enemy might have waiting for them in the dense, maze-like landscape of the French countryside.

Captain Harris led the way, his eyes sharp and focused as he scanned the terrain. He raised his fist, signaling a halt, and the men came to a crouch, spreading out silently along the cover of a hedgerow. Tom dropped low, his rifle at the ready, feeling his heart quicken as he peered through the foliage. In the distance, the faint outline of a farmhouse appeared, its windows dark and empty. A narrow dirt road wound past it, flanked by overgrown fields that swayed in the breeze.

"Looks abandoned," Charlie whispered, crouched beside Tom, his voice barely more than a breath. "Could be they cleared out, or... well, you know."

Tom nodded. Normandy had been under German occupation for years. Many locals had fled, some had been conscripted into forced labor, and others had stayed, their lives overshadowed by the constant threat of violence. Every empty building, every silent road, felt heavy with the weight of stories they would never know.

Captain Harris gestured to a small group of men, including Tom and Charlie. "You five, with me," he said quietly. "We're going to check out that farmhouse. The rest of you, hold position and keep watch. If you see any movement, you know what to do."

They moved out, slipping through the hedgerows and across the narrow field, their steps silent and measured. Tom kept his rifle raised, his finger hovering just above the trigger as his gaze darted from shadow to shadow, every flicker of movement setting his nerves on edge. They reached the farmhouse, pressing up against the stone walls, the cold, rough surface grounding him as he steeled himself.

Captain Harris nodded to Tom, who slowly edged around the corner, peering into one of the shattered windows. The interior was dark, furniture upturned, a thin layer of dust settled over everything. There was no sign of recent activity, no trace of anyone still living there. He let out a slow breath, signaling to the others that it was clear.

They moved inside, spreading out to check each room. The air was stale, the silence thick, broken only by the soft creak of floorboards beneath their boots. Tom felt a strange sense of intrusion, as if they were trespassing in a place that had once been a home, a place filled with life and laughter before the war had left it hollow.

They gathered in the main room, exchanging glances, each man's face marked with the same grim understanding. There was nothing here—just another shell of a place touched by the brutal hand of war.

Captain Harris motioned them back outside, and they regrouped with the rest of the platoon, continuing their cautious advance. They moved from field to field, skirting the edges of overgrown orchards and empty farmsteads, each man alert, listening for the slightest sound. The tension was palpable, stretching between them like a taut wire, every nerve straining under the weight of the unknown.

Then, a sudden crack of gunfire shattered the silence. The first shot rang out from the tree line ahead, followed by a rapid burst of bullets that tore through the hedgerow, sending men diving for cover. Tom hit the ground, pressing himself into the dirt as he scanned for the source of the fire.

"Enemy ahead! Take cover!" Captain Harris shouted, his voice cutting through the chaos.

Tom lifted his head just enough to see a flash of movement among the trees—a squad of German soldiers, dug in behind low stone walls and firing from the shadows. The air was thick with the sharp crack of rifles and the heavier, deeper roar of machine-gun fire. Bullets tore through the hedgerows, ripping leaves and branches apart, filling the air with splinters and debris.

Charlie was beside him, his face tense but focused as he fired into the tree line, each shot measured, precise. Tom followed suit, raising his rifle, steadying his aim, and squeezing the trigger. The recoil jolted through his shoulder, grounding him, sharpening his focus as he watched the enemy lines, waiting for the slightest sign of movement.

The firefight stretched on, each side entrenched, neither willing to give ground. The German soldiers had the advantage of cover, their position fortified, but the Americans had numbers and determination. Bit by bit, they edged forward, moving between patches of cover, their bodies low to the ground, rifles trained on the enemy.

Tom spotted a German soldier breaking from cover, darting between trees. He took aim, his breath steady, and fired. The soldier went down, his body crumpling in the grass. Tom felt a pang of something—a mixture of relief and sorrow—but he pushed it aside, forcing himself to focus. This was survival; this was war.

"Keep pushing forward!" Captain Harris's voice rang out, steady and unyielding.

The platoon moved as one, advancing in short bursts, each step bringing them closer to the enemy line. The air was thick with the smell of gunpowder, the ground littered with spent shell casings and splintered wood. Tom's ears rang, his heart pounding as he ducked behind another hedgerow, his eyes scanning the field, his rifle ready.

The Germans were beginning to fall back, their line breaking as the American advance pressed on. Tom watched as they retreated, their dark figures vanishing into the shadows of the trees, the crack of their rifles fading into the distance. Finally, the gunfire ceased, leaving only the ragged breathing of the men and the distant rumble of artillery somewhere far off.

They held their position, waiting, listening for any sign of another attack. But the silence held, heavy and tense, as if the land itself were holding its breath.

Captain Harris raised his hand, signaling the platoon to regroup. They gathered in the cover of a low stone wall, catching their breath, exchanging looks of exhaustion and relief. Some of the men were shaken, their faces pale, their eyes haunted by the memory of the firefight, by the lives they'd just taken. Others simply looked weary, worn down by the constant strain, the relentless march forward.

Tom felt a mix of emotions, a strange blend of relief, guilt, and determination. He glanced over at Charlie, who gave him a tired grin, his hand shaking slightly as he lowered his rifle.

"First of many, I reckon," Charlie murmured, his voice heavy.

Tom nodded, unable to find the words. This was only the beginning. They had a long way to go, and every step would bring them deeper into enemy territory, closer to the heart of a war that felt both endless and unbearably close.

Captain Harris moved through the group, his voice quiet but firm as he gave them their next orders. They would keep moving, keep pushing inland, securing the path for the rest of the division. There was no time to dwell on what had happened, no time to mourn the men they'd lost or the lives they'd taken. They were soldiers, and their mission lay ahead, drawing them ever forward.

With a final look at the field behind them, littered with the aftermath of their first skirmish, the platoon rose, ready to continue. They moved on, their steps heavy but resolute, their eyes fixed on the path before them, each man steeling himself for the battles yet to come.

The sun was creeping higher in the sky as the platoon moved cautiously through a narrow dirt road flanked by thick hedgerows. The smell of gunpowder had faded, replaced by the earthy scent of tilled fields and wildflowers. They were further inland now, advancing deeper into the French countryside, their footsteps soft on the dusty path. The tension of the morning's firefight lingered, but there was an almost eerie calm here, broken only by the faint chirping of birds in the trees above.

Ahead, a small village came into view, its stone cottages clustered together in a quiet embrace, as if clinging to one another for comfort. The soldiers approached carefully, rifles lowered but still ready, eyes scanning the empty windows and deserted streets. It felt strange, Tom thought, to walk into a place so untouched by the war's immediate violence yet so marked by its presence. The village had a haunted stillness to it, a silence that felt like an echo of something heavy and unseen.

Captain Harris raised his hand, signaling them to pause. The men stopped, watching, waiting, their senses tuned to the slightest sound. Then, from one of the cottages, a door creaked open, and a small figure emerged—a woman, her face worn and weathered, with graying hair pulled back into a loose bun. She held her hands out in a gesture of surrender, her eyes wide with a mixture of fear and relief as she took in the sight of the American soldiers.

Behind her, more villagers began to appear, stepping cautiously out of their homes. There were old men with canes, women holding small children, teenagers peering curiously from behind stone walls. They moved slowly, uncertain, as if they were still waiting for the Germans to return, for the nightmare of occupation to resume.

Captain Harris stepped forward, raising his hand in greeting. "Bonjour," he said, his voice steady but gentle, as though speaking too loudly might shatter the fragile peace of the village.

The woman nodded, her eyes brightening slightly. "Bonjour," she replied, her voice thick with an accent, the single word carrying a world of emotion. She glanced at the other soldiers, her gaze lingering on their uniforms, their weary faces. "Vous êtes Américains?"

Harris nodded. "Yes. We're here to liberate France, to drive the Germans out."

At that, a murmur rippled through the villagers, a mix of relief, disbelief, and gratitude. Tom watched as their expressions shifted, a spark of hope kindling in faces that had long been marked by fear and suffering. One of the older men stepped forward, leaning heavily on his cane, his gaze sharp and assessing as he looked at the soldiers.

"They took everything from us," he said, his voice low and rough, though the emotion in it was unmistakable. "Food, livestock, even the young men. They took my son to work for them in Germany." His voice cracked, and he looked away, his shoulders sagging under the weight of his grief.

Tom felt a lump form in his throat, his own hardships feeling small in the face of the villagers' stories. He could see the toll of the occupation etched into their faces, the hunger and loss that had become a part of their daily lives. Children clung to their mothers, their faces gaunt and eyes wide, and he wondered how long it had been since they'd had a full meal or slept without fear.

One of the women stepped forward, a young mother with a child on her hip, her face lined with exhaustion. She looked at Tom and his comrades with a strange mixture of gratitude and sorrow. "We had no choice but to obey," she said softly. "If we resisted, they... they would punish us. Sometimes they took people, and they never came back."

She looked away, her fingers tightening around her child, who stared at the soldiers with wide, curious eyes. Tom felt a surge of anger and sorrow twist in his chest, a deep ache for the suffering these people had endured, the cruelty they'd faced with no means to fight back.

Charlie, standing beside Tom, leaned down and rummaged through his pack, pulling out a small tin of food. He stepped forward, offering it to the young mother. "Here," he said softly. "It's not much, but... it might help."

The woman's eyes filled with tears as she took the tin, nodding her thanks, her lips trembling as she tried to speak. "Merci," she whispered, clutching the food close to her chest.

Seeing her gratitude, other soldiers followed Charlie's example, digging through their supplies to offer what little they could spare—crackers, chocolate bars, anything that might bring some comfort. The villagers accepted the offerings with quiet dignity, murmuring their thanks, some pressing their hands to their hearts as they looked at the soldiers with eyes that seemed to hold the weight of a thousand unspoken words.

An older woman approached Captain Harris, her hands shaking as she held out a small loaf of bread. "For you," she said, her English halting but clear. "You have come to help us. We... we have little, but please... take this."

Captain Harris looked down at the bread, his face softening as he took it, his voice thick with emotion. "Thank you, ma'am," he replied. "It's an honor."

Tom watched, feeling a strange mix of humility and pride swell in his chest. These people had endured so much, had lost so much, and yet here they were, offering what little they had left as a gesture of thanks. It was a reminder, he realized, of what they were fighting for—not just to win a war, but to restore a sense of humanity, of dignity, to people who had been stripped of it by an enemy's cruelty.

As they continued to talk with the villagers, Tom heard stories of the German occupation—stories of families torn apart, of rationing and curfews, of nights filled with fear and days spent in quiet despair. One man spoke of hiding in the forest to avoid being sent to a labor camp, of watching helplessly as his friends were taken away. A young woman recounted how the German soldiers had taken over her family's farm, leaving them with almost nothing to survive on.

Tom listened, feeling the weight of their stories settle into his bones. He had known why they were here, why they were fighting, but hearing it from these people—seeing the suffering in their faces—made it real in a way that no briefing or command could ever convey.

Captain Harris eventually signaled that it was time to move on, and the soldiers began to gather their gear, saying quiet farewells to the villagers. As they prepared to leave, the young mother with the child approached Tom, reaching out to touch his arm.

"Merci," she said again, her eyes bright with unshed tears. "You give us hope."

Tom nodded, his voice catching as he replied, "It's the least we can do."

The platoon moved out, leaving the village behind, but the memory of the villagers' faces stayed with them, a reminder of the lives that hung in the balance, the people they were fighting to protect. As they moved back into the open fields, Tom found himself feeling more resolved, more determined than ever. The war had taken so much from these people, but it wouldn't take everything. They would fight, not just for themselves, but for those who had no other choice.

As they walked, Charlie fell into step beside him, glancing back at the village one last time. "Makes it feel real, doesn't it?" he murmured, his voice thick with emotion.

"Yeah," Tom replied quietly. "Makes you realize just what we're fighting for."

The French countryside stretched out before them, quiet and green under the morning sun, but Tom knew now that it was more than just a battlefield. It was a place of homes, of families, of lives interrupted and scarred by war. And as they continued their push inland, he felt a new strength in his step, a resolve that would carry him forward through every fight, every hardship.

This wasn't just a mission anymore; it was a promise—to the villagers, to his fallen comrades, to himself—that they would see this fight through to the end.

The countryside was deceptively quiet as the platoon pushed forward through the winding paths and thick hedgerows that crisscrossed the Normandy fields. Each soldier was alert, scanning the landscape for the slightest movement, every shadow a potential threat. They'd seen the look in the villagers' eyes, had heard the stories of German patrols hiding in the dense countryside, ready to spring at any sign of movement. The Germans knew the land well, and they were prepared to defend it fiercely.

Tom kept his head low as they moved, his rifle at the ready, the weight of the tension pressing down on him with every step. He could feel the others around him, their silence as thick as the morning fog, each man focused, their minds sharpened by the knowledge that an ambush could come at any moment. They had faced resistance already, but this was different. Out here, in the unfamiliar terrain, they were vulnerable, moving forward into territory where the enemy had every advantage.

"Stay sharp," Captain Harris murmured, his voice low and steady, carrying just enough authority to keep them grounded. He gestured ahead, motioning for the platoon to fan out slightly, moving in pairs along the narrow path.

Tom and Charlie moved together, keeping close to the hedgerow. The dense foliage offered a semblance of cover, but it also hid any dangers lurking on the other side. Each rustle of leaves, each snap of a twig, made Tom's pulse race, his grip on his rifle tightening with every cautious step.

They were approaching a bend in the path when it happened. A sudden crack echoed through the air—a single, sharp shot, followed by a rapid burst of machine-gun fire. The air erupted in a storm of bullets, tearing through the leaves, sending men diving to the ground. Tom hit the dirt, his heart pounding as he scrambled for cover behind a fallen tree, pressing himself low as the gunfire raked the path.

"Ambush!" Captain Harris shouted, his voice cutting through the chaos. "Find cover and return fire! Keep your heads down!"

Tom peered over the edge of the tree, his eyes scanning the treeline ahead. He caught sight of a flash of movement—a German soldier, ducking behind a low stone wall, reloading his weapon. Tom raised his rifle, steadying his aim, and fired. The shot rang out, and the soldier crumpled, his body slipping behind the wall.

Around him, his comrades were firing back, their faces tense and focused, each man working to hold his ground. The Germans were well-positioned, using the terrain to their advantage, each soldier hidden behind rocks and trees, their fire coordinated and relentless. Tom felt the weight of the odds pressing down on them, the realization that they were outgunned and outmaneuvered.

Charlie was beside him, his face streaked with dirt and sweat, his eyes sharp as he fired into the trees. "They're dug in good," he muttered between shots, his voice tense but steady. "This might take a while."

Tom nodded, ducking as a spray of bullets struck the ground nearby, sending up a cloud of dust and debris. They couldn't stay here; the Germans had them pinned, and every second they waited only increased the risk of more casualties.

"Flank them!" Captain Harris's voice rang out from further down the line. "Tom, Charlie, take the left! We'll keep them occupied from here!"

Without hesitation, Tom and Charlie nodded, exchanging a quick, determined glance. They moved low and fast, slipping along the edge of the path, keeping close to the hedgerow. The gunfire continued, drawing the Germans' attention, allowing them to inch closer to the enemy's position undetected.

They reached a narrow break in the foliage, where they could see the German position clearly. A machine gun was set up behind a low wall, the gunner focused on the main path, unaware of Tom and Charlie's approach. Behind him, a few other German soldiers were crouched, reloading and barking orders to one another in sharp, clipped voices.

Charlie gave Tom a nod, his expression tense but resolute. "On my mark," he whispered, gripping his rifle tightly. "We take out the gunner first."

Tom steadied his breathing, his heart pounding as he focused on the enemy ahead. The moment stretched out, each second a reminder of what was at stake, of the lives hanging in the balance. Then Charlie raised his hand, signaling the mark, and they both opened fire.

The machine-gunner went down instantly, his body slumping forward as the other German soldiers spun around, their surprise evident. Tom and Charlie kept firing, their shots precise, cutting down two more before the others had a chance to react. The remaining Germans scrambled for cover, but the surprise attack had broken their line, leaving them vulnerable.

From the main path, the rest of the platoon pressed forward, seizing the opening created by Tom and Charlie's attack. Captain Harris led the charge, his rifle blazing as they closed in on the remaining Germans, their advance relentless and coordinated. One by one, the enemy soldiers fell, their cries silenced by the fury of the American assault.

Within minutes, the gunfire ceased, leaving only the echo of battle hanging in the air. The silence that followed was thick, heavy with the scent of gunpowder and the lingering tension of close combat. Tom took a deep breath, his body sagging with relief as he lowered his rifle, feeling the adrenaline begin to ebb from his veins.

They regrouped, each man checking on his comrades, exchanging nods of reassurance, quiet words of relief. A few men had been hit, their wounds hastily bandaged, but none were fatal. It was a small victory, but a victory nonetheless.

Captain Harris walked over, his face set in a hard line, though his eyes held a glimmer of pride as he looked at them. "Good work, men," he said, his voice carrying a note of respect. "They tried to catch us off-guard, but we showed them what we're made of."

Tom nodded, his body still humming with the remnants of the fight, the memory of the ambush etched into his mind. They had faced danger head-on, had outmaneuvered an enemy that was better positioned, and they had come out on top. But he knew that this was only the beginning. The Germans weren't going to give up easily, and each step forward would be harder than the last.

Charlie gave him a nudge, a small grin tugging at the corner of his mouth. "Guess we're getting pretty good at this, huh?"

Tom managed a weak smile. "Guess so. Though I wouldn't mind if they stopped trying to kill us for a while."

Charlie chuckled, a tired, knowing laugh that held a trace of the humor that had seen them through so much already. They both knew it wouldn't get any easier, that each day would bring new challenges, new dangers. But in that moment, with the ambush behind them and the strength of their brotherhood carrying them forward, Tom felt a renewed sense of purpose, a resolve that burned brighter than the fear.

Captain Harris gathered them together, his gaze sweeping over the men, his expression solemn yet resolute. "We keep pushing forward," he said, his voice steady. "We've got a long way to go, and the enemy won't give an inch without a fight. But we're here to do a job, and by God, we're going to see it through."

The platoon moved out, their steps heavy but determined, each man carrying the memory of the ambush with him, a reminder of the strength they'd found in one another. They had overcome the first test, had faced death and come out the other side, and now, with every step deeper into Normandy, they knew they were ready for whatever lay ahead.

The narrow streets of Carentan stretched before them like a labyrinth, lined with stone buildings that bore the scars of past battles. Windows were shattered, walls pockmarked with bullet holes, and the air was thick with the scent of smoke and cordite. Tom and the rest of the platoon moved carefully, each step measured, each man on high alert. This was no open field—this was urban warfare, brutal and claustrophobic, where every corner and doorway could hide the enemy.

Captain Harris led them forward, his voice low but urgent as he issued commands. "Stay close to the walls, watch each other's backs, and move carefully. We're not alone in here."

Tom glanced around at his comrades, each of them tense and focused, their eyes darting from shadow to shadow. They had been through hell on Omaha Beach, had pushed through the countryside and fended off ambushes, but this was something different. The close quarters, the confined spaces—it felt like they were walking into the lion's den.

They turned a corner, and the first shots rang out. Bullets ricocheted off the stone walls, sending shards of rock and dust flying. Tom and Charlie dove for cover behind a low stone wall, pressing themselves flat against it as more gunfire erupted. He risked a glance over the edge, catching sight of German soldiers crouched behind makeshift barricades further down the street, their machine guns trained on the platoon.

"Pinned down already," Charlie muttered, his face tight with concentration. "They were waiting for us."

Tom nodded, gripping his rifle, his heart pounding. Urban combat left little room for maneuvering, and the enemy was well-prepared, using the twisted streets and alleys to their advantage. It was a deadly game of hide-and-seek, with each side trying to outmaneuver the other.

Captain Harris was crouched nearby, gesturing to a group of soldiers. "We need to flank them," he said, his voice calm despite the intensity of the situation. "Tom, take your squad through that alley and see if you can get behind their position. We'll keep them distracted from here."

Tom nodded, signaling to Charlie and a few others to follow him. They moved quickly but quietly, slipping into a narrow alleyway that snaked between the buildings. The walls were close on either side, casting deep shadows that made it difficult to see far ahead. Every step felt like a gamble, every corner a potential death trap.

As they reached the end of the alley, Tom paused, peeking out to assess the situation. They were now behind the German position, close enough to see the enemy soldiers crouched behind their barricades, their attention focused on Captain Harris and the others. Tom signaled to his squad, raising his rifle, and they opened fire.

The Germans reacted instantly, turning to return fire, but the surprise attack had left them exposed. One by one, the enemy soldiers fell, their makeshift defense crumbling as the Americans pressed forward. Tom's squad advanced, using the scattered rubble for cover, firing steadily as they closed the distance.

Amid the gunfire and chaos, Tom felt a strange calm settle over him, his training and instincts guiding his movements. He ducked behind a pile of debris, took aim, fired. The world narrowed to the rhythm of his breathing, the recoil of his rifle, the sight of the enemy lines breaking. Around him, his squad moved in sync, each man focused, determined, pushing forward despite the danger.

Captain Harris and the rest of the platoon joined them, their combined firepower overwhelming the remaining German soldiers. Within minutes, the street was silent again, the enemy position secured. The platoon took a moment to catch their breath, their eyes scanning the area, wary of another ambush.

But the battle was far from over. The sounds of gunfire and explosions echoed from deeper within the town, a reminder that Carentan was still contested. Captain Harris gathered them together, his expression hard and resolute.

"This isn't over," he said. "The Germans have dug in across the town, and they're not going to let go without a fight. We need to clear them out, one building at a time."

They moved deeper into Carentan, pushing through narrow alleyways, across open courtyards, and into the heart of the town. Every step was a risk, every street another battleground. The Germans fought fiercely, using sniper nests, machine-gun placements, and barricades to stall the American advance. Each house, each block, became a fortress, and the platoon had to clear them one by one.

Tom and his squad entered a small stone house, moving cautiously through the dimly lit rooms. The air was thick with dust, the silence heavy, broken only by the muffled sounds of fighting outside. They cleared each room methodically, their footsteps soft, their rifles raised. In the kitchen, they found a German soldier crouched behind an overturned table, his eyes wide with fear as he raised his hands in surrender.

Tom hesitated, his rifle trained on the man, and for a moment, their eyes met. The German soldier was young, barely older than a boy, his face streaked with dirt and desperation. Tom's finger hovered over the trigger, but he couldn't bring himself to pull it. He nodded to one of his squadmates, who moved forward to disarm the soldier, guiding him out to be taken as a prisoner.

They pushed on, moving from building to building, the brutal close-quarters combat testing their resolve, their endurance. The Germans fought with the desperation of men who had nowhere else to go, each one determined to hold his ground. The Americans responded with equal ferocity, their losses on Omaha Beach and the long, grueling march inland fueling their determination.

In one particularly fierce engagement, Tom found himself pinned in a stairwell, gunfire raining down from a German soldier hidden in an upper window. He pressed himself against the wall, his breath coming fast, sweat dripping down his face as he tried to think of a way to get out without exposing himself.

Then he heard a shout—Charlie's voice, calling from below. "Tom, I've got you covered! Go!"

Tom didn't hesitate. He darted out from the stairwell, aiming his rifle as he went, just as Charlie fired from below, drawing the German's attention. The enemy soldier turned, and Tom seized the moment, firing a single, precise shot that took him down. He felt a surge of gratitude for Charlie, a silent acknowledgment of the bond that had grown between them through every battle, every close call.

Finally, after hours of grueling combat, the sounds of gunfire began to fade. The Germans were retreating, their forces scattered, their defenses broken. Carentan was theirs. The platoon gathered in a small square, weary and battered but victorious, their faces etched with relief and exhaustion.

Captain Harris addressed them, his voice carrying a note of pride that was rare for the grizzled officer. "You did good today," he said, his gaze sweeping over them. "We took Carentan. This town is a key to linking our forces on the beach, and you made it happen. We're one step closer to driving the Germans out."

Tom felt a wave of satisfaction wash over him, a deep, quiet pride that tempered the exhaustion settling into his bones. They had done it. They had faced one of the fiercest battles yet, had pushed through the nightmare of urban warfare, and they had come out on top. But as he looked around, he saw the toll it had taken—the faces of men who hadn't made it, the empty places where friends had once stood.

He glanced at Charlie, who gave him a tired but triumphant grin. "We're still here, Tommy," he said, clapping him on the shoulder. "That's got to count for something."

Tom nodded, a small smile tugging at his lips. They were still here, still fighting, still pushing forward. And as they moved to secure their hard-won position, he felt a renewed sense of purpose, a resolve that burned brighter with every step. The road ahead would be long, but they were ready for it.

Together, they would carry on.

As the sun began to dip below the horizon, casting a warm, golden light over the battered town of Carentan, the echoes of battle slowly faded into an eerie silence. The sounds of gunfire and explosions were replaced by the quiet murmur of survivors regrouping, by the hollow shuffling of boots over rubble-strewn streets. Carentan was theirs, secured at a steep price, the victory hard-won and bitter.

Tom leaned against a crumbling wall, letting himself slide down to the ground, his back pressing into the rough stone as he closed his eyes for a moment. His body ached with exhaustion, his hands shaking slightly as he tried to process what they'd just been through. The smell of smoke and blood lingered in the air, mingling with the scent of the Normandy countryside, a strange contrast that left a hollow feeling in his chest.

Around him, his comrades were tending to the wounded, their faces drawn and solemn as they moved through the aftermath. The medics worked with quiet efficiency, bandaging wounds, offering water to those who could still sit up, murmuring words of comfort to those who couldn't. Charlie sat a few feet away, his head bowed, his hands stained with dirt and blood, staring at the ground with a distant look in his eyes.

The battle for Carentan had been a brutal one, and the toll it had taken was clear in the empty faces, in the vacant stares of men who had seen too much. They had fought fiercely, had taken every street and every building from an enemy that had refused to surrender, and they had won. But the victory felt hollow, overshadowed by the knowledge of what it had cost.

Captain Harris walked among them, his expression unreadable as he took stock of their numbers, his eyes lingering on the empty spaces where friends had once stood. He paused beside Tom, his gaze heavy with the weight of responsibility, of loss.

"We did it," Captain Harris said quietly, his voice carrying a mixture of pride and sorrow. "We took Carentan. Our forces are connected now, thanks to you men. The beachheads are united."

Tom nodded, swallowing the lump in his throat. "It doesn't feel like a victory, sir," he murmured, his voice barely more than a whisper.

The captain's expression softened, and for a moment, he looked like an old man, worn down by the weight of command. "War rarely feels like victory," he replied. "Every inch we take costs us something. Every battle has its price."

Tom looked away, his gaze drifting over the fallen soldiers who lay in quiet rows along the side of the street, covered with whatever cloth they could find. Some were Germans, some were his own comrades, and in that moment, the difference between them seemed insignificant. They were all young men, all sons, brothers, friends. They had all had dreams and hopes, lives that had been cut short in the name of a cause that felt distant, abstract, and yet so deeply personal.

Charlie shifted beside him, his voice low, filled with a sadness that mirrored Tom's own. "It's strange, isn't it? They were just doing their job, same as us. Fighting for what they thought was right."

Tom nodded, the words sinking into him. The German soldiers they had fought so fiercely were no different from them. They had been given orders, had followed commands, had held their ground with the same courage and determination. In the end, they had been men trying to survive, caught up in the machinery of war that had claimed so many lives.

He looked down at his hands, his fingers stained with dirt, dried blood clinging to his knuckles. The rifle in his lap felt heavier than ever, the weight of it pressing into his bones, a reminder of the violence he had been a part of, the lives he had taken. The thrill of victory, the sense of accomplishment, felt distant, drowned out by the faces that lingered in his mind—the friends who hadn't made it, the enemy soldiers who had fallen by his hand.

Captain Harris cleared his throat, drawing their attention back to him. "We mourn our dead, and we honor their sacrifice," he said, his voice steady but filled with sorrow. "They gave their lives for something greater than themselves, and we carry that forward. But we can't let the loss consume us. We're still here. And we have to keep going, for them."

The words hung in the air, resonating through the quiet square, settling over the men like a solemn vow. Tom felt the truth of them, felt the strength in his captain's voice, the resolve that had carried them this far. But the weight of grief was still there, heavy and unyielding, a shadow that would follow them with every step.

A French woman approached, a small child clutching her hand, her eyes filled with gratitude and sadness. She looked at the men, her gaze softening as she took in their weary faces, her lips trembling as she tried to speak.

"Merci," she said, her voice choked with emotion. "Thank you... for everything. You have given us hope."

Tom managed a faint smile, nodding as he met her gaze. Her words were a balm, a reminder of why they were here, of the lives they had touched. But even as he felt a flicker of pride, the faces of his fallen friends lingered, a quiet reminder of the price they had paid.

As the woman walked away, leading her child down the rubble-strewn street, Tom glanced over at Charlie, who gave him a tired, bittersweet smile.

"We'll carry them with us, won't we?" Charlie said, his voice soft.

"Yeah," Tom replied, feeling the weight of that truth settle into his heart. "We'll carry them. Every step of the way."

Captain Harris gave the order to regroup, to prepare for the next push. The platoon rose, each man moving with a quiet resolve, their faces marked by the memories of the battle they had just survived. They would keep fighting, keep moving forward, but they would never forget. Carentan was theirs, but the victory was etched with loss, with the knowledge that every battle would bring more sacrifice, more faces to remember.

As they marched out of the town, the sun sinking low in the sky, casting long shadows across the fields, Tom looked back one last time, the image of the quiet village etched into his mind. They had fought for this place, had given so much to see it liberated, and in that victory, he found a fragile sense of peace—a reminder that their struggle, their pain, was part of something larger, something worth fighting for.

With every step, they carried the memory of their fallen brothers, their presence a silent strength, a bond that would guide them through the dark days ahead. And as the platoon moved forward, leaving Carentan behind, Tom felt a new resolve settle into his bones.

They would endure, and they would remember. For those they had lost, for those still waiting for them, and for the hope of a world free from the shadows of war.

Chapter 3: The Battle for Saint-Lô

The landscape shifted as the platoon pushed forward, leaving the battered town of Carentan behind. The Normandy countryside stretched out before them, green and quiet under a cloudy sky, a stark contrast to the horrors they'd faced in Carentan. But there was something unsettling about the silence here, a stillness that seemed to seep into their bones as they moved through the dense, maze-like terrain.

The men knew what lay ahead: the infamous bocage—the thick, tangled hedgerows that crisscrossed the fields of Normandy like a natural fortress. These hedgerows, some of them centuries old, formed dense walls of earth, roots, and foliage that rose up to ten feet high in places. They offered perfect cover for the German defenders, transforming the countryside into a brutal battleground where every step forward was fraught with danger.

Tom adjusted his grip on his rifle, his eyes scanning the wall of green ahead, every rustle of leaves, every distant birdcall setting his nerves on edge. The hedgerows were close, almost claustrophobic, and the narrow paths between them left little room for maneuvering. They were walking into a natural ambush, a battlefield where the enemy could lie hidden only a few feet away, invisible until it was too late.

"Stay sharp, and keep your spacing," Captain Harris called out, his voice low but commanding. "We don't know what's waiting for us in there."

The men nodded, each one settling into a cautious, tense silence as they moved forward, weaving through the narrow lanes carved into the dense underbrush. The air was thick and humid, filled with the earthy scent of moss and damp soil. The sounds of their footsteps were muffled by the grass and fallen leaves, giving the impression that they were moving through a world removed from the war raging around them.

Charlie walked beside Tom, his gaze flickering from side to side as they moved deeper into the bocage. "Feels like we're being watched," he muttered, his voice barely a whisper.

Tom nodded, feeling the same unease gnawing at him. The hedgerows created a natural curtain, hiding whatever lay beyond, and he couldn't shake the feeling that eyes were tracking their every movement. The Germans knew this land well, knew every twist and turn of the hedgerows, every hidden nook where they could lie in wait.

They moved slowly, cautiously, their senses heightened, each man keenly aware that a single misstep could mean disaster. They reached a narrow gap between two tall hedgerows, a natural bottleneck where the path narrowed to a few feet wide. Captain Harris raised his hand, signaling for them to stop, his eyes scanning the area.

"Ambush spot," he said quietly, his gaze sharp. "We'll send a scout through first. Tom, you're up."

Tom swallowed, nodding as he moved forward, feeling the weight of his comrades' eyes on him as he approached the gap. His heart pounded in his chest, each beat echoing through his ribs as he crouched low, rifle at the ready. The air was still, the silence oppressive, broken only by the faint rustle of leaves in the breeze.

He took a step forward, and then another, his gaze darting between the hedgerows on either side. He could feel his muscles tensing, his body bracing for the slightest hint of movement, for the telltale glint of a rifle barrel or the dark shadow of a German helmet.

Suddenly, a shot rang out, shattering the silence. The bullet struck the ground inches from his feet, sending up a spray of dirt and grass. Tom dropped instantly, pressing himself flat against the earth as more gunfire erupted, bullets tearing through the leaves, splintering branches, filling the air with a cacophony of noise.

"Ambush! Take cover!" Captain Harris shouted, his voice sharp and urgent.

The men scrambled, pressing themselves against the hedgerows, finding whatever cover they could as the German soldiers opened fire from hidden positions within the dense foliage. Tom felt the ground vibrate beneath him as machine-gun fire raked across the narrow path, the sharp, metallic scent of gunpowder filling his nostrils.

He raised his rifle, peering through the dense wall of green, trying to catch sight of the enemy. But the Germans were well-concealed, their positions hidden within the thick hedgerows, their gunfire relentless and unforgiving.

Charlie slid in beside him, his face pale but determined. "They're all around us," he muttered, firing a quick shot into the underbrush.

Tom gritted his teeth, feeling the frustration and fear gnawing at him. The hedgerows gave the Germans the perfect advantage, allowing them to fire and then slip away, disappearing into the green maze, their movements hidden from sight. It was like fighting ghosts, shadows that vanished as soon as they appeared.

Captain Harris moved along the line, his voice calm but commanding as he issued orders. "We need to flank them! Tom, take your squad and move through the hedgerow on the left. See if you can get around behind them. The rest of us will keep them pinned here."

Tom nodded, signaling to Charlie and a few others to follow him. They crawled along the ground, using the thick underbrush for cover as they edged around the left side of the German position. The going was slow and dangerous, every step forward filled with the knowledge that an enemy soldier could be waiting just feet away, hidden behind the curtain of green.

They reached a gap in the hedgerow and slipped through, moving in a tight formation, each man covering the other. The sounds of gunfire were muffled here, distant, as if the foliage itself were swallowing the noise, but Tom knew they were close, close enough that he could hear the faint murmur of German voices just ahead.

He raised his hand, signaling for his squad to halt, and peered through the leaves. He could see them now—German soldiers crouched behind a low earthen bank, their rifles trained on the main path where the rest of the platoon was pinned down. They were focused on the fight ahead, unaware of the Americans approaching from behind.

Tom steadied his rifle, his breath coming slow and steady as he took aim. He fired, the shot finding its mark, and the German soldier dropped, his body slumping forward. The rest of the squad followed suit, opening fire, catching the Germans off guard, their line breaking as they tried to turn and defend against the surprise attack.

The Germans scrambled, some falling, others fleeing deeper into the bocage. Tom and his squad pressed forward, their gunfire precise and relentless, driving the enemy back. Within moments, the ambush had collapsed, the Germans retreating, their cover no longer able to shield them from the American advance.

The rest of the platoon joined them, moving through the broken ambush site, their faces marked with relief and exhaustion. Captain Harris gave them a nod, his expression grim but approving.

"Good work," he said, his voice steady. "They had us pinned, but you turned the tables on them."

Tom nodded, feeling a mixture of relief and grim satisfaction. They had survived, had outmaneuvered the enemy in terrain that was supposed to favor the Germans. But he knew that this was only the beginning. The bocage was vast, a sprawling maze that stretched for miles, and the Germans had entrenched themselves here, turning every hedgerow into a potential stronghold.

As they regrouped, preparing to move deeper into the countryside, Tom felt the weight of the task ahead settle into his bones. The bocage would be unforgiving, a battle that would test every ounce of strength, strategy, and determination they had. But they were still here, still fighting, and with every step forward, they were one step closer to Saint-Lô.

Together, they would face the maze of hedgerows, the unseen enemy, the relentless ambushes. They would fight, not just for the ground beneath their feet, but for each other, for the friends they'd lost, and for the promise of a victory that felt painfully distant.

They moved forward, slipping back into the cover of the bocage, their bodies tense, their senses sharp. The Germans were waiting, but so were they. And in this green, shadowed battleground, they would find the strength to keep pushing, no matter what lay ahead.

The humid air clung to the soldiers as they pushed further into the bocage, the thick walls of hedgerows rising around them like a living fortress. The silence was heavy, broken only by the occasional rustle of leaves or the distant call of a bird. Every sense was heightened, each man on edge, the tension mounting with every step. Tom could feel it in his bones—that prickling awareness that something was wrong, that they were walking into a trap.

The platoon moved cautiously, their formation tight, rifles raised, eyes darting to every shadow, every patch of dense greenery. The bocage was like a maze, the paths winding and narrow, visibility limited to a few yards in any direction. It was the perfect place for an ambush, and they all knew it.

Suddenly, a single shot rang out, slicing through the air and snapping every man to attention. The silence shattered as an explosion erupted nearby, sending a shower of dirt and debris into the air. Then, as if on cue, a hail of bullets rained down from the hedgerows, tearing through the leaves, pinging off rocks, sending the platoon scrambling for cover.

"Ambush! Take cover!" Captain Harris shouted, his voice barely audible over the deafening gunfire.

Tom dove to the ground, pressing himself against a low mound of earth, his heart pounding as he gripped his rifle. The Germans were hidden, their positions invisible, masked by the dense foliage. Gunfire echoed from all around, making it impossible to pinpoint their exact location. It was as if the very hedgerows had come alive, unleashing a relentless assault from every direction.

Charlie was beside him, his face pale but focused, his eyes scanning the walls of green. "They're all around us, Tommy," he muttered, barely loud enough to be heard over the gunfire. "We're sitting ducks here."

Tom nodded, feeling the weight of their situation press down on him. They were exposed, trapped in a narrow corridor with limited cover, and the enemy had the high ground, firing from concealed positions within the hedgerows. It was a death trap, and they had to find a way out before they were overrun.

"Fall back to the hedgerow!" Captain Harris ordered, waving his arm to signal the platoon to retreat. "We need to get out of the open!"

The men scrambled, crawling and ducking as they moved toward the nearest patch of cover, bullets whizzing past them, tearing through the leaves and dirt. Tom grabbed Charlie's arm, pulling him along as they made their way toward the hedgerow, his body tense, every nerve screaming for him to keep moving.

They reached the hedgerow, pressing themselves against the wall of earth and roots, finding some semblance of shelter from the withering fire. Tom's breath came in shallow gasps, his mind racing as he tried to assess their position. The Germans had them boxed in, firing down from the thick underbrush above, their angles giving them a clear line of sight on the Americans below.

Captain Harris crouched nearby, his face set in a grim expression as he surveyed the situation. "We can't stay here," he said, his voice low but urgent. "We need to establish a defensive line. Tom, you take your squad and hold the right flank. Charlie, cover the left."

Tom nodded, signaling to his squad to spread out along the hedgerow, their rifles trained on the foliage above. They fired in bursts, aiming for any hint of movement, any flicker of a helmet or rifle barrel that might betray the enemy's position. The gunfire from the Germans slowed, but it didn't stop, the sporadic bursts keeping them pinned, forcing them to stay low.

Beside him, one of the younger soldiers, Private Jacobs, was breathing hard, his hands shaking as he tried to steady his aim. Tom reached over, gripping his shoulder. "Stay with me, Jacobs. We're going to get through this."

Jacobs nodded, his face pale but determined, and Tom felt a surge of resolve. They were outnumbered and outgunned, but they weren't helpless. They just had to hold their ground, to keep each other alive long enough to find a way out.

Another burst of gunfire tore through the hedgerow, inches from Tom's head, sending a shower of dirt into his face. He coughed, wiping the grit from his eyes, then returned fire, his rifle kicking against his shoulder. He caught sight of a German soldier ducking behind a tree, his helmet barely visible, and fired. The soldier fell back, disappearing into the foliage.

"Keep firing!" Captain Harris shouted. "Make them think twice about advancing!"

The platoon held the line, each man firing in turn, their bullets ripping into the dense greenery, forcing the Germans to stay back. The gunfire from the enemy slowed, the ambush losing some of its ferocity as the Americans mounted their defense. But Tom knew it wouldn't last. The Germans were regrouping, waiting for the right moment to press forward.

Then, from deeper within the bocage, the sound of a machine gun roared to life, its deadly rhythm filling the air, the bullets slashing through the hedgerow like a scythe. Tom and the others ducked lower, pressing themselves flat against the earth as the gunfire chewed through the branches and leaves above, splintering wood, tearing holes in the greenery.

Charlie crawled over, his face etched with worry. "We need to take that machine gun out, or they'll pin us here until reinforcements arrive."

Tom glanced at Captain Harris, who nodded, his expression grim. "Tom, take a couple of men and see if you can flank it. The rest of us will cover you."

Tom signaled to two men, Private Jacobs and Corporal Lewis, and they moved out, keeping low as they crawled along the hedgerow, their movements slow and deliberate. The machine gun continued its deadly rhythm, the sound pounding in Tom's ears as they inched forward, each second feeling like an eternity.

They reached a break in the hedgerow, a narrow path that led around to the side of the German position. Tom motioned for the others to follow, his heart pounding as they slipped through the gap, creeping closer to the source of the gunfire. He could see the gunner now, crouched behind a makeshift barricade of sandbags and branches, his attention focused on the main path where the rest of the platoon was pinned down.

Tom took a deep breath, steadying himself, then raised his rifle. He aimed carefully, his finger tightening on the trigger. The shot rang out, striking the gunner squarely in the back. The man fell forward, his hands clutching at the gun as he crumpled to the ground.

The rest of the Germans turned, surprised by the sudden attack from their flank. Jacobs and Lewis opened fire, cutting down two more soldiers before the remaining Germans began to retreat, disappearing into the depths of the bocage.

The ambush had broken, the German fire fading as the enemy pulled back, regrouping deeper within the hedgerows. Tom let out a shaky breath, the adrenaline still coursing through his veins as he lowered his rifle. He signaled to Jacobs and Lewis, and they moved back toward the main line, joining the rest of the platoon.

Captain Harris greeted them with a nod, his face set in a look of relief and respect. "Good work, Tom," he said quietly. "You saved us back there."

Tom nodded, feeling a wave of exhaustion wash over him. They had survived, had held their ground in the face of overwhelming odds, but the ambush had shaken them all, a stark reminder of the dangers that lurked within the bocage. They were fighting an enemy who knew every inch of this land, who would use every advantage to hold it.

The platoon regrouped, tending to the wounded, exchanging quiet words of reassurance. They had survived this time, but each man knew that more ambushes lay ahead, that the bocage would continue to test their strength, their resolve.

As they prepared to move forward, Tom glanced at the dense hedgerows, their shadows stretching long and dark over the path. The bocage was unforgiving, a battlefield that offered no mercy, but he felt a spark of determination ignite within him. They would keep going, keep pushing forward, no matter what lay ahead.

Together, they would face the dangers of the bocage, fighting for every inch of ground, for every life beside them. And as they moved out, Tom felt the weight of the battle settle into his bones, a reminder of the resilience and courage that would see them through.

The push through the bocage was relentless, a slow, grinding advance where every step forward felt hard-won, each patch of ground earned at a price that weighed heavily on every man's mind. The ambushes had become a regular occurrence, with German troops melting into the thick foliage only to reappear at the worst possible moments, their knowledge of the terrain an ever-present threat. The narrow paths forced the platoon into single-file lines, making it nearly impossible to cover each angle. Each soldier moved with a growing sense of dread, waiting for the next round of gunfire to cut through the air.

Tom was near the front, moving carefully, his senses sharp. He glanced back, catching sight of Red—a tall, broad-shouldered soldier with a thick shock of red hair that had earned him his nickname. Red was the kind of man who could lighten any situation, his booming laugh often a welcome distraction from the endless grind of combat. Even in the darkest moments, he had been the one to crack a joke, his smile infectious, a reminder of the lives they had left behind.

Today, though, even Red looked worn down, his usual grin replaced with a look of grim determination. Tom gave him a nod, a silent acknowledgment of their shared struggle, and Red returned it, managing a small, weary smile.

The air felt heavy, thick with humidity and the smell of damp earth. The only sounds were the soft crunch of their boots on the ground, the occasional rustle of leaves, and the distant, ominous rumble of artillery. It was almost too quiet, the kind of silence that crawled into the mind, stoking every hidden fear.

Then, in a heartbeat, that silence shattered.

A burst of gunfire erupted from the hedgerow to their right, so close that Tom could feel the rush of air as bullets tore through the foliage. He dove to the ground, pressing himself flat as shouts filled the air, each man scrambling for cover in the narrow space. The Germans had positioned themselves well, their line hidden within the dense underbrush, firing down on the Americans with brutal precision.

"Ambush! Take cover!" Captain Harris's voice cut through the chaos, but there was nowhere to go. The men were pinned, trapped between the thick walls of the hedgerows with no way to maneuver, their only option to press forward or risk being overrun.

In the midst of the gunfire, Tom saw Red, his rifle raised as he fired into the trees, his face set with a fierce resolve. He was closer to the front, exposed, and Tom's heart leapt in his chest as he realized the danger his friend was in.

"Red, get down!" Tom shouted, his voice lost in the roar of gunfire. But Red didn't hear him, or maybe he did and chose to ignore it. He fired another round, taking down a German soldier who had been hidden behind a tree, his expression grim as he advanced, determined to break through the line.

And then, in a flash, it happened.

A shot rang out, sharp and final, and Red staggered, his body lurching forward before he crumpled to the ground. The world seemed to slow, the sounds of battle fading into a muffled hum as Tom watched his friend fall, his heart clenching in a mix of horror and disbelief.

"No!" Tom's voice broke as he scrambled toward Red, his body moving instinctively, driven by a need to reach him, to somehow undo what had just happened. He dropped to his knees beside his friend, his hands shaking as he reached out, his fingers brushing against Red's shoulder.

Red's face was pale, his eyes wide with shock, his breaths shallow and ragged. Blood seeped from the wound in his chest, staining his uniform, pooling beneath him in the dirt. He looked up at Tom, a faint, pained smile flickering across his lips.

"Guess... this is it, huh, Tommy?" he whispered, his voice barely audible over the sounds of the firefight raging around them.

Tom shook his head, his throat tight as he fought back tears. "Don't say that, Red. We're getting you out of here. You're gonna be fine."

Red's smile softened, his eyes losing some of their focus as his grip on Tom's arm weakened. "Just... keep going, Tommy. Get the boys through... you can do that for me, right?"

Tom's chest ached, the weight of Red's words settling into him like a stone. He wanted to promise, to assure his friend that everything would be okay, but the reality of the situation hung heavy between them. Red's breaths were growing weaker, his face ashen, the light in his eyes dimming.

"Yeah," Tom whispered, his voice breaking. "I'll get them through, Red. I promise."

Red gave a faint nod, his hand slipping from Tom's arm, his gaze drifting up to the sky as his breaths slowed, then stopped. Tom stared down at his friend, the numbness settling in, a quiet, hollow ache that felt like it would swallow him whole.

The battle raged on around him, but for a moment, Tom couldn't move, couldn't think. He felt the weight of the loss pressing down on him, the reality of it hitting him like a punch to the gut. Red was gone, a man who had been a constant presence, a friend who had kept them all laughing even in the darkest times. And now, in the mud and blood of the bocage, he was just... gone.

A hand clapped him on the shoulder, jolting him back to the present. It was Captain Harris, his face drawn, his eyes filled with an understanding that needed no words. "We need to keep moving, Tom," he said quietly. "For him, for all of us."

Tom nodded, swallowing the grief that threatened to choke him. He rose to his feet, his body heavy, his heart aching as he took one last look at Red's still form. He wanted to give his friend a proper farewell, to honor him in a way that felt fitting, but there was no time. The fight wasn't over, and they couldn't afford to stop.

As the platoon regrouped, the mood was somber, each man carrying the weight of Red's death, the loss rippling through them like a dark current. His absence was palpable, a reminder of the cost of every inch they gained, every hedgerow they cleared. The laughter that Red had brought, the lighthearted banter, felt like a distant memory, replaced by a quiet, unspoken grief that hung over them like a shroud.

They pressed on, moving forward through the bocage, each man driven by the promise Tom had made, by the memory of their fallen friend. The terrain grew rougher, the ambushes more frequent, but they fought with a renewed sense of purpose, each step a tribute to Red's sacrifice.

Tom felt the weight of it in every breath, every shot fired, the loss cutting deeper than any wound. He carried Red's memory with him, a silent vow to see the mission through, to honor his friend's courage and laughter, his unwavering spirit.

They had lost a brother, but his memory would live on, pushing them forward, binding them together. And as they moved deeper into the bocage, Tom knew that no matter what happened, he would keep going, driven by the promise he'd made on that blood-soaked ground.

Red was gone, but his spirit was with them, a quiet strength that would carry them through the battles yet to come. The cost of progress was steep, but they would bear it together, honoring the lives of those they had lost, each step a testament to their resolve.

The sun was high as Tom and the rest of the platoon approached Saint-Lô, the once-quaint French town now a shadow of its former self. Bombing had reduced many of the buildings to piles of rubble, their jagged remains jutting out like broken bones against the bright sky. Dust hung heavy in the air, mingling with smoke and the smell of charred wood, creating a thick, acrid haze that stung the eyes and clung to the lungs.

Saint-Lô had been a major German stronghold in Normandy, and the enemy was prepared to defend it fiercely. The Americans needed to take it, and every soldier knew the significance of this mission. The fight would be close-quarters, brutal, and unforgiving. Urban warfare was a different beast entirely, and the men could feel the weight of it pressing down on them, the knowledge that every street, every building, could become a battleground.

Captain Harris addressed the platoon, his voice steady but serious. "Listen up, men. The Germans have fortified their positions throughout Saint-Lô. They know the terrain, they know the buildings, and they're ready to die to keep us out. Stick close to your squads, watch each other's backs, and keep moving forward. We don't leave anyone behind."

The platoon nodded, their expressions hardening with resolve. Tom felt the familiar weight of his rifle, the metal cool against his hands, grounding him. Beside him, Charlie gave a nod, a silent assurance that they would get through this, no matter what.

They moved into the town, the quiet eeriness broken only by the faint sound of distant gunfire. The streets were narrow, winding, with rubble piled high, creating natural choke points that forced them into single-file lines. Tom's eyes scanned every window, every doorway, every shadow. The Germans could be anywhere, and he knew they were watching, waiting for the right moment to strike.

It came quicker than he expected.

A burst of gunfire erupted from a nearby alley, bullets pinging off the stone walls, sending shards of rock and dust into the air. Tom dropped to his knees, pressing himself against a crumbling wall, his heart racing as he scanned for the source of the fire. The enemy was hidden, their shots precise, calculated, each burst intended to slow the platoon's advance.

"Snipers!" someone shouted, and the men scattered, ducking behind whatever cover they could find.

Tom spotted the glint of a rifle barrel in a broken window above, and he fired, the shot cracking through the air. The figure in the window jerked back, the rifle slipping from sight. But the sniper was only one of many, and the Germans were well-entrenched, using the high ground and cover to their advantage.

Captain Harris shouted orders, his voice carrying over the noise of gunfire. "We need to clear these buildings! Squad A, take the left side. Squad B, with me. We're going straight through!"

Tom and Charlie's squad moved left, slipping through a narrow alleyway that led to a row of shattered storefronts. They pressed against the wall, creeping forward, rifles ready. The silence was oppressive, every footstep amplified, every breath loud in the confined space. Tom could feel the sweat trickling down his back, his body tensed as he approached the nearest building, its door hanging off the hinges, swaying slightly in the breeze.

He raised his hand, signaling to Charlie and the others, then moved in, sweeping his rifle from side to side as he entered. The interior was dark, the furniture overturned, shelves broken, debris scattered across the floor. It was eerily quiet, but he knew better than to assume they were alone.

A sudden shout echoed from the back of the room, and a German soldier charged, his rifle raised. Tom fired instinctively, the shot striking the man in the chest, sending him sprawling back. More footsteps sounded from above, and he looked up, catching sight of another soldier descending the staircase, his rifle trained on the squad.

Charlie reacted first, firing a quick shot that took the man down. The Germans were everywhere, using the rooms, the floors, even the rooftops to gain an advantage. It was like trying to clear a nest of hornets, each step forward met with resistance, every corner potentially hiding another enemy.

They moved up the stairs, clearing each floor, each room, their movements precise, deliberate. The sounds of gunfire and shouts echoed through the building as they pressed forward, their focus unbroken despite the chaos. Tom felt the familiar adrenaline surge, his senses sharp, his mind tuned to the rhythm of combat. Each shot, each movement, was driven by instinct, by the training that had become second nature.

When they reached the top floor, they found two more Germans huddled near a broken window, their eyes wide with fear as they saw the Americans approaching. They surrendered, raising their hands, and Tom gestured for a squadmate to take them out of the building, moving them back to the platoon's position.

As they cleared the final room, Tom looked out over the town, taking in the sight of Saint-Lô spread out below them. The streets were filled with rubble, the buildings broken and hollow, their windows like empty eyes staring out over the devastation. He could see flashes of movement below, American soldiers advancing, taking cover, pushing forward as the Germans fell back, regrouping, fighting desperately to hold their ground.

Captain Harris's voice crackled over the radio, his tone urgent. "We've got heavy resistance in the town square. I need all squads to converge there immediately."

Tom and the others quickly made their way down the stairs, exiting the building and joining the rest of the platoon as they moved toward the square. The air was thick with dust and smoke, the sounds of gunfire and explosions louder than ever. The Germans had dug in here, turning the square into a fortified position, their machine guns set up behind sandbags, covering every angle.

The platoon took cover along the edges of the square, each man finding a piece of rubble, a doorway, anything that offered protection. Tom crouched behind a low stone wall, his gaze fixed on the German position, his mind racing as he tried to think of a way to break through.

Captain Harris shouted over the din, his voice commanding. "We need to flank them! Tom, take your squad and move along the right side. We'll keep them distracted from here."

Tom nodded, signaling to Charlie and the others, and they moved out, keeping low as they skirted the edge of the square, using the debris and broken walls for cover. The Germans were focused on the main force, their attention fixed on the heavy fire from the center of the square, allowing Tom's squad to get closer.

They reached a narrow alley that opened up behind the German position, and Tom raised his hand, signaling his squad to hold. He peered around the corner, taking in the layout. The machine gunners were focused forward, their backs exposed, their attention elsewhere.

Tom steadied his rifle, taking aim, and opened fire. The rest of his squad joined in, their shots precise, cutting down the German soldiers before they had a chance to react. The machine guns fell silent, and the rest of the platoon surged forward, taking advantage of the sudden gap in the enemy's defenses.

Within minutes, the square was secured, the last of the German soldiers either dead or captured. The Americans held their ground, their breaths coming in ragged gasps, their faces streaked with dirt and sweat. The battle for Saint-Lô had been fierce, brutal, but they had done it. The town was theirs.

Tom leaned against a wall, the adrenaline fading, leaving behind a bone-deep exhaustion. He looked around, taking in the faces of his comrades, each one marked with the same mixture of relief and sorrow. They had won, but the cost had been steep, the fight hard-fought, the memories of the battle etched into each man's mind.

Captain Harris approached, his expression a mix of pride and weariness. "You did good today, men," he said, his voice carrying a quiet strength. "Saint-Lô is ours, and with it, a foothold in Normandy. We're one step closer to ending this."

The platoon nodded, each man feeling the weight of the victory, the significance of what they had achieved. They had secured Saint-Lô, had broken through the German defenses, but the town was a shadow of what it once was, a testament to the cost of war.

As they regrouped, preparing to move out, Tom felt a sense of pride tempered by a deep, quiet sadness. They had fought, they had won, but the cost had been high, and he knew that more battles lay ahead, each one as fierce, as unforgiving as this.

Together, they moved through the broken streets of Saint-Lô, their steps heavy but resolute. They would carry on, each step a tribute to those they had lost, each victory a reminder of the strength they found in one another. And as they left the town behind, Tom felt the weight of the battle settle into his bones, a reminder of the courage, the sacrifice, that would see them through the days to come.

Saint-Lô lay behind them, a battered, silent witness to the violence that had unfolded within its streets. The once-bustling town was now a skeleton of crumbling buildings and smoke-stained walls, and as the platoon moved through its shattered streets, an almost reverent silence settled over the men. They had taken the town, broken through the German defenses, but the victory was bittersweet, its cost etched into the faces of those who walked beside Tom.

They reached a makeshift camp just outside the town, set up in the shadow of an old stone farmhouse that had somehow survived the bombings. The medics were already tending to the wounded, and the men who hadn't been injured gathered in small groups, sharing water canteens, cleaning their weapons, each man quietly reflecting on the battle they had just survived.

Tom sat on a low wall, his rifle laid across his lap as he wiped the dust and grime from the barrel, his hands moving mechanically, the motions grounding him. Around him, the faces of his comrades reflected a similar exhaustion. Some stared into the distance, lost in thought; others murmured in low voices, recounting moments from the battle, their words filled with a mix of relief and sorrow.

Captain Harris moved among them, checking on each squad, offering a quiet word here and there, his presence a steady reminder of the strength that had carried them through. He approached Tom, giving him a nod, his eyes betraying the fatigue he carried.

"Good work out there, Tom," he said, his voice low but filled with respect. "Saint-Lô was a turning point, and you played a big part in making it happen."

Tom managed a faint smile, though the weight of the victory still hung heavy on his shoulders. "Thank you, sir," he replied. "Feels strange to finally be out of there, doesn't it?"

Captain Harris nodded, glancing back at the town, his expression thoughtful. "It does. But we're not done yet. Saint-Lô was only one battle. Command wants us to regroup, reorganize, and prepare for the next phase. There's more ground to cover, more strongholds to take."

Tom looked down, his fingers running over the scratches on his rifle stock, a quiet reminder of the battles they'd fought together. He knew the captain was right—Saint-Lô was only the beginning, a foothold in a long and grueling campaign that would push them deeper into France, closer to German territory. The victory was important, but it was just one step on a path that stretched far ahead.

"We'll be ready," he said, his voice carrying a resolve he hadn't realized he felt.

Captain Harris clapped him on the shoulder, his grip firm. "That's what I like to hear. Get some rest. We'll have our orders soon."

As the captain moved on, Tom settled back, taking a deep breath, letting the weight of the past few days settle into his bones. The exhaustion was overwhelming, pressing down on him with a force he could feel in every muscle, every joint. But there was something else too, a quiet determination, a sense of purpose that had been strengthened by the victory they had achieved together.

Charlie appeared beside him, lowering himself onto the wall with a weary sigh. He held a tin cup of water, his hands shaking slightly as he took a sip, his face marked by the same exhaustion Tom felt.

"Hell of a fight, wasn't it?" Charlie muttered, staring at the ground, his voice filled with a quiet reverence. "Feels like we left a part of ourselves in those streets."

Tom nodded, his gaze drifting to the horizon. "We did," he replied softly. "But we keep moving. We owe it to the guys we left behind, to Red, to all of them."

Charlie nodded, a faint smile tugging at his lips. "Red would've been the first to tell us to quit moping and get on with it. Said he'd give anything for a hot meal right now."

Tom chuckled, a low, tired sound, but it felt good, a reminder of the camaraderie that had kept them going, even in the darkest moments. "Yeah, he would've. Let's make sure we keep that promise to him."

The sun was beginning to set, casting a warm glow over the camp as the men began to settle in for the night. The tension that had gripped them in Saint-Lô was slowly easing, replaced by a sense of calm, of readiness for what lay ahead. They knew the road would be hard, that each mile forward would bring new challenges, new losses, but they were together, bound by the experiences they'd shared, by the unbreakable bonds forged in the fire of combat.

A voice called out, announcing that food was ready, and the men gathered around, sharing tins of rations, breaking bread together in a quiet, almost sacred ritual. Tom ate slowly, his mind drifting back to the streets of Saint-Lô, to the faces of those they had lost. He felt the weight of their memory, a presence that would travel with them, pushing them forward, reminding them of why they fought.

As the sky darkened, Captain Harris called the platoon together, gathering them in a rough circle. His face was lit by the glow of a nearby fire, his expression solemn but resolute.

"Saint-Lô was a victory, but we have a long way to go," he said, his voice carrying across the camp. "Each of you has shown strength, resilience, and courage beyond anything I could have asked for. I'm proud of you. Tomorrow, we'll receive our orders for the next phase. It won't be easy, but I know you'll be ready."

The men nodded, their faces set, each one carrying a quiet resolve. They had been through hell together, had fought, bled, and grieved together, and they would face whatever came next the same way—side by side, as brothers in arms.

Tom felt a surge of pride, a sense of belonging that settled deep within him. They were more than a platoon now; they were a family, each man carrying the weight of the others, each one strengthened by the bond they shared. As they prepared to move forward, to face the unknown challenges that lay ahead, Tom knew they would do it with courage, with honor, and with the memory of those they had lost guiding their steps.

He looked around at the faces of his comrades, each one marked by the trials they had endured, each one a testament to the strength they had found in one another. They would carry on, together, each step a tribute to the sacrifices they had made, each mile a step closer to the end of the war.

The night grew quiet as the men settled in, their bodies weary, their minds steeling themselves for the days to come. And as Tom lay back, his gaze fixed on the stars above, he felt a quiet peace, a sense of purpose that burned bright within him.

They would continue. They would fight. And together, they would see this through to the end.

Chapter 4: Operation Cobra - Breaking Out of Normandy

THE CAMP WAS ALIVE with a tense energy, each soldier moving with purpose as they prepared for the next phase of their campaign. Operation Cobra, the plan to break out of Normandy, was in motion. The objective was clear: shatter the German lines and open a path for the Allied advance into the heart of France. For the men of Tom's platoon, it meant one thing—another push into enemy territory, another battle, another test of their resolve.

Tom stood near his squad's makeshift quarters, carefully checking over his gear. He'd lost count of how many times he'd done this, but each time felt critical, each check a small way to maintain control over the unknown that lay ahead. His rifle was clean and ready, his ammunition stocked, his mind focused. Around him, the sounds of final preparations filled the air—the low murmur of voices, the clinking of metal, the rustle of gear being stowed and weapons being loaded.

Captain Harris approached, his expression as serious as Tom had ever seen it. He carried a map, folded and well-worn, the edges frayed from constant use. The captain spread it out on a small crate, and the platoon gathered around, listening closely as he outlined the plan.

"Listen up, men," Harris said, his voice steady, though a flicker of tension was visible in his eyes. "Operation Cobra is our shot at breaking through the German lines once and for all. The goal is to overwhelm their positions with a massive air and artillery bombardment, creating a gap in their defenses. Once that happens, we're going to move fast and hard, pushing through and taking key positions along the way."

He pointed to a section of the map marked with a red line, indicating the main German defensive line. "Our objective is to secure this high ground here," he explained, tapping a spot on the map. "It's heavily fortified, and the Germans know it's crucial for maintaining their hold on the area. If we can take it, we'll open up a pathway for our tanks and other units to advance."

Tom looked at the map, his gaze fixed on the high ground they'd been assigned. The area was strategically important, an ideal location for the Germans to defend. He knew the assault would be brutal, a fight for every inch. But he also knew that success here would mean a turning point, a chance to finally push beyond the bocage and gain ground.

Charlie stood beside him, nodding as he took in the captain's words, his expression focused. "So it's all or nothing, then," he muttered, glancing at Tom. "They're not gonna give that ground up without a hell of a fight."

Tom nodded, feeling the weight of what lay ahead settle into his bones. "We've made it this far, Charlie. We'll make it through this too."

Captain Harris looked over the group, his gaze serious but resolute. "This isn't going to be easy. The bombardment will create chaos, but it's only the beginning. Once we're in, we'll be facing dug-in machine guns, artillery, and whatever reinforcements they can throw at us. Stick to your squads, follow orders, and keep moving forward. We take that high ground, and we hold it."

The men nodded, each one preparing himself mentally for what was coming. They'd faced fierce resistance before, but this felt different. Operation Cobra was a coordinated, large-scale assault, and they were just one part of a much larger machine. The air around them buzzed with a mixture of anticipation and tension, each man aware of the scale of the mission and the role he would play.

As they broke away to finish preparing, Tom pulled Charlie aside. "You ready for this?" he asked, his voice quiet, though his tone held a hint of determination.

Charlie gave a tired but resolute grin. "Hell, we've been ready since we hit the beaches. Let's go break some lines."

They shared a brief nod, the kind of unspoken understanding that had developed over countless battles, the knowledge that they would face whatever came next together.

The hours ticked by slowly as the platoon prepared. Tom checked and rechecked his gear, his fingers moving over the familiar shapes and textures of his rifle, his canteen, his ammunition pouches. Every item was in place, every detail accounted for, but he could feel the tension building with each passing minute. Around him, the other men did the same, each one focused, their faces set with a grim determination.

In the distance, the rumble of artillery and the hum of aircraft engines began to grow louder. The air strikes were starting, the first wave of bombs already falling on the German lines. The ground shook with the impact, each explosion a reminder of the immense force being brought to bear on their enemy. Dust and smoke rose on the horizon, blotting out the distant treeline, marking the beginning of the assault.

Captain Harris gathered the platoon one last time, his voice firm, his gaze steady. "Remember, stick together, stay focused, and keep moving. We break through their lines, take the high ground, and hold it. No matter what happens, we do not give an inch."

The men nodded, each one carrying the weight of his words, the promise of their mission. They were ready, each one steeling himself for the unknown, for the chaos and violence that awaited them just beyond the line.

As they moved out, the noise of the bombardment grew louder, the ground trembling beneath their boots as the planes roared overhead, dropping their payloads in a relentless assault. The explosions lit up the sky, flashes of light cutting through the smoke and dust, illuminating the battlefield in stark, terrible clarity. Tom felt his heart pounding, his body alive with adrenaline, every sense tuned to the rhythm of the assault.

They reached the edge of the bombardment zone, the ground scarred and cratered, littered with debris and shattered trees. The air was thick with smoke and the acrid smell of burning, each breath filled with the taste of dust and gunpowder. Tom took a deep breath, steadying himself, feeling the weight of his rifle in his hands, the solid presence of his squad around him.

Captain Harris raised his hand, signaling them to hold, his voice calm but intense. "The bombardment is almost over. Once it's done, we move fast. Stay low, keep moving, and don't stop until we've taken that hill."

They waited, every muscle tense, every eye fixed on the smoking horizon. The final wave of bombs fell, a series of deafening explosions that seemed to shake the very ground beneath them. And then, suddenly, there was silence. The planes were gone, the rumble of artillery fading into the distance, leaving only the faint crackling of fires and the distant sounds of battle.

Captain Harris lowered his hand. "Move out!"

The platoon surged forward, their boots crunching over the rubble-strewn ground as they advanced into the wake of the bombardment. The air was thick with smoke, the landscape a twisted mess of broken trees and craters, each step a reminder of the violence that had cleared the path before them.

As they moved deeper into the battlefield, Tom felt the familiar rush of adrenaline, his senses sharp, every movement purposeful. He could see the high ground ahead, the hill that marked their objective, still partially obscured by smoke, but closer with every step. The Germans would be waiting, regrouping, ready to defend their position, and he knew the fight would be brutal, but he felt a surge of determination rise within him.

They had prepared. They had endured. And now, they would break through, together.

The silence that followed the bombardment felt like the calm before a storm, a brief moment of stillness before the next wave of violence. But in that silence, Tom found strength, a quiet resolve that steadied his hand, focused his mind. They were ready.

Operation Cobra had begun. And with it, the fight to break out of Normandy, to push forward, to claim victory one inch at a time.

The air around them buzzed with anticipation, every man tense and silent as they watched the horizon, waiting for the operation to unfold. Operation Cobra was underway, and the air strikes—the bombardment meant to break the German lines—were about to begin. Tom stood among his platoon, his eyes fixed on the distant treeline where the German positions lay hidden, his rifle resting heavily in his hands. The ground was dry and dusty, and each breath carried the faint scent of smoke, the promise of the inferno that was about to descend.

The rumble started low, like distant thunder rolling over the hills. Tom looked up, catching sight of the first wave of American bombers slicing through the sky, their engines a deep, resonant hum that grew louder, closer, until the entire horizon seemed to pulse with the sound. The planes flew in tight formation, dozens of them stretched across the sky, the metallic glint of their wings catching the afternoon sunlight, transforming them into silver darts poised to strike.

"Here we go," Charlie murmured beside him, his voice tense but steady, his gaze locked on the approaching bombers.

Tom nodded, feeling his heart pick up speed, his muscles tensing in anticipation. This was the opening move, the hammer that would smash through the German defenses, clearing the path for their advance. The sheer scale of it was staggering, a reminder of the power they had at their command—but also of the risks. He knew that once the bombardment began, there would be no turning back.

A high-pitched whine pierced the air as the first bombs were released, tiny dark shapes falling from the bellies of the planes, their descent marked by a faint trail of smoke. Tom barely had time to process it before the ground erupted, the horizon lighting up in a series of blinding flashes as the bombs found their marks. The explosions shook the earth, a chain of violent, fiery eruptions that seemed to tear the very landscape apart.

The platoon watched in awe and horror, transfixed by the destruction unfolding before them. The ground rippled with each blast, a distant wall of dust and fire rolling across the German lines. Buildings were obliterated, bunkers collapsed, and the trees that dotted the landscape were stripped of leaves, their trunks splintered and broken.

The bombers continued their assault, wave after wave of them dropping their payloads in precise, relentless succession. The air was thick with the roar of engines, the deep, rhythmic thud of bombs impacting the ground, and the thick plumes of smoke rising into the sky, turning the afternoon sun into a hazy, red-tinged orb.

"Good God," whispered one of the younger soldiers, his eyes wide as he took in the scene.

The destruction was almost surreal, a scene that felt as if it belonged in some other world, some place untouched by reason or restraint. Tom felt a strange mixture of awe and dread settle over him as he watched, the power of the bombardment both exhilarating and terrifying. It was a sight that left no doubt about the scale of their mission, the intensity of the fight they were about to enter.

But he also knew that beneath the smoldering landscape, amid the smoke and chaos, German soldiers were fighting to survive, taking cover, rallying themselves for the oncoming attack. The bombardment was only the beginning. Once the dust settled, they would have to push forward into the ruins, facing an enemy that was battered but not broken.

The noise was almost overwhelming now, a wall of sound that drowned out everything else, the ground trembling beneath their feet. Tom could feel it in his bones, a low, constant rumble that seemed to reverberate through the very earth. He glanced at Charlie, who met his gaze with a grim expression.

"They won't know what hit them," Charlie said, though his voice held no triumph, only the sober understanding of what lay ahead.

Tom nodded. "We'll be moving in soon. The Germans will be disoriented, but they'll be ready. They won't go down without a fight."

As the last wave of bombers passed overhead, releasing their final payloads, the explosions began to slow, the rhythmic thuds giving way to an eerie silence, broken only by the crackling of distant fires and the fading roar of engines. The bombers disappeared over the horizon, leaving behind a scarred, smoking landscape, a scene that looked more like the surface of some desolate planet than the peaceful countryside they'd known only days before.

Captain Harris moved through the ranks, his face set, his gaze sharp as he took in the expressions of his men. "This is it, boys," he said, his voice carrying over the quiet. "We're moving in as soon as the dust settles. Remember, stick close to your squads, keep your heads down, and keep moving. The Germans won't give up that ground without a fight, and we'll need every ounce of strength we have to take it."

The platoon nodded, each man steeling himself, preparing for the next step. They'd watched the landscape transform before their eyes, seen the devastation wrought by the air strikes, but they knew that what came next would be different. This wasn't about watching from a distance; this was about moving into the heart of it, facing the reality of close-quarters combat, of every building and trench potentially hiding an enemy soldier.

As the dust began to settle, the men gathered their gear, checking their rifles, their grenades, adjusting helmets and packs, their hands moving with practiced precision despite the tension in the air. Tom took a deep breath, steadying himself, his mind focused, his body ready. They'd been through hell in the bocage, had fought for every inch, and now they were ready to break free, to push forward with the momentum that Operation Cobra had unleashed.

Charlie gave him a nod, his usual grin replaced by a look of determination. "You ready, Tommy?"

Tom nodded, feeling the weight of his rifle, the familiar heft of his gear. "Let's do this. It's time to break through."

Captain Harris raised his hand, signaling them to advance, and the platoon moved forward, their steps measured but purposeful. The air was still thick with smoke, the smell of burning wood and earth filling their lungs as they pushed toward the remnants of the German lines. The ground was uneven, scarred by craters, and every step felt precarious, a reminder of the destruction they'd just witnessed.

The silence was almost deafening now, broken only by the crunch of their boots on the scorched ground, the faint crackling of fires smoldering in the distance. They moved as one, each man alert, his senses tuned to the shifting shadows, the faintest sign of movement. They knew the Germans were there, somewhere in the ruins, waiting.

And as they drew closer to the edge of the bombed-out landscape, Tom felt a strange calm settle over him, a sense of purpose that steadied his hand, focused his mind. The bombardment had set the stage, and now it was up to them to finish the job.

Operation Cobra was in motion, and with it, the promise of freedom, of progress, of a hard-won victory that lay just beyond the horizon. They would break through, not just for themselves, but for every soldier who had fallen, for every life marked by the shadow of war. They would move forward, one step at a time, carrying with them the strength and courage that had brought them this far.

Together, they advanced into the ruins, prepared to face whatever awaited them. The path to victory was uncertain, but they were ready to see it through, to fight for every inch, for every breath, for the hope that lay ahead.

The platoon advanced cautiously, the dust from the bombardment still hanging thick in the air, clinging to their uniforms and filling their lungs with each shallow breath. The landscape before them was unrecognizable—a scarred, smoking wasteland of craters and shattered trees, the earth torn apart by the relentless rain of bombs that had softened the German defenses. Yet, as they moved forward, Tom knew this was just the beginning. The

Germans had been shaken but not broken, and pockets of resistance waited to meet them.

Captain Harris led them forward, his figure barely visible through the haze. His voice was steady but low, guiding them as they pressed through the twisted remains of what had once been a dense forest. "Stay sharp and keep an eye out for cover," he murmured, his words punctuated by the crunch of boots over loose rubble. "They're scattered, but they're still here."

Tom scanned the horizon, his rifle held at the ready, every nerve tingling with the knowledge that the enemy could be lying in wait just beyond the next ridge, behind the next pile of debris. Around him, the men moved silently, their steps careful, their eyes alert. They'd been trained for this, had fought through close-quarters battles and ambushes, but there was a quiet dread that settled over them now—the understanding that each inch forward would be earned with sweat and blood.

They reached the remnants of a German trench line, the earthworks shattered but still discernible amid the chaos. Tom dropped to his knees, peering over the edge, scanning for any sign of movement. The silence felt almost unnatural, a quiet before the inevitable storm. He glanced at Charlie, who gave him a nod, his face grim but focused.

Then, the silence was broken.

A single gunshot rang out, sharp and sudden, and a bullet kicked up dirt inches from Tom's face. He ducked instinctively, pressing himself against the ground as the crack of machine-gun fire erupted from the far side of the trench. The Germans had regrouped, their positions hidden among the rubble, and the platoon was caught in the open.

"Get to cover!" Captain Harris shouted, his voice cutting through the chaos.

Tom scrambled, his heart pounding as he threw himself behind a twisted section of metal that had once been part of a German bunker. Around him, his comrades did the same, taking cover behind craters and debris, their bodies pressed low as bullets whizzed overhead. He felt the impact of each shot, the ground trembling beneath him as the enemy dug in, refusing to let them advance any further.

He glanced over the edge of his cover, spotting the source of the machine-gun fire—a fortified position dug into the far side of the trench, the barrel of the gun sweeping back and forth, its deadly rhythm unyielding. Tom raised his rifle, taking aim, and fired, but the distance and smoke made it impossible to tell if his shot had connected. The Germans were well-concealed, their fire coordinated, each burst forcing the platoon to stay low.

"Tom! We need to flank them!" Charlie called, his voice barely audible over the gunfire.

Tom nodded, gesturing to a few nearby soldiers to follow him. They crawled along the edge of the trench, moving carefully, keeping their bodies low to avoid the enemy's line of sight. Each movement felt painfully slow, each second a reminder of the danger that pressed in around them.

As they neared the side of the German position, Tom could hear the shouts of the enemy soldiers, their voices tense and hurried. He exchanged a glance with Charlie, who nodded, his eyes narrowing as he readied his weapon.

"On my signal," Tom whispered, his voice steady despite the pounding of his heart. "We go in hard and fast."

Charlie and the others gave a nod, their grips tightening on their rifles. Tom raised his hand, counted to three, then dropped it, signaling the attack.

They rose as one, moving forward in a burst of controlled aggression, their rifles trained on the enemy position. Tom fired, his shots finding their mark, taking down a German gunner as he turned to react. The others joined in, their fire swift and precise, overwhelming the Germans in a matter of seconds. Within moments, the machine-gun nest was silenced, the enemy soldiers sprawled among the rubble, their weapons lying still.

The rest of the platoon surged forward, taking advantage of the break in fire to press into the trench. They moved quickly, clearing each section, flushing out any remaining resistance. Tom felt the rush of adrenaline surge through him, his senses sharp, his mind focused as he swept his rifle from side to side, each step calculated, purposeful.

But as they advanced, the resistance intensified. German soldiers emerged from hidden bunkers, firing down from elevated positions, their faces set with a grim determination that spoke of desperation. Each corner, each rise in the ground, held a new challenge, another deadly pocket of resistance that the platoon had to root out, neutralize, and overcome.

Tom ducked as another round of gunfire tore through the air, the bullets slicing into the dirt beside him. He returned fire, his shots precise, each one driving the enemy back, forcing them to retreat further into the ruins. Around him, the sounds of battle filled the air—the sharp cracks of rifles, the roar of grenades, the shouts of men caught in the intensity of the fight.

Captain Harris moved through the ranks, his voice a steady anchor amid the chaos. "Keep pushing forward! We break through here, or we don't break through at all!"

The men pressed on, their bodies aching, their minds focused, each one fueled by the drive to see the mission through. They moved with a relentless rhythm, clearing each position, securing each inch of ground, their unity unbroken despite the mounting resistance.

They reached a final stretch, a narrow corridor that led to an elevated position where the last German soldiers had entrenched themselves. Tom's squad approached carefully, using the cover of a fallen tree to conceal their movements. He signaled for a grenade, nodding to one of the younger soldiers, who tossed it expertly into the enemy stronghold.

The explosion rocked the air, sending a plume of dust and debris into the sky. When the smoke cleared, the German position was silent, the resistance finally broken. Tom took a deep breath, his shoulders sagging with relief as he lowered his rifle, the realization settling in—they'd done it. They'd broken through.

The platoon regrouped, gathering in the trench as they took stock of the battlefield, the landscape a grim testament to the brutal fight they had endured. Bodies lay scattered among the craters, the remnants of German defenses reduced to rubble and twisted metal. The smell of smoke and burnt earth hung heavy in the air, a reminder of the intensity of the battle.

Captain Harris addressed them, his voice carrying a note of respect and pride. "You did good today, men. We broke through their lines, and with this ground secure, we're one step closer to liberating France. You've shown courage, resilience, and determination. I'm proud of each and every one of you."

The men nodded, their faces weary but marked with a quiet pride. They had fought for every inch, had faced a fierce and unyielding enemy, and they had come out on top. The cost had been high, but they had achieved their objective, had broken through the lines that had once seemed impenetrable.

As they moved to secure their positions, Tom looked out over the battlefield, his gaze lingering on the fallen German soldiers, the men who had fought just as hard, with the same determination to defend their ground. There was no triumph in their victory, only the sober understanding of the sacrifice, the lives lost, on both sides.

Charlie appeared beside him, his expression thoughtful as he looked out over the scene. "We did it, Tommy. We're breaking out of Normandy."

Tom nodded, a faint smile tugging at his lips. "Yeah. We are. But there's a long way to go."

They stood in silence, each man carrying the weight of the battle, the memory of the friends they had lost, the promise of what lay ahead. They had broken through, had faced the fire and come out the other side, but the road was far from over.

Together, they moved forward, each step a tribute to their resilience, their unity, their shared purpose. They were breaking through—not just the German lines, but the barriers that had held them back, the weight of the past. And as they advanced, Tom felt a quiet resolve settle within him, a determination that would carry him through whatever lay ahead.

The platoon advanced through the churned-up fields, the broken ground and scattered remnants of the German defenses marking their path forward. They were pressing toward Avranches, and with each mile gained, they moved deeper into territory the enemy was desperate to reclaim. The resistance was fierce, as the Germans launched counterattacks to slow their progress and reestablish control. It was a test of endurance, of unity, and of the resolve that had been forged through every battle since the Normandy landings.

Tom felt the weight of exhaustion pressing down on him, his body weary from days of near-constant movement and combat. But he pushed it aside, his focus unwavering, his grip on his rifle steady. Around him, his comrades moved with the same determination, each one carrying the unspoken understanding that they were all in this together. They had come too far, fought too hard, to let anything break their line now.

Captain Harris led them forward, his voice calm and firm, his commands clear. "Stay close, eyes on each other. They're going to try to split us up, isolate us. Don't let them. We move as one."

They spread out, each squad watching the flanks, their eyes scanning the dense hedgerows and broken tree lines that could easily conceal an enemy force. The Germans had an advantage here, knowing every inch of the terrain, using the thick vegetation and uneven ground to launch hit-and-run attacks, their tactics sharp and unpredictable.

The first counterattack came suddenly, a burst of gunfire slicing through the quiet, tearing through the leaves and branches with brutal precision. The Germans had entrenched themselves in a ridge up ahead, a well-defended line that they held with grim determination. Bullets kicked up dirt and leaves as the Americans hit the ground, finding whatever cover they could in the exposed field.

"Cover fire!" Captain Harris shouted, raising his rifle. "Tom, take your squad and flank the ridge. We need to break this line."

Tom nodded, signaling to Charlie and the rest of his squad to follow. They moved quickly, crawling through the grass and underbrush, keeping low to avoid drawing fire. Every movement felt tense, every sound magnified as they inched their way along the ridge, their hearts pounding with the knowledge that the Germans were waiting just above them.

As they neared the edge of the ridge, Tom raised his hand, signaling for them to hold. He could see the German positions now, dug into the high ground, the barrels of their machine guns trained on the open field below. They were focused on the main line, their attention fixed on the Americans who were holding the enemy fire at bay.

Tom took a deep breath, feeling the adrenaline surge as he counted down in his mind. *Three... two... one...*

He dropped his hand, and they surged forward, rifles raised, firing in unison as they broke through the cover and advanced on the German line. The enemy soldiers turned, caught off guard by the flanking maneuver, and the ridge erupted in chaos. Tom's shots found their mark, the sharp crack of his rifle cutting through the noise as he and his squad pushed up the ridge, their movements synchronized, each man covering the other.

Charlie was beside him, his face set with a fierce resolve as he fired, his aim steady, each shot a reminder of the bond they shared, the unity that had carried them through every battle. They moved together, their footsteps falling in rhythm, each man drawing strength from the others as they pressed the Germans back, step by step, clearing the ridge with a relentless determination.

The rest of the platoon joined them, the counterattack crumbling as the Germans fell back, retreating to regroup. The ridge was theirs, but there was little time to celebrate. Captain Harris gave a quick nod, a flash of pride in his eyes as he looked at Tom and the others.

"Good work, men," he said, his voice steady but urgent. "But we're not done yet. They'll be back, and they won't make it easy. Set up defensive positions, keep your eyes sharp."

The men moved quickly, digging into the ridge, setting up a line of defense in preparation for the inevitable counterattack. The air was thick with tension, every man keenly aware of the threat that loomed, the knowledge that the Germans would strike again, more determined than ever.

They didn't have to wait long.

The sound of engines rumbled in the distance, and Tom spotted a line of German soldiers advancing through the tree line, their movements quick and coordinated, their faces set with grim determination. The enemy was bringing everything they had, throwing fresh troops into the fight, determined to reclaim the ground they had lost.

"Hold steady!" Captain Harris commanded, his voice carrying over the ridge. "Wait until they're in range."

The men braced themselves, rifles aimed, fingers steady on the triggers as they watched the advancing line. The Germans moved closer, their figures blending into the landscape, their pace quickening as they neared the ridge. The tension was electric, each second stretching out as they waited, their breaths held, their bodies coiled, ready to respond.

"Now!" Captain Harris shouted.

The ridge erupted in gunfire, the sharp crack of rifles and the roar of machine guns filling the air as the platoon opened fire. Tom's world narrowed to the rhythm of his rifle, the steady recoil grounding him, his mind focused, his aim precise. Around him, his comrades held their ground, each man firing in turn, their line unbroken despite the intensity of the assault.

The Germans pressed forward, their determination fierce, but the Americans held firm, each man fighting not just for himself but for the brother beside him. They were a single, unified force, each shot a testament to their resolve, each movement a reminder of the bond that had carried them through the worst of the war.

Charlie was beside him, his face streaked with sweat and dirt, his expression fierce. "They're not giving up, are they?"

Tom shook his head, his grip tightening on his rifle. "No. But neither are we."

The Germans fell back, retreating into the tree line, their assault broken, their forces scattered. The platoon let out a collective sigh of relief, the tension easing as they took stock of the situation. The ridge was theirs, and for the moment, the line held.

Captain Harris moved through the ranks, his voice quiet but filled with a pride that resonated through each man. "You held your ground. You showed them what we're made of. They're going to throw everything they have at us, but we're not going anywhere."

The men nodded, their faces marked with exhaustion but also with a quiet strength, a resolve that would carry them forward, no matter the cost. They had faced the worst of the German counterattacks, had stood shoulder to shoulder in the face of overwhelming odds, and they had come out on top.

Tom looked around at his comrades, at the faces of the men who had fought beside him, each one marked by the battles they had endured, the hardships they had faced together. They were more than a platoon—they were a family, bound by a unity that could not be broken.

As they prepared to move forward, to push deeper into enemy territory, Tom felt a renewed sense of purpose, a strength that came from the men beside him. They would face whatever came next, would push toward Avranches with the same determination that had brought them this far.

They were soldiers, brothers, united by a shared resolve, and as they moved out, leaving the ridge behind, they knew that nothing could break them. Together, they would carry on, each step a testament to their courage, each victory a reminder of their unity.

And as they pressed forward, Tom felt a quiet, unshakable resolve settle within him. They would make it to Avranches. They would see this through.

The platoon's steady advance toward Avranches had been marked by relentless firefights, ambushes, and counterattacks, each encounter chipping away at their numbers, their strength, and their resolve. Now, as they approached the final stretch, they could see the German line—the last stronghold standing between them and victory. But this victory, they knew, would come at a cost.

The air was thick with tension as Captain Harris gathered the men in a small clearing, his voice low and urgent. "This is it," he said, his gaze sweeping over each man, his tone carrying a gravity they all understood. "We break through here, and we open the path to Avranches. But the Germans know what's at stake. They won't let us take this ground easily."

The men nodded, their faces set with a quiet resolve. They'd come too far, fought too hard, to turn back now. Each one of them knew that they were all-in, that there would be no retreat, no room for hesitation. Tom tightened his grip on his rifle, his gaze fixed on the line ahead, the fortified bunkers and trenches where the Germans waited, ready to defend their ground to the last.

"Stay low, keep close, and watch each other's backs," Captain Harris continued, his voice steady. "We're going in hard and fast. We take this line, or we don't come back."

They moved out, each squad in formation, their steps careful and quiet as they approached the German defenses. The landscape was a scarred, smoking expanse, littered with the remnants of earlier battles, the ground torn up and uneven. Every inch forward was a reminder of the fight they'd endured to get here, of the sacrifices that had brought them to this moment.

As they drew closer, the silence shattered. The Germans opened fire from their bunkers, the sharp crack of rifles and the heavy thud of machine guns cutting through the air. Tom hit the ground, pressing himself into the dirt as bullets whizzed overhead, tearing through the leaves and kicking up plumes of dust. Around him, the men found cover, each one moving with a precision born of necessity, their bodies tense, their faces set.

"Move up! Keep pressing!" Captain Harris shouted, his voice carrying over the roar of gunfire.

The platoon pushed forward, advancing in short bursts, moving from cover to cover as they inched closer to the enemy line. Tom could feel his heart pounding, the familiar adrenaline sharpening his senses, focusing his mind. Each step felt perilous, each movement a risk, but there was no time for fear, no room for doubt.

He glanced over at Charlie, who was moving beside him, his face streaked with sweat and dirt, his gaze locked on the enemy ahead. They shared a brief nod, a silent acknowledgment of the bond that had carried them through every battle, every close call. They were in this together, as they had been from the start.

As they neared the first bunker, Tom saw the flash of a rifle barrel and fired, his shot finding its mark, taking down a German soldier who had been crouched behind the sandbags. The rest of the squad surged forward, throwing grenades, clearing the bunker in a swift, brutal assault. The Germans fought fiercely, but the Americans were relentless, each man driven by the need to see the mission through, no matter the cost.

They pushed deeper into the line, moving from bunker to bunker, trench to trench, the fight intensifying with every step. The Germans were entrenched, their defenses formidable, but the platoon pressed on, each man drawing strength from the others, their unity unbroken.

But then, amid the chaos, Tom heard a shout—a sound that cut through the noise and pierced him to his core. He turned, his heart clenching as he saw Charlie fall, his body crumpling to the ground, his face pale, his rifle slipping from his grasp.

"Charlie!" Tom's voice broke as he scrambled to his friend's side, his hands reaching out, his heart pounding as he knelt beside him.

Charlie's eyes flickered, his breaths shallow, his face etched with pain. He managed a faint smile, a shadow of his usual grin, his gaze meeting Tom's with a quiet resignation.

"Guess... I'm out of luck, huh?" he murmured, his voice barely more than a whisper.

Tom shook his head, his throat tight. "No. You're going to make it, Charlie. We're almost there. Just hold on."

Charlie's smile softened, his hand reaching out to grip Tom's arm. "Get them through, Tommy. Finish this."

Tom felt the weight of his friend's words settle into his bones, a promise that anchored him even as his heart ached. He wanted to say more, to find the words that could somehow make this right, but the sounds of the battle pulled him back, the urgency pressing down on him.

With one last, pained look, Tom rose to his feet, his resolve hardening, his mind focused. He turned back to the line, the sight of the German defenses sharpening into clarity. This was for Charlie, for Red, for every man who had given everything to see this mission through.

"Move up!" he shouted, his voice carrying over the gunfire. "For Charlie!"

The platoon surged forward, their movements fierce, their aim precise. They fought with a renewed determination, each man driven by the sacrifices they had witnessed, by the memory of those who had fallen. The German line began to buckle, their defenses cracking under the relentless assault, their will to hold the ground faltering in the face of the Americans' unbreakable unity.

Tom's squad pushed through the final trench, their steps steady, their faces set. They reached the last bunker, clearing it with a precision born of necessity, the last German soldiers falling back, their resistance finally broken. And then, in the quiet that followed, the realization settled over them—they had done it. They had broken through.

The men gathered, their breaths coming in ragged gasps, their faces marked with exhaustion and grief. The sight of the open ground before them, the pathway cleared, brought a bittersweet sense of victory. They had won, but the cost was staggering, the weight of their losses pressing down on them like a shadow.

Captain Harris approached, his gaze sweeping over the men, his expression a mix of pride and sorrow. "You did it," he said, his voice steady, though his eyes betrayed the grief he carried. "You broke the line. Avranches is within reach, thanks to each of you."

The platoon nodded, each man feeling the weight of his words, the understanding that their victory was built on sacrifice. They had given everything, had fought for each other, for the brothers who had fallen, and now, as they stood on the edge of the battlefield, they felt the bittersweet taste of success tempered by loss.

Tom knelt, his gaze fixed on the ground, his mind drifting to Charlie, to the smile that had been a constant presence, the laughter that had carried them through so many dark moments. He knew he would carry that memory with him, that each step forward would be a tribute to the friend he had lost, to the bond they had shared.

The platoon regrouped, each man gathering his gear, preparing to move forward. They would press on, would continue the fight, but they would do so with the memory of those they had lost, the knowledge that their victory had come at a price.

As they left the battlefield, the open ground stretching out before them, Tom felt a quiet resolve settle within him. They would honor the fallen by carrying on, by seeing the mission through, by standing together, no matter the cost.

They had succeeded, but it was a success marked by sacrifice. And as they moved toward Avranches, each man carried the weight of that sacrifice, a reminder of the courage, the unity, that had brought them here.

Together, they would finish the fight.

Chapter 5: The Liberation of Paris

The atmosphere in the camp shifted as the news swept through the ranks: the liberation of Paris was within reach. For months, the platoon had slogged through hedgerows, towns, and fields, fighting inch by inch across France. They'd endured ambushes, counterattacks, and brutal losses, each battle a testament to their resolve. And now, Paris—the heart of France, the symbol of hope and freedom—was nearly theirs.

Tom felt a strange lightness settle over him as he processed the news, a sensation he hadn't felt in what seemed like a lifetime. Around him, his comrades mirrored that energy, their faces lighting up with something they hadn't allowed themselves to feel in a long time: optimism. Paris wasn't just another objective; it was a symbol, a promise of the end of the occupation and the beginning of something new.

Captain Harris called the platoon together, his own expression softened by the news. Even his normally serious demeanor carried a hint of excitement as he addressed them. "Men, I know it's been a long and grueling campaign, but we're close. We've been ordered to push forward, to be among the first units to reach the outskirts of Paris. This is the moment we've all been waiting for. We're bringing liberty back to this country."

A cheer rose up from the men, a sound that was as much relief as it was exhilaration. For the first time, their objective felt tangible, a goal they could almost touch. The liberation of Paris wasn't just a strategic victory; it was something that would live on in history, something that would be remembered, and each one of them felt the weight—and the honor—of being part of it.

Tom exchanged a grin with Charlie's replacement, Private Foster, a young but resilient soldier who had quickly found his place among the platoon. "Can you believe it, Tommy?" Foster said, his eyes wide with the thrill of the news. "Paris. We're actually going to see Paris."

Tom nodded, a smile breaking through the stoic front he'd maintained for so long. "Yeah. It feels almost... unreal. We've been through so much, and now... this is it. The chance to make history."

They spent the rest of the day preparing, checking their gear, making sure their rifles were clean, their ammunition stocked. There was a renewed sense of purpose in every movement, a spring in their steps as they went about the familiar routines. For once, the exhaustion that weighed on them felt lighter, tempered by the excitement of what lay ahead.

The evening brought a quiet sense of camaraderie as the men gathered around, sharing stories of home, of friends and family waiting for them. The thought of seeing Paris—the famed city of light, with its grand boulevards and historic monuments—lifted their spirits, bringing them back, even if just for a moment, to the lives they had left behind.

Captain Harris joined them by the fire, his usual stern gaze softened by the moment. "I know you're all excited, but remember, we're still at war," he said, though even he couldn't suppress the small smile tugging at the corners of his mouth. "We'll be moving in as part of a larger push, and the Germans won't let Paris go without a fight. Stay sharp, and don't lose focus."

The men nodded, their faces serious but still carrying that spark of hope. They knew the reality—they had fought long enough to understand that every victory came with a price. But Paris was different. The liberation of the city was more than just another battle; it was a beacon, a symbol of everything they'd fought for.

As night fell, Tom lay on his back, staring up at the stars, his mind drifting to thoughts of the city. He'd heard stories of Paris all his life, tales of its grandeur, its culture, the way it had captured the hearts of so many before the war. And now, to be part of its liberation felt surreal, like something out of a dream.

He thought of his fallen friends, of Red and Charlie, of the laughter and courage they'd shared, the moments that had carried them through the hardest times. He felt their presence with him, a quiet reminder of the sacrifices that had brought him here, of the promises he had made. They had given everything, and now, standing on the cusp of liberation, he knew that their spirits would march with him into Paris.

Around him, the camp settled into a restful silence, each man lost in his own thoughts, his own memories. They were soldiers, bound by duty, by loyalty, but they were also men with dreams, hopes, and a longing for peace. The thought of Paris, of seeing its streets and standing in the shadow of its monuments, brought those dreams to life, if only for a fleeting moment.

The first light of dawn began to creep over the horizon, casting a soft glow over the camp, and Tom rose, feeling a quiet resolve settle within him. The day had come. They were going to Paris.

Captain Harris assembled the platoon, his voice carrying the weight of the moment. "Today, we march toward history. Remember who you're fighting for. Remember those who have fallen. We are doing this for them, for France, for freedom. Now, let's go make history."

With those words, the platoon moved out, their steps confident, their hearts filled with a new purpose. They were soldiers, each one hardened by the battles they'd fought, but today, they marched with hope, with a renewed sense of purpose that lifted them beyond the pain, the weariness, the scars.

The road to Paris stretched out before them, lined with the remnants of war, the land scarred but resilient. As they moved closer to the city, civilians began to appear along the road, their faces lighting up as they saw the American soldiers, their expressions filled with gratitude and joy. They waved, some holding out flowers, others cheering, their voices carrying a message that needed no translation: *Welcome. Thank you. You're our heroes.*

Tom felt a lump rise in his throat as he watched the faces of the people they'd come to liberate. They were the reason they had fought, the reason they had endured, and now, as they approached the city, he felt a sense of fulfillment that reached beyond words.

The Eiffel Tower appeared on the horizon, a distant silhouette rising above the city, a symbol of hope, of freedom, standing tall against the sky. The sight of it brought a hush over the men, a collective intake of breath as they realized just how close they were. Paris was within reach, and with it, the end of their long, grueling journey across France.

As they moved toward the city, Tom felt the weight of every step, the presence of those who had fallen, of the friends he had lost. They were with him, a quiet strength that bolstered his resolve, that carried him forward. He knew that this was their victory too, that every life lost, every sacrifice made, had led them here.

Together, they would enter Paris, bringing with them the promise of liberation, the hope of peace. And as they approached the city, Tom felt a quiet pride settle within him, a gratitude that he had been a part of this, a witness to history.

Paris was waiting. And they were ready.

The platoon moved carefully along the outskirts of Paris, each man on high alert as they approached the city's edge. Although the news had spread that the Germans were beginning to withdraw, there was still a lingering tension, a quiet wariness in the air. The soldiers knew better than to trust rumors of an easy advance; they'd fought long enough to understand that until the city was officially secure, every street, every building, could hide unseen danger.

Tom glanced around, taking in the sight of the first Parisian buildings, their facades scarred from years of occupation. Even in their faded grandeur, they carried an elegance that struck him as both beautiful and haunting, reminders of a world untouched by war. As they moved deeper into the city, the grandeur of Paris began to reveal itself—a city filled with history and culture, now poised to reclaim its spirit of freedom.

Captain Harris kept his voice low but steady as he directed them forward. "Stay sharp, men. We don't know what to expect, but let's make sure we don't get caught off guard. Watch each other's backs, and keep your eyes open."

They advanced cautiously, weaving through the narrow streets, their footsteps soft on the cobblestone. The air was thick with anticipation, a quiet that was broken only by the distant hum of vehicles and the faint crackle of a radio from a nearby building. The civilians who had stayed behind peered out from behind curtains and doorways, their faces filled with a mixture of hope and apprehension.

Then, as they rounded a corner, Tom saw the first signs of German forces retreating. A line of trucks moved slowly down a side street, loaded with weary, resigned soldiers who cast glances over their shoulders at the advancing Americans. They made no move to engage, simply watching with hollow expressions as they left the city they had occupied for so long.

The sight filled Tom with an unexpected mix of relief and disbelief. After all the fierce battles, the brutal defenses, to see the Germans retreating was almost surreal. But there was no celebration yet; they still had to make sure the city was clear, secure. He exchanged a cautious glance with Private Foster, who nodded, his face a blend of anticipation and tension.

As they moved further into Paris, the civilians began to emerge from their hiding places. They stepped out into the streets, cautiously at first, as if still uncertain that the nightmare was finally over. Then, slowly, cheers began to rise, soft at first, but growing louder with each step the platoon took. Parisians gathered along the sidewalks, waving handkerchiefs, some holding small French flags that had been hidden away, waiting for this very moment.

The men of the platoon felt a shift, an energy they hadn't felt in months. The fatigue and weariness seemed to fade as the faces of the civilians filled with joy, relief, and overwhelming gratitude. People began to approach them, clasping their hands, murmuring words of thanks, their eyes glistening with tears of happiness.

Tom felt someone tug at his sleeve, and he looked down to see a young girl with wide, curious eyes. She held out a single flower, a daisy with petals slightly crumpled but still bright, a small token of gratitude. He took it gently, his throat tight as he smiled at her, a simple gesture that carried a depth of meaning he couldn't fully express. The people of Paris weren't just grateful; they were free.

The platoon moved carefully down one of the main avenues, the famous Parisian architecture towering above them, every building a reminder of the history they were now part of. In the distance, the Eiffel Tower rose against the sky, its silhouette iconic and unyielding, a symbol of resilience and beauty.

As they approached the center of the city, Captain Harris gave the signal to halt, his eyes scanning the crowd that had gathered. Parisians filled the street, their expressions jubilant, their voices rising in song and cheers. Some waved flags, others clapped their hands, the sound growing louder, echoing through the narrow streets and filling the air with a sense of liberation that felt almost tangible.

Then, a man stepped forward from the crowd, his suit slightly rumpled, a tricolor armband on his sleeve—a member of the French Resistance. He approached Captain Harris, his expression serious but grateful, and extended his hand.

"Merci," the man said simply, his voice thick with emotion. "Merci, to all of you."

Captain Harris nodded, clasping the man's hand. "The honor is ours," he replied quietly. "Paris is yours once again."

The man nodded, his gaze sweeping over the soldiers, his eyes filled with respect and gratitude. He stepped back, raising his fist in the air, a gesture of unity and resilience. The crowd responded with a cheer, their voices rising in unison, a collective cry of joy that reverberated through the city.

The men of the platoon took in the sight, their expressions a mixture of pride and relief. They had fought, bled, and lost friends along the way, but seeing the joy on the faces of the Parisians made it all feel worth it. This was the reason they had fought, the reason they had endured the hardship and the horror of war—to see this moment, to witness the rebirth of hope.

Tom glanced around, his eyes catching the sight of his comrades, each one marked by the battles they had fought, the scars they carried. He thought of Red, of Charlie, of the friends who hadn't made it to see this moment, and felt a quiet ache settle within him. But he knew they were here, in spirit, a part of the liberation, woven into the fabric of this victory.

The crowd began to move forward, surrounding the soldiers, embracing them, shaking their hands. Women kissed their cheeks, children climbed onto their shoulders, and old men clasped their hands, murmuring words of thanks, their voices thick with emotion. Tom felt overwhelmed, his heart full as he took in the faces of the people they had come to liberate, the people who were now free.

For the first time in months, a true sense of peace washed over him. The war wasn't over yet, but this victory, this moment in Paris, was a taste of what they had all been fighting for—a world free from oppression, a future where people could live without fear.

As the sun began to set, casting a warm glow over the city, the platoon continued their advance, moving carefully through the streets, ensuring that every corner, every building, was clear. But with each step, they were met not with resistance, but with open arms, with voices lifted in gratitude, with faces filled with joy.

And as Tom looked out over the city, the Eiffel Tower standing tall against the fading light, he felt a quiet pride settle within him. They had done it. They had brought freedom back to Paris, and with it, a piece of hope, a glimpse of the future they had all fought for.

Paris was free. And so were they.

As dusk settled over Paris, the streets came alive in a way Tom had never seen. Parisians poured into the streets, their voices rising in songs of celebration, their faces lit with smiles, laughter, and tears. The tension and fear that had held the city captive for years melted away, replaced by a wave of joy and relief so profound it was almost palpable. The platoon moved through the crowd, their hearts full as they took in the scenes unfolding around them, scenes that spoke to the resilience and strength of the people they had come to liberate.

The men of the platoon were swept up by the crowd, locals surrounding them, shaking their hands, clapping them on the backs, thanking them in voices thick with gratitude. Tom was nearly pulled off his feet as he was hugged by an elderly woman who, with tears in her eyes, thanked him over and over, calling him a hero. He didn't have words to respond, only managing a quiet "You're welcome" as he hugged her back, moved by her emotion.

A small boy darted out from the crowd, waving a tiny tricolor flag, his eyes bright with wonder as he approached the soldiers. Tom knelt down, smiling as the boy extended the flag to him, his face beaming with pride.

"Merci, monsieur," the boy said, his voice a mix of shyness and excitement. "Thank you for bringing us freedom."

Tom accepted the flag, his throat tight, and he ruffled the boy's hair. "Thank you," he replied softly. "You're braver than you know."

Nearby, Captain Harris was surrounded by a group of young men and women from the French Resistance. They embraced him and his men, their eyes alight with respect and gratitude. The captain, normally so composed, looked visibly moved, his shoulders relaxing as he spoke with them, nodding as they recounted stories of their struggle, of the hardships they had endured under occupation. There was a mutual understanding in their voices, a recognition of shared sacrifice.

The evening wore on, and the celebration only grew. Someone produced a bottle of champagne, and as it was passed around, the pop of the cork was met with cheers. Laughter filled the air, mingling with the sound of singing, as locals and soldiers alike toasted to the liberation of Paris. Tom found himself laughing with them, his heart lighter than it had been in months, the weight of the war momentarily forgotten.

He looked around, catching sight of Foster dancing with a young woman who had placed a wreath of flowers on his head, her laughter echoing through the street as she spun him in circles. Nearby, another soldier had his arms around two elderly men, who were singing an old French folk song, their voices slightly off-key but filled with joy. The resilience of the people, their ability to find happiness after everything they had endured, moved Tom deeply. They were stronger than any army, their spirits unbreakable.

As the night deepened, candles and lanterns began to appear in the windows of homes and shops, casting a warm glow over the streets. It was a quiet, defiant act, a return to light after years of darkness. The sight of it, the simple act of lighting a candle, brought a lump to Tom's throat. For so long, these people had lived in the shadows, but tonight, they reclaimed their city, their lives, and their hope.

A man approached Tom, carrying a battered accordion, its paint chipped but its sound rich and soulful. With a nod, he began to play, the notes soft and mournful, carrying a melody that spoke of resilience, of survival, of the quiet courage that had kept Paris alive. The crowd fell silent, each person lost in the song, their faces reflecting memories of hardship, of loss, but also of hope.

The accordion player finished, and for a moment, there was only silence, a quiet respect for all that had been lost, for all that had been endured. Then, as if on cue, the crowd erupted in applause, the cheers rising again, louder and more joyful than before. Paris was alive, its spirit unbroken, and the people celebrated not just the end of occupation, but the beginning of something new.

Tom felt a hand on his shoulder and turned to see Captain Harris, who gave him a small, knowing smile. "We did good here, Tom," he said, his voice low but filled with pride. "This... this makes it all worth it."

Tom nodded, unable to find words, his heart full as he looked out over the crowd, the faces of the people they had freed. He thought of those who had fallen along the way, of Red and Charlie, of the friends who hadn't made it to see this day, and felt a quiet gratitude settle over him. They were here in spirit, a part of this victory, woven into the joy and resilience of the people around them.

The celebration continued late into the night, the streets filled with music, laughter, and song. As the first light of dawn began to break over the city, casting a soft glow over the buildings, the people of Paris began to drift back to their homes, their voices quieting, their faces carrying a contentment, a peace that had been absent for too long.

Tom stood with his comrades, watching as the city settled into the early morning calm. The Eiffel Tower stood tall against the pink and orange sky, a symbol of endurance, of beauty, of a city that had weathered the storm and emerged stronger. They had fought for this, for the freedom to live without fear, for the right to celebrate, to hope, to love.

As they prepared to return to their camp, Tom took one last look at the city, at the people who had welcomed them with open arms, who had shown them the true meaning of resilience. He knew that this night, this memory, would stay with him forever—a reminder of why they had fought, of the strength of the human spirit.

Paris was free, and so were they. And in the faces of the people, in the warmth of their embraces, Tom felt a sense of peace that would carry him forward, a reminder that even in the darkest times, there was light. They had been part of history, but more than that, they had been part of something deeply human, something that transcended borders and battlefields.

As the sun rose over Paris, Tom and the platoon made their way back, their hearts full, their spirits renewed. They had seen the resilience of a city, the courage of a people, and they carried that strength with them, a strength that would guide them through whatever came next.

As the days passed in Paris, the American platoon found themselves working side by side with members of the French Resistance, helping to secure the city and clear out any remnants of German forces that lingered in hiding. It was a task that brought the two groups together, forging a bond that went beyond language or nationality—a kinship born from shared struggle, resilience, and sacrifice.

In a quiet courtyard one evening, the Americans gathered with the French fighters, the tension of battle giving way to a rare moment of camaraderie. Lanterns flickered around them, casting soft shadows over faces that were marked by both exhaustion and relief. A few crates had been pulled together to form makeshift tables, and someone had managed to find a bottle of wine, its label faded but its contents filling their cups with a warmth that cut through the autumn chill.

Captain Harris sat with a Frenchman named Jacques, a tall, wiry man with a rough face and sharp eyes that spoke of years spent fighting in the shadows. Jacques had been a leader in the Resistance, organizing missions, gathering intelligence, and helping his people survive under the harsh grip of occupation. His voice carried a quiet authority as he recounted stories of daring raids, of late-night sabotage, of whispers exchanged in darkened alleys.

"We did what we could with what we had," Jacques said, his accent thick but his words clear. "Sometimes, all we had was a handful of bullets and a bit of courage. But that was enough. We knew we had to fight, even if it cost us everything."

Tom listened intently, his heart heavy with respect. He had seen firsthand the price of war, but hearing Jacques' story, he felt a new appreciation for the strength it took to resist, to keep fighting even when surrounded by an enemy that seemed insurmountable.

Jacques turned to Tom, his gaze steady. "And you, my friend. You've seen much, I'm sure. The beaches, the towns, the fields... You have fought your own battle, and it has brought you here, to our city."

Tom nodded, his gaze dropping to his cup. "Yeah... we've been through a lot. Lost good men along the way." He paused, a flicker of memory flashing in his mind—Red's laughter, Charlie's steady hand on his shoulder. "But I think they'd be proud to see this. To know that, somehow, we've all made it here."

A woman from the Resistance, Isabelle, nodded from across the table. Her eyes were tired, but they held a fierce pride. "We owe you our gratitude, all of you," she said, her voice carrying a quiet strength. "You gave us hope, showed us that we weren't alone. For years, we felt forgotten. But when we saw you coming... it felt like a miracle."

Foster, sitting beside Tom, raised his cup with a grin. "Here's to miracles, then," he said, his voice light but his expression sincere. "And here's to all of you—the bravest folks I've ever met."

The Americans and the French lifted their cups in a toast, a quiet but powerful gesture of unity, of mutual respect. As the wine flowed, so did the stories, each man and woman sharing memories, both bitter and sweet, their voices filling the courtyard with a warmth that was rare in times of war.

One of the younger Resistance fighters, Philippe, leaned forward, his eyes bright with admiration as he spoke to Tom and Foster. "You know, when I was a boy, I dreamed of being a soldier. But when the Germans came, that dream became something different. I didn't want to be a soldier anymore. I just wanted to be free."

Tom nodded, understanding the weight of Philippe's words. "I think that's what we all wanted," he replied softly. "To be free. To live without looking over our shoulders, without worrying about what's around the corner."

Isabelle's expression softened as she looked at Tom, her gaze filled with an understanding born from shared pain. "And now, because of you, we can do that again. We can walk through our own streets without fear. You gave us that gift, and for that, we can never thank you enough."

They fell into a companionable silence, the weight of her words settling over them like a blanket, warm and comforting. The Americans and the French shared looks, each side seeing in the other a reflection of their own resilience, their own sacrifices. They were different in many ways, but they were bound by the same purpose, the same desire for peace, for a life where they could leave the darkness of war behind.

Jacques raised his cup again, his voice carrying a quiet solemnity as he spoke. "To those who have fallen," he said, his gaze sweeping over the group, his eyes softening. "To the friends we've lost, the loved ones who will never see this day. We carry them with us, each and every one."

The men and women around him nodded, their faces reflecting memories of those they had left behind. Tom thought of Red and Charlie, of the laughs they'd shared, the silent promises they'd made to each other. They were gone, but they were here too, in the resilience of the French, in the unity of the moment, in the quiet pride that had brought them all to this place.

They toasted to the fallen, each sip a quiet tribute to those who had given everything, a vow to honor their memory by fighting for the peace they had dreamed of. The night grew darker, but the warmth of the fire, the shared stories, and the unspoken bond between them kept the chill at bay.

As the evening wore on, they shared more stories, exchanged more laughs, and in the quiet moments, they reflected on all that had brought them to this point. They were soldiers, yes, but they were also people—people who had fought, bled, and sacrificed for a future they could only glimpse.

Before parting for the night, Captain Harris placed a hand on Jacques' shoulder, his voice filled with respect. "We may come from different places, but tonight, we're brothers. We've shared a journey, and we won't forget it."

Jacques nodded, his face solemn but his eyes alight with gratitude. "Nor will we, Captain. No matter what comes next, we will always remember this night, and those who made it possible."

As the platoon and the Resistance fighters exchanged farewells, Tom felt a quiet peace settle within him. They were not alone; they had never been alone. In every face he saw that night, in every handshake and embrace, he found a piece of himself, a reminder of the strength that had carried him this far.

Together, they had faced the darkness. Together, they would carry the memories of those they had lost, the friendships they had forged, and the hope that had brought them through. And as they returned to their quarters, he knew that this bond, this brotherhood, would stay with him forever—a light that would guide him, no matter where the road might lead.

In the days following the liberation of Paris, the platoon was granted a brief respite. They were housed in a small, quiet barracks on the outskirts of the city, away from the noise and excitement of the celebrations. For the first time in months, the men found themselves with a rare luxury—time to rest, to sleep, and to simply be.

Tom woke to sunlight streaming through a window, the warmth gentle against his face. He lay there for a moment, savoring the softness of the bed beneath him, the quiet calm of the morning. The sounds outside were peaceful—the occasional distant laugh, the chirping of birds, the soft hum of voices in conversation. It was a stark contrast to the gunfire and explosions that had filled his days for so long, and he felt almost disoriented by the stillness.

He sat up slowly, stretching, his muscles sore and tired, a reminder of the months he'd spent pushing himself to the edge. Around him, his comrades were stirring, each one waking with a similar mixture of relief and disbelief. It was strange to have nothing immediate to prepare for, no orders waiting, no sense of impending danger. They had a chance to breathe, if only for a moment.

After breakfast, Tom wandered outside, drawn by the quiet beauty of the day. He found a small, shaded spot beneath a tree and sat down, his gaze drifting over the landscape, the rooftops of Paris visible in the distance. The Eiffel Tower stood tall against the skyline, a symbol of endurance, a reminder of the resilience that had brought them here. He could hardly believe they'd made it, that after all they'd been through, they were finally able to see the city in peace.

Captain Harris joined him after a while, settling down beside him with a weary sigh. The captain's face was lined with exhaustion, but there was a glimmer of satisfaction in his eyes, a quiet pride that hadn't been there before.

They sat in silence for a while, each man lost in his own thoughts, the weight of the journey they'd shared settling between them.

"It feels strange, doesn't it?" Harris said eventually, his voice low and thoughtful. "To be here, to have time to rest. Part of me keeps waiting for the next call to action."

Tom nodded, his gaze fixed on the skyline. "Yeah. I can hardly believe it's real. Paris was... it was everything we'd been fighting for. It makes all the sacrifices feel worth it, but..."

He trailed off, and Harris nodded, understanding the unspoken words. "But we know it's not over. We still have a long way to go, and more battles to face."

The reality of it settled heavily on them. The liberation of Paris was a monumental victory, but it was just one part of a larger war, a struggle that stretched across continents and showed no signs of ending soon. Tom knew that they would be called back into the fray, that there would be more blood, more loss, and more sacrifices. The thought was sobering, a reminder that their journey was far from complete.

Around them, the other men were similarly lost in reflection. Some were sharing quiet conversations, voices soft as they spoke of friends lost, battles endured, and memories that would stay with them forever. Others sat alone, their faces turned toward the sun, eyes closed as they soaked in the warmth, holding on to this brief moment of peace.

Foster approached, sitting down beside Tom and Harris with a faint smile. "Can't remember the last time I just sat like this," he murmured. "Feels... good, you know? Like we've found a bit of ourselves again."

Tom smiled, a small but genuine expression. "Yeah. Feels like we're human again. Not just soldiers."

They sat in a comfortable silence, each man reflecting on what they'd been through, what they'd lost, and what they'd gained. For Tom, the memories of Red and Charlie were close, their voices, laughter, and steady presence etched into his mind. They were gone, but he carried them with him, a quiet strength that would guide him through whatever came next.

As the afternoon wore on, the men found small ways to pass the time. Some wrote letters, their words filled with stories of Paris, of the joy they had felt in liberating the city. Others played cards, laughing and joking, their camaraderie strengthened by the knowledge of all they had shared. There was a lightness in the air, a sense of renewal, of hope that hadn't been there before.

In the evening, as the sun began to set, the platoon gathered around a small fire, sharing stories in low voices. They spoke of home, of the people they missed, of the simple pleasures they dreamed of—hot meals, warm beds, the embrace of family. The war had taken so much from them, but it hadn't taken their dreams, their hopes, or their resilience.

Captain Harris addressed them, his voice steady but filled with a quiet resolve. "We've been given this time to rest, to find ourselves again. But remember, this isn't the end. The war isn't over. We have a duty to finish what we started, to see it through, for all those who can't."

The men nodded, their faces reflecting a mix of determination and acceptance. They understood the truth of his words, the reality that awaited them beyond this moment. But they also understood that they would face it together, that they were more than soldiers—they were a brotherhood, bound by shared sacrifice, by courage, and by a commitment to each other.

As the night deepened, Tom looked around at his comrades, each one marked by the battles they'd endured, the friends they'd lost, the memories that would stay with them. They were warriors, yes, but they were also men who had tasted freedom, who had seen the light at the end of the tunnel, if only for a fleeting moment.

And in that moment, Tom felt a quiet peace settle within him, a resolve that would carry him through the trials yet to come. He would fight for those who couldn't, for those he had lost, for the dream of a world free from war.

They had a long road ahead, but they would walk it together, side by side, their bond unbreakable, their purpose clear. They were soldiers, brothers, and they would see it through to the end. And as he looked out over the city of Paris, its lights shimmering against the night sky, Tom knew that they would endure, that they would carry this moment with them, a light that would guide them through whatever darkness lay ahead.

Chapter 6: Crossing the Siegfried Line

The chill of autumn had settled over the countryside as the platoon gathered for their latest briefing, their faces a mix of determination and apprehension. They had celebrated the liberation of Paris, had shared a few brief days of rest, but now, the reality of the war's next stage weighed heavily on them. Ahead of them lay the Siegfried Line, Germany's formidable defensive barrier, stretching across the western border and bristling with concrete bunkers, tank traps, and artillery emplacements.

Captain Harris stood before a large map pinned to a makeshift easel, his face lined with tension. He traced the thick, red line that marked the German border, his fingers lingering over the maze of symbols indicating defensive positions. The Siegfried Line was known among soldiers as the "Westwall"—a series of interconnected fortifications stretching hundreds of miles, built to repel any attempt to invade German soil.

Harris's voice was steady, but there was no mistaking the gravity in his tone. "The Siegfried Line is unlike anything we've faced before. This isn't a city we can liberate or a village we can sweep through. It's a fortress, built to keep us out. The Germans know we're coming, and they're prepared to hold this line to the last man."

The men listened intently, their expressions shifting as the reality of the challenge ahead settled over them. The Siegfried Line was not just a defensive wall; it was Germany's final stronghold, a barrier that represented the line between occupied Europe and the heart of the Reich. Each soldier understood that crossing it would not only be dangerous but would also be a test of their resolve, their strength, and their ability to face fear head-on.

Foster leaned over, whispering to Tom, "I've heard stories about that line. Hundreds of bunkers, artillery everywhere, and enough tank traps to stop an army. They say even air support has a hard time breaking through it."

Tom nodded, his gaze fixed on the map. He'd heard about the Siegfried Line too, back home, stories of its towering "dragon's teeth"—pyramidal tank traps that jutted from the ground like rows of teeth, designed to immobilize armored vehicles. He'd heard of the bunkers dug into hillsides, hidden within dense forests, and the narrow trenches that snaked across the countryside. It was a fortress meant to repel invaders, to break the spirit of any who dared to cross it.

Captain Harris continued, his eyes scanning his men, gauging their reactions. "Our intelligence suggests that the Germans have reinforced their positions along this line, and they're digging in. They know this is their last defense. They've set up minefields, sniper nests, and anti-tank positions. Every step forward will be a fight, and every inch will be contested."

The weight of his words settled over them like a cold fog. The men exchanged glances, each one grappling with the challenge they were about to face. They had survived Normandy, had pushed through France and liberated Paris, but the Siegfried Line was different. It was Germany's last stand, a fortress that would test them in ways they hadn't yet experienced.

Harris's gaze softened, his tone shifting to one of quiet determination. "But I know you, men. I've seen what you're capable of. We've fought through hell together, and I know that each one of you has the courage, the grit, and the heart to face this. The Siegfried Line may be fortified, but it's not invincible. We will find a way through."

The platoon nodded, their faces set with a newfound resolve. They'd faced impossible odds before, had pushed through lines that had seemed unbreakable. The Siegfried Line was daunting, but they had each other, and that was the one thing that Germany's defenses couldn't weaken.

Captain Harris gestured to the map, pointing to a small town just east of the line. "Our objective is to breach the line near this area. The terrain is rough—dense forests, steep hills, and little cover. We'll be advancing under artillery fire, and we'll have to move fast to avoid being pinned down. Once we're through, we'll need to secure a foothold inside Germany, something we can hold and defend until reinforcements arrive."

Foster shifted uneasily, his voice quiet but firm. "So we're the tip of the spear."

"That's right," Harris confirmed, his eyes meeting Foster's. "We'll be among the first to cross into German territory. This line has held back every assault so far, but we're going to break through it, no matter what it takes."

Tom felt a surge of determination rise within him. They were being asked to do the impossible, to face an enemy entrenched in one of the most fortified lines in history. But he knew that this was the task they had trained for, the mission they had signed up to complete. They were soldiers, each one prepared to do whatever it took to see this war through to the end.

As the briefing concluded, the men began to prepare, checking their weapons, loading ammunition, adjusting their gear with a focus born from both fear and courage. Tom took a deep breath, his mind drifting to the memories of battles past, of friends lost, and of the promises he had made—to Red, to Charlie, to every man who had fallen along the way. They had all given so much to see this war through, and he knew that they would give even more before it was over.

Foster approached him, his face set with resolve. "Think we'll make it, Tommy? Think we'll break through?"

Tom looked at him, his expression serious but calm. "We've made it this far, Foster. We're not stopping now. That line might look unbreakable, but nothing's stopping us from getting through. We just have to stay sharp, stay together."

Foster nodded, a faint smile tugging at his lips. "Right. Together."

As they moved out, marching toward the edge of the forest that concealed the first defenses of the Siegfried Line, a quiet determination settled over the platoon. They knew that each step forward was a step closer to the heart of Germany, to the end of the war, to the peace they all longed for. But they also knew that this would be their hardest fight yet, a test of everything they had learned, every bond they had formed.

The dragon's teeth rose ahead, jagged concrete barriers jutting out of the earth, their presence stark and ominous against the autumn sky. Beyond them, the dark outline of bunkers and machine-gun nests loomed, silent but foreboding, waiting to unleash the fury of a nation defending its borders.

Tom took a deep breath, feeling the chill of the air, the weight of his rifle, the steady presence of his comrades beside him. They had faced fear before, had fought through it, and they would do it again. The Siegfried Line was just another obstacle, another line in the sand.

As they moved forward, Tom felt a sense of purpose settle within him, a resolve that burned bright against the shadow of the fortified line ahead. They would break through. They would see this war to its end, no matter what lay between them and victory.

The early morning mist clung to the ground as the platoon moved forward, their footsteps muffled by the damp earth. They were at the edge of the Siegfried Line, the German defensive stronghold that stretched out before them like a menacing labyrinth of concrete and steel. It was quiet, almost eerily so, as if the entire line were holding its breath, waiting for the Americans to make the first move. Each man knew that within minutes, that silence would erupt into a cacophony of gunfire and explosions.

Captain Harris raised his hand, signaling the platoon to halt. He pointed ahead to a series of pillboxes and machine-gun nests, their grey concrete structures barely visible amid the trees and brush. The pillboxes were half-buried in the earth, with small, narrow slits facing outward, allowing the Germans to fire while remaining nearly impervious to return fire. They were positioned strategically, with overlapping fields of fire, creating deadly kill zones that would be nearly impossible to cross without heavy casualties.

Tom scanned the landscape, his heart pounding as he took in the defensive positions. He could see the jagged rows of dragon's teeth in front of the pillboxes—concrete barriers designed to stop tanks and funnel troops into areas covered by machine guns. There was no easy way forward, no clear path that didn't leave them exposed to the enemy's guns.

Captain Harris's voice was low but steady as he gave the orders. "Listen up. We need to take out those pillboxes if we're going to make any progress. They've got overlapping machine-gun nests, so we'll be moving in teams. Squad A, you'll go left, drawing their fire. Squad B, you'll circle right and hit them with grenades. Squad C, stay here and provide cover."

Tom was part of Squad B, and he felt a surge of adrenaline as he prepared to move. The plan was risky; they'd have to get close enough to toss grenades into the pillboxes, all while avoiding the deadly fire from the machine guns. But they didn't have a choice. If they couldn't neutralize those defenses, they'd be pinned down indefinitely, and the line would hold.

"Stay low and move fast," Captain Harris said, his voice a quiet command that carried the weight of urgency and resolve. "Good luck, men."

With a nod, Squad A began to advance on the left, moving quickly and quietly through the brush, keeping low to the ground. Within seconds, the air erupted as the Germans opened fire, the sharp rattle of machine guns tearing through the silence. Bullets kicked up dirt and leaves, splintering branches, filling the air with the scent of gunpowder and the harsh clang of metal.

"Go, go!" Harris shouted, and Squad B surged forward, using the distraction to circle around the right side, moving closer to the pillboxes. Tom kept his head down, his heart hammering as he darted from cover to cover, feeling the rush of air as bullets sliced past him. Around him, his comrades moved with practiced precision, each man focused, each step calculated.

They reached a low ridge, just out of sight of the nearest pillbox, and crouched behind it, catching their breath as they prepared for the next push. Foster was beside Tom, his face pale but determined, his grip tight on his rifle. They exchanged a look, a brief moment of understanding, a silent promise to watch each other's backs.

"Grenades ready," Tom whispered, pulling one from his belt. He felt the familiar weight of it in his hand, the rough metal cool against his palm. He knew they'd have to time it perfectly; one mistake, and they'd be exposed to a deadly barrage of gunfire.

He signaled to the others, counting down with his fingers—three, two, one—and then they rose as one, each man pulling the pin and tossing his grenade toward the pillbox in a single, fluid motion. The grenades sailed through the air, landing just in front of the structure, their detonations erupting in a cloud of smoke and shrapnel.

The explosion rattled the pillbox, and for a moment, the machine-gun fire ceased. Seizing the opportunity, Tom and his squad advanced, pressing forward under the cover of the smoke. He could hear shouts from inside the pillbox, the sounds of the Germans scrambling, caught off guard by the sudden assault.

As they neared the pillbox, Tom dropped to one knee, his rifle trained on the narrow firing slit. A German soldier appeared, his face contorted with surprise, and Tom fired, the shot finding its mark. The soldier crumpled, and Tom moved forward, signaling to his squadmates to keep pressing.

They reached the pillbox, securing the entrance as the remaining Germans inside surrendered, their faces etched with fear and exhaustion. The fight had been quick, brutal, but they had taken the position. Tom felt a surge of relief, tempered by the knowledge that this was only the beginning. There were more pillboxes ahead, more machine-gun nests, more soldiers waiting to defend their homeland.

The rest of the platoon advanced, taking up positions around the captured pillbox. Captain Harris approached, nodding in approval as he assessed the scene. "Good work, men," he said, his voice steady. "But we're not done yet. There's another line of defenses up ahead, and they'll be ready for us."

The men nodded, each one feeling the weight of the task ahead. They had taken one pillbox, one small piece of the Siegfried Line, but the path forward was still treacherous, filled with obstacles and heavily fortified positions.

Every inch they gained would come at a cost, and they knew that the worst was yet to come.

As they moved out, the German defenses grew more concentrated, the fire more intense. They encountered another machine-gun nest, hidden behind a low stone wall, its gunner firing in controlled bursts, pinning down Squad A as they tried to advance. Tom and his squad circled around, using the trees for cover, moving carefully as they crept closer to the nest.

The gunfire was deafening, the rounds cutting through the air with deadly precision. Tom could feel the vibration of each shot in his bones, a constant reminder of the danger that pressed in around them. He signaled to Foster, who nodded, raising his rifle, his expression tense but focused.

They reached the edge of the wall, and Tom took a deep breath, counting down once again. Three, two, one—and then they sprang into action, tossing another set of grenades over the wall, the blasts sending plumes of dirt and smoke into the air. The gunfire ceased, and they moved in, rifles at the ready, securing the nest as the Germans inside surrendered.

Around them, the battlefield was a chaotic mix of smoke, fire, and shattered concrete. The Siegfried Line was a fortress, and every position was fortified, every bunker defended with a grim determination. The Germans fought with the desperation of men defending their homeland, their resistance fierce and unyielding.

But the platoon pushed on, each man driven by a resolve that matched the enemy's, a determination to see the line broken, to bring the war one step closer to its end. They moved from one position to the next, taking out pillboxes, clearing trenches, advancing inch by inch through the labyrinth of defenses.

By the time the sun began to set, they had made progress, but the cost had been high. They had lost men along the way, their faces now etched in memory, their sacrifice woven into the fabric of the battle. The line had been breached in places, but the fight was far from over, and they knew that the days ahead would be just as grueling, just as deadly.

As they regrouped, Tom looked around at his comrades, their faces marked by exhaustion, by the weight of what they had endured. They had faced the initial assault, had tasted the fury of the Siegfried Line, but they were still standing, still pushing forward.

Captain Harris's voice cut through the quiet, his tone a mix of pride and resolve. "We're breaking through, but we're not done yet. Rest while you can. We'll hit them again at first light."

The men nodded, their expressions determined. They had faced the worst the Siegfried Line had to offer, and they had come out on the other side. But they knew that the fight was far from over, that each day would bring new challenges, new losses, and new tests of their courage.

As Tom settled in for a brief rest, he felt a quiet resolve settle within him. They would keep fighting, keep pushing, no matter what lay ahead. The Siegfried Line was a fortress, but they were soldiers, and they would see it through to the end. Together, they would break this line.

The Siegfried Line was proving to be as formidable as its reputation suggested, with each bunker, trench, and tank trap meticulously designed to hold back the Allied advance. By the third day of battle, the platoon was feeling the strain, their numbers reduced, their bodies worn from the unrelenting combat. But they knew there was no turning back; they had to find a way through. Their survival—and the success of the mission—depended on it.

Captain Harris gathered the platoon in a shallow depression, hidden from the line of sight of nearby pillboxes. His face was grim, etched with exhaustion, but his eyes held a determined spark. "We need to think outside the box here, men. These fortifications were designed to repel any direct assault. We've lost good men trying to brute-force our way through, and that's not sustainable. We need to adapt."

The men listened intently, their expressions a mix of exhaustion and resolve. Each one understood that this wasn't just about firepower; it was about outthinking the enemy, finding ways to turn the seemingly impenetrable defenses of the Siegfried Line against itself.

Tom glanced over at Foster, who gave a small nod, as if to say he was ready for anything. They'd been through countless firefights, but this was different. This was a test of ingenuity, of strategy, and they'd have to dig deep to break through.

Captain Harris began outlining the plan. "We've got enough explosives left to make some real progress if we can place them strategically. But we're not going to use them just to blow up pillboxes. Instead, we're going to use the terrain—and the defenses themselves—to our advantage. Our goal isn't just to destroy, but to destabilize."

He gestured to a nearby hill, where the Germans had constructed a series of bunkers connected by trenches. "If we can breach the ground between those bunkers, we can use their own trenches to move through their line. We'll also rig some of the dragon's teeth with explosives to create openings wide enough for our vehicles."

Tom felt a spark of excitement. It was a bold plan, but it just might work. By creating gaps in the defensive line itself, they could move through without having to confront every fortified position head-on.

"Foster, Tom—you're on demolition detail," Captain Harris continued. "Your job is to plant charges on the first row of dragon's teeth. We'll use the resulting breach to move some of our forces forward under cover."

The two men exchanged a look of grim determination. It would be dangerous work, moving so close to the enemy line, but it was the best way forward.

As darkness fell, Tom and Foster gathered their explosives, each man carrying a satchel of carefully packed charges. They moved low and quiet, using the shadows to conceal their approach, their footsteps muffled by the damp earth. The dragon's teeth loomed ahead, their jagged concrete forms stretching out like rows of stone sentinels. Each one represented a carefully placed obstacle, designed to stop any vehicle or foot soldier from advancing unchallenged.

They reached the first row and crouched, pressing themselves against the cold concrete as they assessed their position. Tom signaled to Foster, and they began setting charges, working with quick, practiced movements, their fingers steady despite the tension that hung heavy in the air. Each charge was placed with precision, angled to maximize the impact and create a gap wide enough for their vehicles.

As they worked, a distant rumble of German artillery reminded them of the stakes, a low, ominous sound that reverberated through the ground. The Germans were dug in, but they were also nervous; the sounds of their movement and sporadic fire made it clear they knew the Allies were close.

With the charges in place, Tom gave Foster a nod, and they retreated to a safe distance. The rest of the platoon was waiting, their faces tense as they prepared for the next phase. Captain Harris raised his hand, signaling to detonate.

The explosions erupted in quick succession, a controlled but powerful series of blasts that shook the ground and filled the air with dust and debris. The dragon's teeth shattered, fragments flying as the gap opened in the line. They'd done it—there was now a breach wide enough for their vehicles to pass through, a way to penetrate deeper into the line.

But the Germans were quick to react. Almost immediately, machine-gun fire erupted from the bunkers above, cutting through the darkness, the bullets tearing through the air with deadly precision. The Germans had spotted the breach, and they were determined to defend it.

Captain Harris motioned to Squad C to lay down suppressive fire while Tom, Foster, and a few others prepared to advance. The platoon moved forward, using the newly created gap as cover, ducking low as they crept closer to the bunkers.

"Stay low," Tom whispered to Foster as they moved, his eyes fixed on the dark silhouettes of the bunkers ahead. They'd have to be quick, using the element of surprise before the Germans could fully regroup.

The platoon spread out, taking cover behind the remnants of the dragon's teeth and the uneven terrain, advancing with caution. Using the German trenches as Harris had planned, they slipped through the defenses, flanking the first machine-gun nest. Tom lobbed a grenade over the edge of the trench, the explosion sending a plume of smoke into the night. The machine gun fell silent, and the platoon pressed forward, clearing each position with calculated efficiency.

As they pushed deeper, they encountered another line of bunkers, these ones reinforced with thicker walls and overlapping fields of fire. Captain Harris signaled to change tactics. "We'll use their own tunnels. Get to the rear entrances."

The platoon split into small teams, each one moving along a separate trench, advancing toward the rear entrances of the bunkers. It was risky, moving through German-constructed trenches, but it offered cover and allowed them to bypass the main defenses.

Tom and Foster reached the rear of one of the larger bunkers, pressing themselves against the cold stone wall as they prepared to enter. Foster held his breath, his hand gripping his rifle tightly, as Tom checked the entrance. With a nod, they slipped inside, moving quickly and quietly.

The Germans inside were caught off guard, scrambling to respond as the Americans appeared in their midst. Tom and Foster fired, their shots precise, taking down the remaining defenders. Within moments, the bunker was theirs.

Outside, the rest of the platoon had done the same, securing each bunker, clearing each trench. They regrouped, each man feeling the thrill of their success tempered by the exhaustion that weighed heavily on them.

Captain Harris surveyed the ground they'd gained, his expression a mix of pride and exhaustion. "We adapted. We found a way through. That's what's going to get us past this line. Not brute force, but strategy."

The men nodded, their faces marked by a quiet satisfaction. They had outsmarted the defenses, turned the Siegfried Line's own fortifications against it. The line had been pierced, but they knew this was just the beginning. Each victory would demand new tactics, new strategies, and the willingness to adapt to whatever the enemy threw their way.

As they moved forward, preparing for the next assault, Tom felt a renewed sense of purpose. They were soldiers, yes, but they were also thinkers, problem-solvers, men who could adapt and overcome. The Siegfried Line was formidable, but they had proven that it was not unbreakable.

Together, they would continue, inch by inch, using every tactic, every skill, every ounce of ingenuity they had. And as they moved deeper into enemy territory, Tom knew that no wall, no line, could hold them back.

The advance through the Siegfried Line was brutal, a relentless gauntlet of fortified bunkers, machine-gun nests, and booby traps designed to halt their progress at every turn. The line had been pierced, but each step forward came with fierce resistance, and the ground they gained was paid for in blood.

Captain Harris led the platoon forward with a steady determination, his commands concise, his gaze sharp as he directed the men through the shifting landscape of debris, trenches, and half-collapsed bunkers. Every piece of cover was used, every inch of ground scrutinized. The air was thick with the smell of smoke and gunpowder, and the sounds of battle were relentless—the deafening crack of rifle fire, the thunderous blasts of artillery, the shouts and cries of men caught in the heat of combat.

Tom moved in tandem with Foster, both of them covered in mud and grime, their faces set with grim focus. The camaraderie they shared had become something unspoken, each of them reacting to the other's movements without needing words. They had fought side by side for so long that they knew each other's instincts, and it was that bond, that trust, that kept them alive as they pushed deeper into the line.

They approached a heavily fortified bunker, its concrete walls thick and weathered, with narrow firing slits that allowed the Germans inside to unleash a steady stream of gunfire on anything that moved. Captain Harris signaled for the men to take cover as he surveyed the position. There was no clear approach; the bunker was strategically positioned to cover all angles, and attempting a direct assault would be suicide.

"We'll need to flank it," Harris said, his voice steady. "Tom, Foster, you're with me. We'll circle around to the right while the others provide covering fire."

Tom nodded, checking his rifle, his fingers moving over the familiar grooves and scratches on the stock. They had done this countless times before, but the stakes always felt just as high. As the covering fire erupted, he and Foster moved swiftly, keeping low, using every scrap of cover they could find as they inched toward the bunker's blind spot.

The ground around them was littered with debris shattered concrete, broken weapons, the remnants of past assaults that had been repelled. They slipped into a shallow trench that led toward the rear of the bunker, pressing themselves against the walls as bullets whizzed overhead, the machine gun inside roaring with unrelenting fury.

When they reached the rear entrance, Tom held up a hand, signaling Foster and Captain Harris to hold. He listened, his heart pounding as he tried to gauge the movements inside. The Germans were focused on the front, their attention drawn by the covering fire from the rest of the platoon. With a nod, Tom moved forward, gripping his rifle tightly, and the three of them entered the bunker in swift, practiced movements.

The Germans inside turned in shock, scrambling to react, but Tom, Foster, and Harris moved quickly, firing with deadly precision. Within seconds, the bunker fell silent, the enemy soldiers slumped against the walls, their rifles slipping from their hands. The three men took a moment to catch their breath, the reality of the assault settling in, and then they signaled to the others, who advanced to secure the area.

But the victory was short-lived.

No sooner had they regrouped than the air was shattered by the scream of incoming artillery. The Germans, knowing their line was faltering, were throwing everything they had to halt the American advance. Shells exploded around them, sending plumes of dirt and shrapnel into the air, filling their ears with a deafening roar. Tom threw himself to the ground, his arms over his head as the blasts shook the earth.

He looked up to see some of his comrades lying motionless, their bodies broken by the relentless barrage. A wave of grief and anger surged through him, but there was no time to process it, no time to grieve. They had to keep moving, had to press forward before the Germans could regroup.

Captain Harris shouted over the noise, his voice filled with urgency. "Get up! We need to keep pushing forward!"

The platoon rallied, each man rising with a mixture of determination and exhaustion etched into their faces. They moved forward in staggered formations, darting from cover to cover as the artillery continued to rain down. The losses were mounting, each casualty a painful reminder of the cost of their progress, but they could not afford to stop.

They reached another line of dragon's teeth, their jagged edges barely visible through the smoke and dust. Foster looked at Tom, his face smeared with dirt, his expression weary but resolute. "How much more of this can we take, Tommy?"

Tom shook his head, his voice steady but grim. "As much as we have to, Foster. We didn't come this far to turn back now."

They worked quickly to place charges on the dragon's teeth, creating another breach for their vehicles to move through. As the explosions tore through the concrete, the men surged forward, using the smoke for cover as they advanced. But the Germans were waiting, and the gunfire resumed almost immediately, cutting through the haze with brutal precision.

The next few hours were a blur of chaos and blood, each moment a desperate struggle to survive, to take just one more step forward. They cleared trench after trench, bunker after bunker, their bodies weary but their spirits unbroken. The Siegfried Line was exacting a heavy toll, but they refused to be stopped.

Tom found himself fighting in close quarters, his rifle empty, his hands reaching for his bayonet as he faced a German soldier in a narrow trench. The man's face was contorted with fear and determination, a mirror of Tom's own, and for a brief second, their eyes met, each one recognizing the humanity in the other. But there was no choice, no hesitation—they were soldiers, and they fought with a brutal efficiency that left little room for mercy.

When the trench was clear, Tom leaned against the wall, his chest heaving, his hands stained with dirt and blood. Around him, his comrades moved with the same weary resolve, each one battered but unyielding. The line was breaking, inch by inch, but at a cost that weighed heavily on each of them.

By the time the sun began to dip below the horizon, they had made progress, but the losses were staggering. Men they had laughed with, shared meals with, were gone, their faces now etched in memory. The Siegfried Line had been breached, but the price had been high, and each man felt the weight of it pressing down on him like a shadow.

Captain Harris gathered the remaining men, his voice steady but filled with sorrow. "We've done what we came here to do. We've broken through, but we carry with us the memories of those who didn't make it. They fought with everything they had, and we honor them by finishing what they started."

The men nodded, their faces set with a quiet, shared grief. They had lost brothers, friends, men who had become family in the crucible of war. But they had also gained ground, had pushed through one of the most fortified lines in history, and they knew that their sacrifices had not been in vain.

As they settled in for a brief rest, Tom looked around at his comrades, their faces marked by exhaustion and loss, but also by a fierce determination. They had come so far, had endured so much, and they would carry on, if only to honor those who had fallen.

The Siegfried Line was behind them, but the journey ahead was still long, still filled with unknown challenges. They would face it together, with the strength they had found in each other, with the resilience that had carried them through the darkest moments.

And as Tom looked out over the shattered landscape, he felt a quiet resolve settle within him. They had paid a heavy price, but they would continue, one step at a time, until the end.

The Siegfried Line had fallen, its imposing fortifications now reduced to rubble, its bunkers emptied, its trenches abandoned. The platoon had broken through, pushing past the last line of German defenses that had once seemed insurmountable. The road ahead was clear, leading into the heart of Germany—a path they had fought and bled to open. And yet, as they stood on the battered ground of their hard-won victory, there was no cheer, no celebration. Only a heavy silence filled with the weight of all they had lost.

Tom stood with Foster near what had been the final stronghold, a half-destroyed pillbox jutting from the earth like a broken tooth. Around them, the remaining members of the platoon moved with a quiet purpose, checking weapons, gathering supplies, tending to wounds. They were a shadow of the force that had first approached the Siegfried Line, and each man's face was marked by grief, exhaustion, and a lingering disbelief that they had actually made it through.

Captain Harris walked among them, his steps slower, his gaze somber as he took in the aftermath. He stopped near Tom and Foster, giving them a nod—a small gesture, but one that carried a quiet pride and acknowledgment of all they had endured.

"We did it," Harris said, his voice low, the words more for himself than for anyone else. "We broke through the line. We did what they said couldn't be done."

Tom nodded, feeling the weight of those words settle in his chest. They had done it, had achieved what had seemed impossible. But as he looked around at the faces of his comrades, at the vacant expressions of those who had survived but would never be the same, he felt no triumph. Victory was theirs, but it came with an emptiness he hadn't expected.

The silence was broken by the distant rumble of artillery, a reminder that the war wasn't over, that there were still battles ahead. They had breached the Siegfried Line, yes, but Germany was not yet defeated. There was no end in sight, only the knowledge that they would be moving deeper into enemy territory, facing unknown challenges that would test them even further.

Foster leaned against the ruined pillbox, his gaze fixed on the horizon, his face etched with fatigue. "Doesn't feel like we won, does it?" he murmured, his voice heavy with sorrow. "Feels more like... we just survived."

Tom looked at him, nodding slowly. "Yeah. I thought breaking through would feel different. Like we'd feel... I don't know, some kind of relief. But all I can think about are the faces of the men who didn't make it."

They both fell silent, each man lost in memories of friends who had fallen along the way—Red, Charlie, and the others whose laughter, whose voices, now lingered as faint echoes in their minds. They had paid the ultimate price, their lives woven into the fabric of this victory, and Tom knew he would carry them with him, that each step forward would be a tribute to their sacrifice.

Captain Harris turned to address the platoon, his face marked with the same mix of pride and sorrow that they all felt. "We've accomplished something monumental here. Each one of you has fought with courage, with resilience, with a strength that goes beyond words. But I know that this victory comes with a cost, and that the weight of that cost is something we'll carry with us. We honor our brothers by moving forward, by finishing what they started."

The men nodded, their faces reflecting a shared understanding. They had come through the worst, had survived the impossible, but they were different now, changed in ways that went deeper than wounds or scars. They were bound not just by camaraderie but by a mutual grief, a kinship forged in the fires of war.

As they gathered their gear, preparing for the next phase of the mission, the sounds of distant cheers drifted toward them from the nearby lines where news of the breakthrough was spreading. Other units were celebrating, the sense of victory spreading like a wave through the ranks. But for Tom and his comrades, those cheers felt hollow, like the echoes of a joy that was out of reach.

They moved out, each man silent, his steps heavy as they left the shattered remains of the Siegfried Line behind. The path ahead was uncertain, a road that stretched into the unknown, and Tom felt a quiet unease settle over him—a feeling that this victory, as hard-fought as it was, would not be the end. There would be more battles, more losses, more moments that would test the limits of their strength.

As the platoon made its way down the road, Foster looked over at Tom, his expression serious. "Do you think we'll ever feel like ourselves again, after all this?"

Tom took a deep breath, his gaze distant. "I don't know, Foster. Maybe. But I think... I think we'll carry this with us for the rest of our lives. Every step, every victory—it's a part of us now. But maybe, when this is all over, we'll find some kind of peace. Maybe we'll make sense of it somehow."

They fell silent again, the weight of his words settling between them, a quiet acknowledgment of the truth they all shared. They were different now, each one changed by the battles they had fought, the friends they had lost, the memories that would stay with them forever.

As they walked, Tom felt a flicker of resolve—a promise to honor those who had fallen, to carry their memory forward, to see this war through to its end. The victory over the Siegfried Line was theirs, but it was a victory marked by loss, a triumph shadowed by grief. And though they marched on, there was a part of them that would always remain on that shattered ground, a part that had been left behind in the name of duty, of honor, of brotherhood.

They had broken through, but they would never be the same. And as they moved forward, each step filled with both pride and sorrow, they carried with them the quiet understanding that true victory would not come on the battlefield—it would come, someday, when the guns fell silent, when they could finally lay down their arms and remember those who had given everything for the cause of freedom.

Until then, they would continue, each step a tribute to the men they had lost, each battle a reminder of the cost of war, each victory a hard-won moment of resilience amid the darkness.

Chapter 7: The Battle of the Hürtgen Forest

<hr>

The Hürtgen Forest loomed ahead, its dense canopy casting long shadows over the narrow trails that snaked through the trees. The forest was thick with ancient pines and oaks, their branches interwoven like the bars of a cage. As the platoon made its way into the dense woods, the once-open fields of the Siegfried Line gave way to a dark, claustrophobic terrain that felt more like a trap than a battlefield.

The weather had taken a turn for the worse. Cold, damp air seeped through their uniforms, and a thin, unrelenting drizzle had begun to fall, coating everything in a fine mist that blurred the edges of their vision and dampened their spirits. The forest floor was uneven, tangled with roots and fallen branches that made each step treacherous. Mud clung to their boots, thick and heavy, sapping their energy with every movement.

Captain Harris led them forward, his face tense as he scanned the thick undergrowth, alert for any sign of movement. "Stay close and keep your eyes open," he ordered in a low voice. "Visibility's limited in here, and we're going to have to move slowly."

Tom kept his rifle ready, his gaze sweeping from side to side as he followed in line. Every sound seemed amplified in the silence of the forest—the snap of a twig, the rustle of leaves, the faint drip of water from the branches above. It was a far cry from the open battlefields they'd become accustomed to. Here, the enemy could be anywhere, hidden among the trees, watching them from the shadows.

Foster trudged beside him, muttering under his breath, "They didn't tell us we'd be fighting a whole forest too."

Tom gave a grim smile. "Feels like it's trying to swallow us whole."

The forest was a natural fortress, its thick canopy blocking out most of the light, casting everything in a dull, gray twilight. The dense trees offered endless cover for German snipers and machine-gun positions, creating a labyrinth of hidden dangers. The mud made it nearly impossible to keep their footing, and the cold seemed to settle in their bones, sapping their energy as they pushed forward.

As they advanced, they came across the remnants of earlier battles—abandoned foxholes, twisted barbed wire, and shattered helmets half-buried in the mud. It was a grim reminder that they were not the first to attempt this advance, and that the forest had already claimed many lives.

Captain Harris paused, gesturing for the platoon to take cover behind a cluster of fallen trees. "This place is crawling with defenses," he said, his voice barely more than a whisper. "The Germans have been dug in here for months. They know this terrain, and they're going to use every inch of it to their advantage."

The men exchanged wary glances, each of them feeling the weight of those words. The Hürtgen Forest wasn't just a battlefield; it was a natural fortress, one that the Germans had spent months fortifying. Every tree, every shadow, every patch of undergrowth could hide a trap, a sniper, or a machine-gun nest.

As they moved deeper into the forest, the drizzle turned into a steady rain, the drops cold and heavy as they seeped through their clothes. The path became slick, and the mud turned thicker, clinging to their boots, making every step a struggle. Visibility dropped even further, the mist swirling around them like a shroud, muffling sounds and distorting shapes in the distance.

Tom strained to see through the fog, his eyes constantly scanning the dense undergrowth, his body tense with the anticipation of an ambush. The forest was deathly quiet, the usual sounds of birds and rustling leaves conspicuously absent. The silence was unnatural, oppressive, pressing down on them like a weight.

Captain Harris raised a hand, signaling for them to halt. He listened, his face set, his eyes narrowed as he tried to pick out any sound, any movement that might signal the presence of the enemy.

Then, out of the silence, a sharp crack echoed through the trees—the distinct sound of a rifle shot.

"Down!" Harris shouted, and the men dropped to the ground, pressing themselves into the mud as another shot rang out, the bullet thudding into a tree trunk just feet away.

The Germans had been waiting.

The platoon scrambled for cover, ducking behind trees and fallen logs, their eyes darting through the mist as they tried to locate the enemy. The fog and rain made it nearly impossible to see more than a few feet in any direction, and the echo of the gunfire bounced off the trees, making it hard to pinpoint where the shots were coming from.

Tom pressed himself against a tree, his heart racing as he scanned the forest, searching for any sign of movement. The forest was a sniper's paradise, with countless vantage points and endless cover. He could feel the tension building, each man waiting, watching, knowing that the next shot could come from anywhere.

Captain Harris signaled for a small team to flank left, hoping to locate and neutralize the sniper. Tom, Foster, and a few others moved quietly through the underbrush, their footsteps muffled by the wet ground. Every step felt like a risk, every shadow a potential threat.

Suddenly, a burst of machine-gun fire erupted from a nearby thicket, sending splinters flying as bullets tore into the trees. Tom and Foster dropped to the ground, pressing themselves into the mud as the gunfire raked over them. They were pinned down, unable to move without exposing themselves to the deadly fire.

"Stay low!" Tom shouted over the roar of gunfire, his voice barely audible. "We need to find another way around!"

Foster nodded, his face pale but determined. "Feels like they're everywhere."

Captain Harris crawled over to them, his face set with grim resolve. "We need to smoke them out. If we stay here, we're sitting ducks."

He signaled to another soldier to toss a smoke grenade, the small canister sailing through the air and landing near the thicket. Thick plumes of smoke billowed out, creating a temporary screen that gave them a sliver of cover. Under the blanket of smoke, they moved forward, creeping through the underbrush as they advanced toward the machine-gun nest.

The smoke provided only temporary relief, and as it began to dissipate, the gunfire resumed, cutting through the haze with deadly precision. But the platoon pressed on, using the limited cover to inch closer to the enemy position.

Tom could feel his pulse pounding in his ears, his muscles tense as he moved. The forest felt alive around him, each tree and shadow holding its breath, waiting. He knew that the Germans were just as tense, their nerves on edge, their fingers on the triggers.

They reached the edge of the thicket, and Tom caught sight of the machine gun—a hulking piece of metal hidden behind a makeshift barricade of logs and branches. He signaled to Foster, and together they moved into position, preparing to strike.

In one swift motion, Tom tossed a grenade over the barricade, the explosion shattering the silence and sending debris flying. The machine-gun fire stopped, and they rushed forward, securing the position, finding the German soldiers inside either dead or wounded.

The rest of the platoon regrouped, their faces marked by relief but also by a growing apprehension. They had made it through the first encounter, but they all knew it was just the beginning. The Hürtgen Forest was vast, and the Germans had had months to prepare. Every inch of ground they gained would be contested, every step forward fraught with danger.

Captain Harris looked over his men, his expression a mix of pride and concern. "We keep moving," he said, his voice steady but weary. "This forest is unforgiving, but so are we. Stay close, stay alert, and don't let your guard down. We'll get through this, together."

The platoon nodded, each man bracing himself for the days ahead. They were in the heart of the Hürtgen now, and there was no going back. The forest loomed around them, its shadows deep, its silence heavy, and Tom felt a chill settle over him—a sense that the real battle was only just beginning.

They moved forward, each step a test of their resolve, each moment a reminder that they were entering one of the most grueling battles of the war.

The Hürtgen Forest was a place of shadows, of shifting shapes and whispered dangers. The dense trees pressed in on the platoon from all sides, their thick branches forming a canopy that blocked out the sky, leaving the forest in a permanent state of twilight. As the men pushed deeper into the woods, it became clear that this was more than just difficult terrain; it was a sniper's paradise, a place where every tree, every patch of undergrowth, could conceal a deadly threat.

Tom kept his rifle at the ready, his gaze sweeping constantly from side to side, his body tense with the anticipation of unseen danger. The forest felt alive with menace, each creak of wood, each rustle of leaves a potential threat. The Germans knew this terrain intimately and had taken full advantage of it, embedding themselves in the trees, using the natural cover to turn the forest into a deadly maze.

Captain Harris raised a hand, signaling the platoon to spread out and move with caution. They moved slowly, each step deliberate, their eyes scanning the treetops and shadows, every man aware that a single misstep could make him a target.

The first shot rang out with a sharp, echoing crack, breaking the silence and sending the men diving for cover. The bullet struck a soldier near the front of the line, and he crumpled without a sound, his body falling limp against the tree trunk. The men froze, pressing themselves against the ground or against the nearest tree, their faces pale as they tried to determine the sniper's location.

"Stay down!" Captain Harris shouted, his voice low but urgent. "They're watching us. Move slowly, use the trees for cover."

Tom's heart pounded as he pressed himself against a fallen log, his body hidden from view. He peered into the canopy, searching for any sign of movement, any hint of the sniper's position. But the forest was dense, the shadows deep, and the sniper was invisible—a ghost hidden among the branches.

Another shot cracked through the air, followed by a muffled scream as another soldier was hit. The men stayed low, fear tightening their throats as they tried to make sense of the attack. The sniper was skilled, his shots precise, each one finding its mark with deadly accuracy. It was clear they were dealing with someone who knew the forest intimately, who had spent months perfecting his craft.

"Tom, Foster—flank left," Harris ordered, his voice a calm anchor in the chaos. "Try to draw him out. The rest of you, keep moving forward. Stay low, and don't make yourself a target."

Tom nodded, signaling to Foster as they moved cautiously to the left, creeping from tree to tree, their movements slow and deliberate. They kept their bodies pressed against the ground, their rifles at the ready, each step a test of patience and nerve. The sniper could be anywhere, hidden among the branches, watching their every move.

They advanced in silence, inching their way around the trees, trying to circle behind the sniper's possible position. Every muscle in Tom's body was tense, his senses on high alert, his mind racing with possibilities. The forest was thick with hiding spots, each one a potential nest for the sniper who was picking them off one by one.

Suddenly, another shot cracked through the air, closer this time, and Tom saw a flash of movement high in the trees. He froze, signaling to Foster, his gaze fixed on a dark shape partially obscured by branches. The sniper was perched high above, concealed by leaves and branches, his rifle trained on the platoon below.

Tom raised his own rifle, steadying his aim, his finger tightening on the trigger. He took a slow, steady breath, blocking out everything but the shape of the sniper, his focus narrowed to a single point. With a calm precision born from experience, he squeezed the trigger.

The shot rang out, echoing through the forest, and the dark shape shifted, slumping slightly. The sniper fell, his body crashing through the branches before landing with a dull thud on the forest floor below.

Tom let out a shaky breath, relief flooding through him as he lowered his rifle. But the relief was short-lived; even as he turned back to the platoon, another shot cracked from somewhere deeper in the woods, the Germans revealing that they had more than one sniper hidden among the trees.

The platoon was pinned, each man pressed against the ground or crouched behind a tree, their faces pale as they scanned the shadows. The snipers had them at a disadvantage, the dense foliage offering little in the way of clear targets. Tom could feel the tension building, the weight of the forest pressing down on them, each moment filled with the knowledge that they were being hunted.

Captain Harris crawled over to Tom and Foster, his face set with grim determination. "We need to keep moving, keep changing position," he said quietly. "If we stay in one place, we're sitting ducks."

Tom nodded, glancing around, his gaze sweeping over the scattered shapes of his comrades. "How many of them do you think there are?"

Harris's jaw tightened. "Enough to make this hell for us. But they can't cover every angle. We'll split into smaller groups, try to flush them out."

The platoon split into pairs, each team moving carefully through the undergrowth, their movements slow and controlled, their eyes scanning every shadow. The forest felt alive with menace, each patch of darkness a potential threat. Tom and Foster crept forward, staying close to the ground, their nerves on edge.

As they moved, they heard the crack of another shot, followed by the faint rustle of movement as the Germans repositioned. The snipers were moving, shifting between vantage points, making it nearly impossible to pin them down. It was a deadly game of cat and mouse, and the Germans held the advantage.

Tom spotted a glint of metal through the trees—a rifle barrel, barely visible among the branches. He raised his own weapon, signaling to Foster, and together they moved into position, each one covering the other as they advanced. They were close, the sniper's position just ahead, but each step felt like a risk, each movement filled with the knowledge that one misstep could make them the next target.

They reached a patch of thick brush, positioning themselves on either side. Tom counted down silently, his heart pounding as he prepared to move. Three, two, one—and then he stepped out, raising his rifle, firing a quick, precise shot.

The sniper fell, his body slumping against the tree trunk, his rifle slipping from his hands. Tom let out a breath, the tension easing slightly, but he knew they weren't done yet. The Germans were well-prepared, and they wouldn't give up the forest easily.

The platoon regrouped, each man's face marked by exhaustion, by the weight of what they'd endured. They had made progress, had taken out some of the snipers, but the forest was vast, and there were more Germans hidden among the trees.

Captain Harris gathered them, his voice low but resolute. "We're going to keep moving, keep pushing forward. They have the advantage here, but we're not going to let them hold us back. Stay alert, watch each other's backs, and keep your heads down. We're not losing anyone else."

The men nodded, their faces set with grim determination. They knew the forest was deadly, that each step forward could bring them face-to-face with hidden enemies, but they had no choice. The only way out was through, and they would push forward, no matter the cost.

As they moved deeper into the forest, the shadows grew darker, the air colder. The Hürtgen was unforgiving, its dense foliage concealing threats that lurked just beyond sight, but they were soldiers, and they would see this through. They had survived snipers and ambushes, had pushed through the terror of the unknown, and they would continue, step by step, until they had cleared the forest or fallen trying.

And as they moved forward, each man felt the weight of the forest pressing down on him, a reminder that the Hürtgen was not just a battlefield—it was a test, one that would demand everything they had to give.

The days in the Hürtgen Forest began to blur together, each one a test of endurance, of willpower, of sheer survival. The constant, unyielding cold had seeped into their bones, the damp chill wrapping around them like a second skin, gnawing away at their strength. Every breath was a struggle, every movement a reminder of how exhausted they were, how depleted their bodies had become in this unforgiving landscape.

Tom pulled his coat tighter around him, but the thin fabric did little against the relentless cold. His fingers were numb, stiff from gripping his rifle for hours on end, his knuckles raw from crawling over rough ground and gripping cold steel. Around him, his comrades moved like ghosts, their faces pale, their eyes hollow with fatigue. They were all running on empty, their bodies weakened by days without proper rest, their spirits worn down by the constant threat of enemy fire and the gnawing fear of an unseen sniper's bullet.

Captain Harris crouched beside Tom, his voice low, steady. "We keep moving," he said, though even his voice carried a tremor of exhaustion. "We stay together and keep moving. We can't afford to stop for long, not here."

The platoon nodded, too tired to respond. The forest was as much their enemy as the Germans; the terrain, the weather, the isolation—they all worked together to wear them down, to make each step feel like a monumental effort. The rain had turned the ground into a thick, cloying mud that clung to their boots, slowing them down, making every step an exhausting effort. Their uniforms were soaked through, the fabric heavy with mud and water, adding extra weight to every movement.

Foster stumbled beside Tom, his face pale, his breath coming in short, ragged bursts. "How much further do you think we have to go?" he whispered, his voice barely more than a breath.

Tom shook his head, his own voice hoarse from days of cold air and quiet orders. "I don't know. Feels like we're barely making any progress."

They moved through the dense trees in single file, each man watching the back of the soldier in front of him, every sense tuned to the faintest sound, the slightest movement. The forest was alive with subtle noises—the rustling of leaves, the soft crack of a distant branch, the quiet patter of rain hitting the trees. It was a soundscape that kept them constantly on edge, a reminder that danger could strike at any moment.

The weight of the pack on Tom's shoulders felt unbearable, the straps digging into his shoulders as he trudged forward, his steps dragging through the mud. The cold had settled deep into his bones, sapping his energy, dulling his senses. He could see the exhaustion mirrored in the faces of his comrades, each one of them barely holding on, each step an act of willpower.

Captain Harris raised a hand, signaling for them to stop, and the men sank to the ground, their breaths visible in the frigid air. They didn't speak, each one too tired to waste energy on words. Instead, they focused on the simple act of staying warm, of holding onto what little strength they had left.

Tom took a shaky breath, feeling the cold air fill his lungs, sharp and biting. He tried to ignore the hunger gnawing at his stomach, the ache in his muscles, the constant, unyielding pain in his joints. He could feel himself reaching the limits of what his body could endure, but he pushed the thought aside, forcing himself to focus on survival, on putting one foot in front of the other.

A sound echoed through the trees—a distant crack, followed by the unmistakable rumble of an approaching storm. The men looked at each other, their expressions a mix of dread and resignation. A storm meant more cold, more rain, more misery. It was the last thing they needed, but they had no choice but to endure it.

Captain Harris motioned for them to set up a makeshift camp, knowing that they couldn't afford to keep moving in the worsening weather. The men huddled together beneath what little cover they could find, trying to shield themselves from the icy rain that had begun to fall, each drop piercing like needles against their exposed skin.

Tom sat with his back against a tree, pulling his coat as tight as he could around himself. His hands were shaking, his body shivering uncontrollably as he tried to keep warm. Foster sat beside him, his head bowed, his face drawn and pale.

"I don't know how much more of this I can take," Foster muttered, his voice barely audible over the sound of the rain.

Tom didn't respond. He didn't have the words, didn't have the energy to offer any comfort. All he could do was sit there, his eyes unfocused, his mind numb with fatigue. The forest felt endless, a prison that trapped them in a cycle of cold, hunger, and exhaustion, with no escape in sight.

The night wore on, the rain continuing to fall, the wind howling through the trees, adding to their misery. The ground was soaked, turning their temporary shelter into a muddy, freezing mess. Sleep was impossible; every time Tom's eyes closed, he was jolted awake by the cold, by the discomfort, by the fear of letting his guard down for even a second.

By dawn, the rain had stopped, but the cold remained, a biting chill that gnawed at them as they gathered their gear and prepared to move. Captain

Harris addressed them, his voice steady but weary. "We keep going. The sooner we get out of this forest, the better."

The men nodded, their faces set with grim determination. They were beyond hope, beyond comfort; all that remained was the drive to survive, to push forward one step at a time. They moved through the forest in silence, each man lost in his own thoughts, his own struggle to keep going.

As they advanced, the terrain grew steeper, the ground littered with roots and rocks that made every step treacherous. The mud clung to their boots, the weight pulling them down, slowing their progress. They stumbled often, their bodies weakened by days of cold and hunger, but each time, they picked themselves up, gritting their teeth and pushing forward.

The forest remained silent, oppressive, a place that seemed to swallow them whole, draining their energy, their hope. Tom could feel himself fading, his vision blurring, his mind clouded by exhaustion. But he forced himself to keep going, his steps steady, his focus narrowed to the single goal of survival.

They reached a small clearing, and Captain Harris signaled for them to stop, allowing them a few moments of rest. The men sank to the ground, their bodies slumping as they closed their eyes, taking shallow breaths as they tried to regain some strength.

Tom leaned back, his gaze fixed on the treetops above, the pale morning light filtering through the branches. He felt a strange sense of detachment, as if he were watching himself from a distance, a quiet acceptance of the harsh reality of their situation. They were trapped in this forest, fighting not just the enemy but the elements, their own exhaustion, their own limits.

But despite everything, they kept going. They were soldiers, bound by duty, by camaraderie, by the unspoken promise to survive together. And as they rose, gathering their gear, preparing to face another day of cold, of hunger, of unrelenting struggle, Tom felt a flicker of resolve—a quiet, unbreakable strength that came from the simple act of putting one foot in front of the other.

They would survive. They would keep moving, keep fighting, keep pushing forward through the Hürtgen Forest. Because that was all they had, the one thing they could hold onto in this dark, unforgiving place.

And as they disappeared once more into the shadows of the trees, they knew that they would keep going, no matter how many steps it took.

The Hürtgen Forest seemed to close in tighter with each passing hour, its thick trees and tangled underbrush forming an unyielding labyrinth of shadows. Visibility was limited to mere feet in front of them, the dense canopy blocking out most of the light, and the constant mist shrouding the forest in an eerie gloom. Every sound echoed off the trees, each rustle of leaves or snap of a twig keeping the men on edge. The fog drifted through the woods like a living thing, distorting shapes, turning every branch and shadow into a potential threat.

Tom moved carefully, his gaze fixed on the shifting shapes in the mist, his rifle at the ready. Around him, his comrades advanced with the same cautious steps, each man's face drawn and pale, their eyes hollow with exhaustion. They were soldiers, battle-hardened, but this was different. The Hürtgen was not just a battlefield; it was a place of psychological warfare, where the enemy was not always visible but was always present, always watching.

Captain Harris's voice was a low murmur as he gave orders, his tone calm but tense. "Keep tight, stay close to cover. They know we're here. Don't give them an easy target."

The Germans were using the forest to their advantage, launching ambushes from unseen positions, then melting back into the trees before the Americans could counterattack. It was a constant, relentless assault that sapped their energy, fraying their nerves. The feeling of being hunted settled over the platoon, pressing down on them like a weight.

A sudden burst of gunfire shattered the silence, the bullets tearing through the trees and splintering branches above their heads. The men dropped to the ground, pressing themselves against the mud as they searched for the source of the attack. The shots had come from somewhere deep within the fog, the muzzle flashes barely visible through the mist.

"Return fire!" Captain Harris shouted, his voice cutting through the chaos. The men opened fire in the direction of the attack, their shots piercing the fog, but the Germans had already repositioned, their figures disappearing into the shadows.

Tom's heart pounded as he scanned the trees, his grip on his rifle tight. He could feel the fatigue in his arms, the sting of his cold-numbed fingers, but he pushed it aside, focusing on survival. The forest was a maze, the fog turning each step into a risk, each movement a potential target. They were fighting blind, shooting at phantoms, each gunfight as disorienting as the last.

The Germans struck again from a different angle, their shots carefully timed to catch the platoon off guard. A soldier near Tom cried out and fell, clutching his shoulder as blood seeped through his fingers. Foster was beside him in an instant, dragging him behind cover as the rest of the men returned fire, their shots a futile attempt to pin down an enemy that moved like shadows.

Tom felt a surge of frustration rise within him, a helpless anger at the situation they were trapped in. The Germans were using guerrilla tactics, striking swiftly and fading away before the Americans could get a fix on their positions. It was a constant, unrelenting game of cat and mouse, and the platoon was losing men to an enemy they could barely see.

Captain Harris crawled over to Tom, his face set with grim determination. "They're trying to break our line, keep us off balance. We need to keep moving, stay unpredictable."

Tom nodded, understanding the logic even as exhaustion weighed on him. They had to keep pushing forward, keep changing their position, even if it felt like they were stumbling blind through a nightmare. Staying still meant giving the Germans an advantage, allowing them to set up their next ambush.

They moved in small groups, each man covering the other as they advanced through the dense forest. The fog grew thicker, wrapping around them like a shroud, muffling sounds, turning even the closest trees into indistinct shapes. Tom's eyes strained to see through the mist, his senses heightened by the ever-present threat.

The Germans attacked again, this time from an elevated position, the bullets raining down from above. The men scrambled for cover, pressing themselves against trees and rocks, their faces tight with fear and frustration. The enemy seemed to be everywhere and nowhere at once, using the forest as both shield and weapon.

Tom raised his rifle, scanning the treetops, searching for any sign of movement. He caught a glimpse of a figure, barely visible through the branches, and fired, the shot echoing through the forest. There was a faint cry, and the figure slumped, disappearing from view.

But there was no time to process the small victory. Another shot rang out, and another soldier fell, his body collapsing into the mud. The platoon was scattered, each man isolated, relying on instinct and training as they navigated the deadly maze of the forest.

The fog was thickening, turning the world into a monochrome haze where friend and foe alike were reduced to shapes and shadows. Tom felt his grip on reality slipping, the constant fear and fatigue clouding his mind, making it hard to distinguish between what was real and what was imagined. Every shadow felt like an enemy, every sound a potential threat.

"Stay together!" Captain Harris shouted, his voice barely audible over the gunfire and the crackling of branches. "Don't lose sight of each other!"

But it was easier said than done. The forest was swallowing them, breaking them apart, isolating them. Tom could barely see Foster, who was only a few feet away, his figure blurred by the fog, his face strained as he fought to stay focused.

They pressed on, each step an act of willpower, each movement a struggle against exhaustion and fear. The Germans continued their attacks, their shots precise, each one claiming another member of the platoon. It felt like a battle against the forest itself, as if the trees and mist were conspiring with the enemy to wear them down, to drain them of every last ounce of strength.

Tom's breath came in shallow gasps, his chest tight with a mix of terror and fatigue. He could feel his body reaching its limits, his mind teetering on the edge. But he pushed forward, driven by a stubborn determination, a refusal to give up.

At last, they reached a small clearing, a brief reprieve from the relentless assault of the trees and shadows. The men collapsed, dropping to the ground, their faces marked by exhaustion, their eyes hollow. They had survived, but just barely, each one of them bearing the scars of the day's battle.

Captain Harris moved among them, his voice calm but weary. "We're going to keep pushing, but we can't afford any more losses. We're fighting blind out here, so we stay close, we stay alert, and we move as one. We can't let them break us."

The men nodded, their faces set with a grim determination. They had come too far to give up now, even if it felt like the forest itself was working against them. They would continue, one step at a time, fighting blind, relying on each other to survive.

As they prepared to move out, Tom glanced around at his comrades, their faces barely visible through the fog, each one marked by the strain of survival. They were exhausted, battered, but they were still here, still fighting.

And as they stepped back into the forest, back into the shadows and the mist, Tom felt a flicker of hope—a quiet resolve that no matter how relentless the enemy, how unforgiving the terrain, they would endure. They would keep going, keep fighting, until they found their way out of the Hürtgen, or until they could go no further.

The order to pull back came just after dawn, when the fog was at its thickest, clinging to the forest like a shroud. The Hürtgen had proven too costly, its dense woods and hidden enemy positions turning every inch of ground into a deadly fight. The platoon had endured days of relentless ambushes, sniper fire, and brutal close-quarters combat, but the losses were staggering. They could no longer sustain the advance. The forest was claiming them, and it was time to retreat.

Tom felt a cold pit form in his stomach as Captain Harris delivered the order in a hushed, heavy tone. "We're pulling out," Harris said, his face marked by exhaustion and grief. "We can't hold this ground any longer. We leave immediately. Stay quiet, stay close, and keep moving."

The remaining men gathered their gear in silence, each one weighed down by the losses they had endured. The platoon that had entered the Hürtgen was nearly unrecognizable now, thinned and battered, their spirits as scarred as their bodies. Some faces were missing altogether, the absence of fallen friends a silent testament to the cost of the forest.

Tom glanced at the empty spots where men he had fought beside, men he had laughed with, should have been. Red, Charlie, Stevens, and others who had come into this place full of life and resolve were now memories, left behind in the mud and shadows of the Hürtgen. He felt the ache of their loss like a physical weight, a constant reminder of the price they had paid for every step they had taken.

As they began the slow, painful withdrawal, Tom kept his gaze forward, his rifle clutched tightly in his hands. He was too numb to speak, his mind dulled by exhaustion and grief. Around him, the survivors moved with the same heavy silence, their eyes hollow, their faces pale. They had come through hell, but not all of them had made it.

The fog was thick, swirling around them, obscuring their vision as they retraced their steps through the dense undergrowth. The forest seemed more oppressive than ever, the trees towering above them like silent witnesses to the carnage they had witnessed. The quiet was unnerving, broken only by the occasional distant crack of gunfire—a reminder that the Germans were still out there, still watching.

Captain Harris led the way, his steps steady but slow, his gaze constantly scanning the trees for any sign of movement. He was a man carrying the weight of command, the responsibility of every man he had lost pressing down on him. His face was set, his expression hard, but there was a sadness in his eyes that none of them had seen before.

As they moved, Foster fell into step beside Tom, his face pale and drawn, his gaze distant. "I can't believe we're leaving them," he whispered, his voice thick with emotion. "All those guys... just left out here."

Tom swallowed, the words catching in his throat. "I know. But we don't have a choice. We'd be leaving more behind if we tried to stay."

They pressed on, each step taking them farther from the battleground that had become their graveyard. The ground was littered with the remnants of the fight—abandoned helmets, spent casings, the broken branches and churned mud where men had fallen. Every so often, they passed a familiar face, a comrade who had given everything in the fight to hold the line. There was no time to stop, no time to pay respects, only a brief, silent acknowledgment before they had to keep moving.

The Germans, sensing their retreat, began harassing them with sporadic gunfire, shots ringing out from the trees. Each crack sent the men scrambling for cover, the instinct to survive kicking in even as their bodies cried out for rest. It was a slow, painful march, each encounter with the enemy a reminder that they weren't yet free of the forest's grasp.

Tom's legs felt like lead, his vision blurred by exhaustion, his mind numb with grief. But he forced himself to keep moving, to put one foot in front of the other. Around him, the men were doing the same, each one driven by the quiet determination to survive, to make it out of the Hürtgen alive.

As they neared the edge of the forest, the fog began to lift slightly, revealing patches of open ground where the trees thinned out. The sight of the clearing brought a faint flicker of hope, a reminder that the nightmare was almost over. They were so close to freedom, to leaving the Hürtgen behind, even if it meant leaving so much of themselves within its shadowed depths.

Captain Harris stopped at the edge of the tree line, turning back to look at the men who had made it, his expression a mixture of relief and sorrow. "We're out," he said quietly, his voice heavy. "But we don't leave them behind. We carry them with us. Every one of them."

The men nodded, each one feeling the truth of his words settle deep within them. They had come through the Hürtgen, but they would never truly leave it. The memories of those they had lost, the friends they had buried in the mud, would stay with them, woven into their very souls.

As they moved into the open ground, leaving the forest behind, Tom felt a wave of conflicting emotions—a mixture of relief, grief, and guilt. They had survived, but at a cost that weighed on him more heavily than any battle he had fought. The Hürtgen had taken so much, and though he was free of its grasp, he knew he would carry the scars forever.

Foster walked beside him, his gaze fixed on the ground. "Feels like we're leaving a piece of ourselves back there," he murmured.

Tom nodded, his throat tight. "We are. But we're carrying them with us too. We won't forget."

They reached the safety of the Allied lines, where medics and other soldiers waited, their faces grim as they took in the battered, hollow-eyed men emerging from the forest. The survivors were given water, blankets, a brief respite from the cold. But even as they settled, each one felt the weight of the losses they had endured, the knowledge that they had left friends behind in that dark, unforgiving place.

As Tom sat, clutching a tin cup of lukewarm coffee, he looked back at the Hürtgen, its shadow stretching out across the land. The forest was quiet now, the fog drifting through the trees like a lingering ghost, a reminder of all that had happened within its depths. He knew that the men they had left behind would forever be a part of that place, their sacrifice woven into the soil, their memory a silent tribute to the cost of war.

They had made it out, but they would never truly leave the Hürtgen. It was a place that would live on within them, a memory they would carry for the rest of their lives—a reminder of courage, of sacrifice, of the friends they had lost.

And as Tom looked out over the forest one last time, he felt a quiet resolve—a promise to honor those who had fallen, to carry their memory forward, even as he left the Hürtgen behind. The battle was over, but the cost would linger, a weight that would remain long after the war had ended.

Chapter 8: The Battle of the Bulge

The winter had settled in with brutal force, blanketing the Ardennes forest in thick layers of snow and ice. The biting cold permeated everything, turning each breath into a cloud of frost, each movement into a struggle against the numbing chill. The men were exhausted, having just barely survived the ordeal in the Hürtgen Forest. The promise of a brief respite brought some relief, but the harsh winter conditions made even rest difficult.

Tom huddled in his foxhole, wrapped in every layer of clothing he could find. He clutched his rifle close to his chest, feeling the icy metal through his gloves. The cold was relentless, creeping into his bones, settling into his muscles, making every movement feel sluggish. Around him, the other men in the platoon sat in silence, their breaths visible in the frigid air, their faces drawn and pale.

Foster was beside him, rubbing his hands together to keep them warm. "Feels like this winter's never going to end," he muttered, his voice a soft rasp in the cold. "And we've barely got enough supplies to last through the week."

Tom nodded, his gaze drifting over the snow-covered landscape. "At least it's quiet," he replied, his voice low. "After the Hürtgen, I'll take any peace I can get, even if it's freezing."

The platoon was stationed in a small, isolated clearing near the Belgian border, positioned to hold the line as part of the wider Allied front. They'd been told that German forces were in retreat, that the war was winding down. Rumors circulated that the Germans were out of resources, out of morale, and that victory was within reach. It was a comforting thought, even if the brutal conditions made it hard to hold on to any sense of optimism.

But in the early hours of December 16th, that illusion of safety shattered.

It began with a distant rumble, so deep and muffled that at first, the men thought it was thunder rolling over the mountains. But the rumble grew louder, the ground trembling beneath them as the noise intensified. Tom's heart quickened, a sense of unease settling over him as he scanned the darkened horizon.

Then, from somewhere beyond the tree line, the night exploded into light and sound. Artillery shells began to rain down, their impacts sending up geysers of snow and earth, the roar of the blasts tearing through the quiet. Tom threw himself to the ground, pressing his face into the frozen dirt as shrapnel and debris flew through the air.

"Take cover!" Captain Harris shouted, his voice barely audible over the thunderous barrage. The men scrambled to find shelter, each one diving into foxholes or pressing themselves against the ground as the shells continued to fall, the bombardment unrelenting.

Tom's ears rang from the blasts, his vision blurring as he huddled in his foxhole, bracing himself against the relentless onslaught. The Germans were pouring artillery down on them with a ferocity they hadn't seen in months. This was no retreat—this was a full-scale assault.

As the shelling subsided, the platoon barely had a moment to catch their breath before they heard it—the sound of engines, of tank treads grinding through the snow, of boots crunching over the frozen ground. The Germans were advancing, and they were bringing everything they had.

Captain Harris crawled over to Tom and Foster, his face set with grim determination. "This is it, boys. They're coming right at us. Hold your positions and prepare to repel the assault. We don't let them through."

Tom nodded, gripping his rifle tightly, his heart pounding as he braced himself for the fight. Around him, the men steeled themselves, their faces a mix of fear and resolve. They were outnumbered, outgunned, and caught off-guard, but they would hold the line. They had no other choice.

The first German soldiers appeared through the trees, dark shapes moving quickly over the snow, their breaths visible in the cold air. The American platoon opened fire, the crack of rifles and the roar of machine guns filling the night, bullets tearing through the darkness as they fought to hold back the advancing wave.

The Germans pressed forward with a relentless determination, their figures barely visible through the thickening snow and smoke. Tanks rolled into view, their massive forms looming over the battlefield, their cannons firing shells that sent more explosions rocking through the line. The men were scattered, forced to fight in small groups, each one struggling to hold its ground against the overwhelming force bearing down on them.

Tom aimed at a German soldier moving through the trees, firing a quick, precise shot that brought the man down. He barely had time to register the impact before another figure appeared, and then another. It felt like the entire German army was pouring through the forest, an endless tide of men and machinery, each one determined to break the Allied line.

Foster was beside him, firing his rifle in quick bursts, his face pale, his breaths coming in short, sharp gasps. "There's too many of them," he shouted, his voice edged with panic. "They're going to overrun us!"

Tom grit his teeth, forcing himself to focus, to keep firing, even as the Germans advanced with brutal efficiency. "We just have to hold," he replied, his voice steady despite the fear gnawing at him. "We don't let them through."

The Germans closed in, their figures nearly indistinguishable in the snow and darkness. The ground was littered with bodies, both American and German, the snow stained with blood, the air thick with smoke and the scent of gunpowder. The platoon was being pushed back, inch by inch, each man struggling to hold his position against the relentless assault.

Captain Harris moved among them, shouting orders, his face set with grim resolve. "Hold your ground! We're not giving an inch!"

But it was clear that the line was faltering. The Germans were pressing harder, their tanks moving closer, their machine guns ripping through the American positions with deadly precision. The men were being pushed to their limits, their ranks thinning as more and more of them fell, each one a reminder of the cost of the battle.

A shell exploded nearby, the blast sending Tom sprawling into the snow. His vision blurred, his ears ringing as he struggled to regain his bearings. Around him, the battle raged on, the sounds of gunfire and explosions blending into a chaotic roar. He forced himself to his feet, his rifle clutched in his hands as he took in the scene.

The line was breaking. The Germans were pushing through, their tanks and infantry overwhelming the American defenses, forcing the platoon to fall back. Tom looked around, searching for familiar faces, for any sign of his comrades, but the battlefield was a blur of smoke and shadows.

He spotted Captain Harris nearby, his face streaked with dirt and blood, his expression one of fierce determination. "Tom! Get to the ridge! We're regrouping there!" he shouted, his voice barely audible over the din.

Tom nodded, signaling to Foster as they began to retreat, each step a struggle against the overwhelming force pressing down on them. They moved through the snow, their breaths coming in ragged gasps, their bodies weary but driven by the need to survive. Around them, other soldiers were doing the same, each one falling back, regrouping, fighting to hold the line.

They reached the ridge, the high ground offering a brief reprieve, a moment to catch their breath. Captain Harris was there, rallying the men, his voice a steady anchor in the chaos. "We're not out of this yet," he said, his gaze fierce. "We hold here. This is where we make our stand."

The men nodded, their faces set with a mixture of fear and determination. They had been caught off-guard, overwhelmed, but they were still standing, still fighting. The Germans may have launched a surprise attack, but they would not break their resolve.

As they prepared to face the next wave, Tom looked out over the battlefield, his heart heavy with the weight of the battle they were facing. The snow was falling thicker now, covering the fallen, concealing the blood-soaked ground. The Battle of the Bulge had only just begun, and already it was testing them in ways they had never imagined.

They were cold, exhausted, outnumbered, but they would not give in. They would hold the line, no matter the cost, because that was all they could do.

The cold was relentless, biting through every layer of clothing as the platoon braced themselves for another wave. They were surrounded, outnumbered, and cut off from reinforcements. The Germans had launched a massive, unexpected counteroffensive, pushing through the Ardennes with overwhelming force, and the American lines were buckling under the pressure. But here, on this ridge, Captain Harris and his men were determined to hold their ground. They would make their stand, no matter the odds.

Tom lay in a shallow trench, his fingers numb around his rifle, his breath fogging in the icy air. He could barely feel his feet, his toes stinging with the cold, but he forced himself to ignore it, to stay focused. Around him, his comrades were doing the same, their faces tight with exhaustion and fear but set with grim determination.

Captain Harris moved along the line, his voice low but commanding as he checked each man's position. "We're holding this ridge, boys," he said. "There's nowhere else to go. We hold, or we don't come out of this. Remember what we're fighting for. Remember why we're here."

The men nodded, each one feeling the weight of his words settle into their bones. They had faced impossible odds before, had fought through hell in the Hürtgen Forest, but this was different. This was a battle for survival, a fight to keep the enemy from breaking through.

The sound of German tanks rumbled through the trees, a low, ominous growl that made the ground tremble beneath them. Tom clenched his jaw, his heart pounding as he peered over the edge of the trench. In the distance, he could see the dark shapes of German infantry advancing through the snow, their figures blurred by the falling flakes, their movements steady and unyielding.

Foster huddled beside him, his face pale, his eyes wide with fear. "We're not getting out of this, are we?" he whispered, his voice barely audible.

Tom shook his head, forcing himself to sound calm, even though he felt the same fear clawing at his insides. "We just have to hold. If we can keep them here, hold this ridge, reinforcements will come. We just need to give them time."

The German forces advanced, their dark uniforms contrasting sharply against the white snow. As they closed in, Captain Harris gave the signal, and the platoon opened fire, the crack of rifles and the rattle of machine guns filling the air. The first wave of Germans faltered, some dropping to the ground as bullets tore through their ranks, but others pressed on, using the terrain to their advantage, moving closer with every step.

Tom fired, his shots precise, each pull of the trigger a fight against his frozen fingers. He aimed for the advancing soldiers, watching them stumble and fall, only to be replaced by more. The Germans were relentless, pushing forward despite the losses, their determination as fierce as the Americans' resolve to hold.

A German tank emerged from the trees, its turret swiveling as it searched for targets. Tom felt a surge of panic as he watched it rumble toward them, its cannon lowering, aimed directly at their position. He ducked down, pressing himself against the cold earth as the tank fired, the shell exploding nearby, sending a spray of snow and debris into the air.

"Hold your positions!" Captain Harris shouted, his voice cutting through the chaos. "We can't let them take this ridge!"

The men dug in, their faces set with grim determination as they held their ground, each one understanding the cost of failure. The German forces were closing in, their numbers overwhelming, but the Americans fought with everything they had, each shot, each moment, a testament to their resolve.

Tom reloaded, his hands shaking from the cold, his fingers clumsy as he struggled to load the bullets. He could feel the weight of exhaustion pressing down on him, his body aching from days without proper rest, but he forced himself to focus, to keep firing. Around him, his comrades did the same, their faces etched with fatigue but unyielding.

The Germans reached the edge of the ridge, and the fighting turned brutal, close and chaotic. Tom found himself in hand-to-hand combat, his rifle now a bludgeon as he fought off a German soldier who had broken through their line. The man's face was twisted with desperation, his movements fierce, but Tom managed to fend him off, using every ounce of strength he had left.

Foster was beside him, grappling with another soldier, his face pale, his eyes wide with terror. Tom lunged, helping him subdue the enemy, the two of them fighting with a desperation born from survival.

The air was thick with gunfire, with the shouts and cries of men locked in combat, each one struggling to hold the line, to push the enemy back. The ground was littered with bodies, the snow stained with blood, the once-pristine landscape transformed into a brutal battleground.

Captain Harris moved along the line, rallying his men, his voice a steady anchor in the chaos. "We're holding, boys! Don't let them through!"

The Germans fell back briefly, regrouping, but it was clear they weren't done. More soldiers emerged from the trees, more tanks rumbled forward, their presence a grim reminder of the overwhelming force bearing down on them.

As the next wave approached, Tom felt a pang of despair. They were outnumbered, exhausted, and their ammunition was running low. But he looked at the faces of his comrades, at Foster, at Captain Harris, and he knew they would keep fighting, no matter the odds. They had come too far, had lost too much, to give up now.

The Germans charged again, and the platoon met them with the same fierce determination, every man fighting as if his life depended on it. The line was buckling, their numbers thinning, but they held, each one drawing strength from the others, each one refusing to yield.

As night began to fall, the Germans finally pulled back, retreating into the trees, their dark shapes disappearing into the gathering shadows. The ridge was still theirs, but the cost had been high. The ground was littered with the bodies of friends and enemies alike, the snow stained red with the blood of those who had fallen.

Captain Harris gathered the remaining men, his face lined with exhaustion and grief. "We did it," he said quietly, his voice steady but heavy. "We held the line."

The men nodded, each one feeling the weight of his words settle over them. They had survived, had kept the Germans from breaking through, but it had come at a terrible cost. They were fewer now, each one bearing the scars of the battle, each one marked by the losses they had endured.

Tom sat in the snow, his rifle resting on his knees, his breath visible in the cold air. He looked around at his comrades, at the weary, battered faces of the men who had fought beside him, and felt a deep, quiet pride. They had held the line, had done what needed to be done, but the price of victory weighed heavily on them all.

Foster slumped beside him, his face pale, his body trembling from exhaustion and cold. "We made it," he whispered, his voice barely more than a breath. "But at what cost?"

Tom nodded, his throat tight. "We held, but we lost so much." He looked out over the ridge, over the bodies of friends who hadn't made it, who had given everything to keep the line from breaking.

As darkness settled over the forest, the men huddled together, their breaths mingling in the cold night air. They had fought with everything they had, had held the line against impossible odds. But as they sat in the snow, surrounded by the silence of the night, each one knew that the battle was far from over. They had survived another day, but the cost of holding the line would stay with them forever.

The winter had fully descended upon the Ardennes, transforming the forest into a frozen, white wasteland. The trees stood bare and brittle, their branches coated in frost, and the ground was covered in thick layers of snow that seemed to mute all sounds. Temperatures plummeted, dropping to levels that turned every breath into a plume of steam, every movement into a struggle against the biting cold. The soldiers were locked in a battle not just with the enemy but with the unyielding winter itself, fighting to survive conditions that were as brutal as the combat.

Tom huddled deeper into his foxhole, his body numb from head to toe despite every piece of clothing he had layered on. His gloves had long since lost their warmth, the fingers stiff and cracked from the cold, and his feet were a constant ache of frostbitten pain. The platoon was on high alert, aware that another German assault could come at any moment, but they were just as focused on staying warm, on keeping their bodies from freezing in place.

Beside him, Foster shivered, his breath visible in the air, his face pale and drawn. "I can't feel my hands anymore," he muttered, his voice trembling. "Feels like the cold is eating right through me."

Tom nodded, barely able to muster the energy to respond. He was fighting the same battle, every muscle in his body tense as he tried to keep moving, keep his blood flowing. The cold had a way of sapping their strength, of settling into their bones and draining them of energy. It was as if the winter itself had become an enemy, pressing down on them, testing their resilience.

The men had resorted to huddling together in groups, sharing body heat as best they could, but the frost was relentless, creeping into every crevice, seeping through their clothes, turning their foxholes into icy tombs. Supplies were dwindling, and what little food they had was frozen solid, each bite an effort that felt more like chewing ice than nourishment.

Captain Harris made his rounds, his face as haggard and weary as the men he commanded, his breath visible as he spoke. "Keep moving as much as you can," he urged, his voice hoarse. "We can't let the cold take us. Keep your fingers and toes moving. Stay alert."

The men nodded, though they could barely move their limbs, the cold having robbed them of flexibility, of coordination. Even the simple act of gripping a rifle was a struggle, their fingers so stiff they could hardly pull the trigger if it came to it. They were soldiers, hardened by months of combat, but this—this was different. This was a battle of endurance, a test of survival against an enemy they couldn't shoot or repel.

Nightfall brought an even more intense chill, the temperatures dropping so low that frost formed on their faces, on their eyelashes, every exposed patch of skin stinging from the icy air. The stars shone bright and clear above them, a beautiful but indifferent backdrop to their suffering. Tom looked up, feeling a strange sense of isolation, as if the universe itself had turned its back on them, leaving them to fight for their lives in this frozen, desolate place.

Sleep was impossible. Every time Tom closed his eyes, he was jolted awake by the sharp bite of the cold, by the knowledge that if he let himself drift off, he might not wake up again. Around him, the other men sat huddled in their foxholes, each one fighting his own private battle against the urge to give in, to let the cold overtake him.

"Think about home," Foster murmured, his voice barely a whisper. "Think about warmth. The sun... beaches. Whatever you can. Just don't think about this damn place."

Tom tried to conjure memories of warmth, of summer days and sunlit fields, but they felt distant, almost unreal. All he could feel was the cold, pressing down on him, filling every corner of his mind. The Hürtgen Forest had been brutal, but this... this was an endurance test that seemed to have no end, no reprieve.

Their rations had been cut to the bare minimum. The once-hot coffee they'd cherished had become a luxury of the past, replaced by ice-cold water that only served to chill them further. What little food they had was hard as rock, and eating became a chore, each bite requiring effort just to chew through the frozen bread and jerky. But they forced themselves to eat, to keep their strength up, knowing that giving in to the cold was not an option.

Captain Harris called a meeting, gathering the men in a small, huddled circle. His face was set with grim determination, his eyes bloodshot from lack of sleep. "I know it feels like hell out here," he said, his voice steady despite the tremor in his hands. "But we're still holding. We're still here. The Germans are suffering too—they're dealing with the same conditions we are. We just have to outlast them."

The men nodded, each one feeling the weight of his words. They were all fighting the same battle, trying to stay alive long enough for reinforcements to arrive, long enough to hold the line against the enemy and the elements. But they could see the toll it was taking on each other—the haunted look in their eyes, the slow, shuffling movements, the way they all spoke in low, measured tones as if to conserve every ounce of energy.

Some of the men began to show signs of frostbite, their skin turning a sickly shade of gray, their fingers and toes numb and swollen. Tom knew that if they didn't get relief soon, some of them wouldn't make it. The thought haunted him, the knowledge that even the strongest among them could be brought down by something as insidious as the cold.

One night, as the temperature dropped to what felt like its lowest yet, the Germans launched another assault, using the cover of darkness and snow to mask their approach. The sudden crack of gunfire jolted the men to attention, each one struggling to raise their rifles, their movements sluggish from the cold.

Tom aimed at the advancing figures, his fingers so stiff that it was a struggle just to pull the trigger. He fired, watching as a German soldier fell, but there was no time to process the shot. The Germans kept coming, their faces set with the same desperation as the Americans, their breaths visible in the freezing air as they pressed forward.

The battle was chaotic, each man fighting as much against the cold as against the enemy. The snow became a battlefield, littered with bodies, the blood staining the white ground in stark contrast. The sound of gunfire echoed through the trees, muffled by the snow but still sharp, each shot a reminder of the deadly stakes.

Captain Harris shouted orders, his voice barely carrying over the noise, his breath visible in short, sharp bursts. "Hold the line! Don't let them through!"

The men dug in, their faces grim as they held their ground, their rifles cracking in the frigid air. They were outnumbered, outgunned, but they fought with a desperation that came from knowing that survival was their only option. They could not retreat, could not fall back. This ridge, this line in the snow, was all they had.

After what felt like hours, the Germans finally pulled back, retreating into the shadows, leaving the Americans to regroup in the freezing silence. The men slumped in their foxholes, their breaths coming in ragged gasps, each one grateful just to be alive. But the relief was short-lived, tempered by the knowledge that the cold would be waiting for them, that it was as much their enemy as the Germans.

As Tom sat in the snow, his body numb, his face stinging with frostbite, he realized that this was what war had become—a test of survival against forces that were beyond their control. The cold, the hunger, the exhaustion—they were enemies that could not be fought with bullets, that could not be driven back. All they could do was endure, to hold on to whatever slivers of hope they had left, to survive one more night, one more hour.

And as he looked around at his comrades, each one a ghostly figure in the snow, he felt a quiet resolve settle within him. They would hold this line, they would survive, because that was all they had left. The winter had turned them into shadows, into men fighting not just for victory, but for life itself. And as they huddled together, sharing what little warmth they had, they knew that they would face whatever came next, because they had no other choice.

The dawn brought little warmth, just a dull, gray light that seeped through the clouds and illuminated the snow-covered landscape. The men were huddled in their foxholes, faces pale and hollow, eyes bloodshot from sleepless nights. Every breath felt labored, every muscle screamed with fatigue. But even in their exhaustion, they were on edge, knowing that the quiet never lasted long. The Germans were relentless, and each moment of calm only served to tighten the tension, the anticipation of another assault.

Captain Harris moved along the line, his voice low but firm. "This is it, boys. They're coming at us hard. Reinforcements are on the way, but we need to hold this ground until they get here."

Tom nodded, his jaw set with determination even as his hands trembled from cold and fatigue. He adjusted his rifle, his eyes scanning the barren, snow-covered trees ahead. The German forces were close, preparing for another wave, and he knew that this would be no ordinary assault. They were outnumbered, exhausted, and facing an enemy just as desperate as they were.

The first sounds were faint—the crunch of snow, the quiet murmur of voices, the distant clank of equipment. Then, without warning, the forest erupted with gunfire and explosions as German forces charged forward, using the snowy landscape for cover. The crack of rifles and the thud of mortars filled the air, sending snow and dirt flying as the men braced themselves for the onslaught.

"Open fire!" Captain Harris shouted, his voice barely audible over the roar of the battle. The men responded, their rifles cracking in unison, bullets slicing through the frosty air, aiming for the dark shapes advancing through the trees.

Tom fired at the first figure he saw, watching as the soldier stumbled, disappearing into the snow. But there was no time to register the shot. The Germans kept coming, pushing forward with a fierce determination, their numbers seemingly endless. The ground around them erupted with explosions, sending up showers of snow and ice, the shockwaves rattling their bones.

Beside him, Foster was firing as fast as he could, his face tight with concentration, his breaths coming in short, visible gasps. "We can't hold them back!" he shouted, his voice tinged with desperation. "There's too many of them!"

"We have to try!" Tom shouted back, forcing himself to keep firing, to ignore the fear gnawing at him. Every shot was an effort, his muscles aching from the cold, his fingers stiff and numb around the trigger. But he pushed on, driven by the knowledge that this line was all that stood between them and disaster.

The Germans reached the edge of their position, and the fighting turned brutal, close-quarters combat erupting as both sides grappled in the snow. Tom found himself face-to-face with a German soldier, their breaths mingling in the frigid air, each one struggling for survival. The man lunged at him, and Tom reacted on instinct, using the butt of his rifle to fend off the attack. They grappled, slipping and sliding on the icy ground, their movements desperate and raw.

Foster was beside him, fending off another German soldier, his face a mask of concentration and fear. The two friends fought side by side, their every movement a testament to the bond they had formed, the unspoken promise to watch each other's backs. They fought with everything they had, pushing their bodies to the breaking point, each moment a struggle to survive.

Captain Harris's voice cut through the chaos, steady and unyielding. "Hold the line! We can't let them break through!"

The men rallied, each one fighting with a desperation born from exhaustion and resolve. They were battered, outnumbered, and nearly broken, but they held their ground, refusing to yield even an inch. The Germans were fierce, relentless, but the platoon met them with equal ferocity, each man fighting as if his life depended on it—because it did.

The air was thick with smoke and the acrid smell of gunpowder, the sounds of battle muffled by the snow but still overwhelming. The ground was littered with bodies, both American and German, the once-pristine landscape turned into a battlefield of blood and ice. Each man was pushed to his limit, fighting with a grim determination that defied the exhaustion etched into their faces.

Tom's arms felt like lead, his vision blurring from fatigue, but he forced himself to keep going, to keep pushing back the waves of soldiers that kept coming. His body was screaming for rest, his mind numb with the horror and chaos around him, but he knew that stopping wasn't an option. The line had to hold.

A mortar shell landed nearby, the explosion sending him sprawling into the snow, his vision flashing white as the shockwave hit. His ears rang, and for a moment, he couldn't tell up from down, his mind reeling from the impact. But he forced himself to his knees, his fingers clutching at the cold ground, his gaze fixed on the dark shapes still moving through the snow.

He looked around, catching sight of Foster, who was struggling to his feet, his face streaked with blood but his eyes fierce. Captain Harris was still shouting orders, rallying the men, his voice a steady anchor in the chaos, even as the Germans continued to press forward.

Tom staggered back to his position, raising his rifle and firing at the nearest figure, his mind and body operating on pure instinct. The Germans were faltering, their advance slowing, but they were still coming, still pushing, each one determined to break the line.

Finally, as the afternoon wore on, the German forces began to pull back, retreating into the trees, their figures disappearing into the shadows. The men watched, each one too exhausted to feel anything other than a dull relief as the enemy finally withdrew. The line had held, but at a cost that was painfully evident.

Tom slumped against the edge of his foxhole, his rifle slipping from his hands as he struggled to catch his breath. Around him, the other men were in similar states, their faces pale, their bodies slumped from exhaustion. The ground was littered with the bodies of their comrades, men who had fought and fallen, their sacrifice etched into the frozen ground.

Captain Harris moved among them, his face marked with exhaustion but also with pride. "We did it," he said quietly, his voice barely audible over the quiet that had settled over the battlefield. "We held the line."

The men nodded, each one too tired to speak, each one feeling the weight of his words. They had survived, had pushed back the Germans, but they all knew that the battle had left them forever changed, had tested them in ways they hadn't thought possible.

Foster sank down beside Tom, his face pale, his breaths coming in shallow gasps. "I didn't think we'd make it," he whispered, his voice shaking. "I thought... I thought this was it."

Tom nodded, his throat tight as he looked out over the battlefield, the snow stained red, the bodies of friends and enemies alike lying in silent testament to the cost of their survival. "We came close," he replied, his voice hollow. "Too close."

They sat in silence, each man lost in his own thoughts, in the memories of the friends they had lost, the moments of terror and desperation that would stay with them long after the war was over.

The battle had pushed them to their limits, had shown them the depths of their own resilience, but it had also shown them the fragility of life, the thin line between survival and death. And as they sat in the freezing snow, each one feeling the weight of what they had endured, they knew that they had been changed forever, their lives marked by the desperate battle they had fought, the line they had held.

The winter was still pressing down on them, the cold as fierce as ever, but they were still here, still standing. They had fought, had held their ground, and in doing so, they had forged a bond that would carry them through whatever came next.

But as they looked out over the silent, bloodstained landscape, they understood that they had paid a price that could never be forgotten. And as the sun set over the Ardennes, casting a pale glow over the frozen battlefield, they knew that this moment, this desperate battle, would live on in their memories, a reminder of the cost of survival.

The morning after the desperate battle brought a quiet that felt almost surreal. The snow lay undisturbed over the battlefield, covering the horrors of the previous day in a layer of stark, white silence. Tom sat in his foxhole, his mind numb, his body aching from exhaustion and cold. Around him, the other men were silent as well, each one lost in his own thoughts, weighed down by the events that had nearly broken them.

Then, from beyond the tree line, a sound began to emerge—a low rumble, unmistakable even from a distance. At first, Tom thought it was his imagination, a trick of the mind after days of brutal combat. But as the sound grew louder, a murmur passed through the line of weary soldiers. Faces turned toward the noise, eyes widening as they began to recognize the steady, rhythmic clank of tank treads, the hum of engines.

"Reinforcements," Foster whispered, his voice filled with awe and disbelief. "They're here."

Tom's heart surged with a feeling he hadn't allowed himself to feel in days: hope. Reinforcements. They had made it through the night, held the line against overwhelming odds, and now, finally, help had arrived. Around him, the other men began to stir, their tired faces lifting as they watched the column of Allied tanks and trucks approach through the snowy landscape. The rumble of engines filled the air, a reassuring sound that drowned out the silence that had haunted them.

Captain Harris stood up, his face etched with relief as he watched the reinforcements roll in. He looked around at his men, a faint, tired smile tugging at his lips. "We did it, boys. We held out long enough. Help's here now."

The men let out a collective breath, the tension that had held them tightly bound finally beginning to release. Some of them exchanged smiles, others simply closed their eyes in silent gratitude. The relief was palpable, a weight lifting from their shoulders as they realized they weren't alone anymore, that they wouldn't have to face another wave without support.

The first soldiers to disembark from the trucks approached the exhausted platoon with wide-eyed respect, taking in the sight of the men who had fought through freezing cold, exhaustion, and relentless enemy attacks. These soldiers had heard stories of the Battle of the Bulge, of the desperate stand in the Ardennes, but to see these men in person, hollow-eyed and battered but unbroken, was something else entirely.

One of the medics approached Tom, kneeling beside him, his face filled with concern. "You look like you've been through hell," he said, his voice gentle. "Let's get you warmed up."

Tom managed a small smile, his voice hoarse. "Feels like we have."

The medic handed him a steaming cup of coffee, the warmth seeping through the metal into Tom's frozen fingers. He held it carefully, savoring the heat, taking a slow sip that brought a flood of warmth to his body, a sensation he had almost forgotten. Around him, other medics moved through the line, offering blankets, food, and hot drinks, small comforts that felt like luxuries in the wake of what they had endured.

As he sipped the coffee, Tom looked around at his comrades, his gaze lingering on each weary, dirt-streaked face. Foster was huddled in his own foxhole, cradling his cup as if it were the most precious thing in the world. Captain Harris was speaking quietly with some of the new officers, his expression a mixture of pride and exhaustion. They had all been pushed to their limits, had fought with every ounce of strength they had, and now, finally, they could breathe.

But beneath the relief, Tom felt something else—a quiet, steely resolve that seemed to settle over him like armor. They had fought through the worst the enemy had thrown at them, had held the line when it seemed impossible, and now they were still standing. They had seen the depths of their own courage, had tested the strength of their bond, and they had come out the other side stronger for it.

Captain Harris gathered the men, his voice steady as he addressed them. "We've been through hell together, and I know each one of you has seen things no one should have to see. But we're still here. We held this ground, and because of you, we're pushing the Germans back. This line held because you were willing to fight for it, and I couldn't be prouder of you all."

The men nodded, each one feeling the weight of his words, the pride and respect they shared for one another. They were soldiers, yes, but they were more than that now. They were brothers, bound not just by duty but by the trials they had endured, by the sacrifices they had made.

As the reinforcements prepared to move forward, to push the Germans out of the Ardennes, Tom felt a surge of determination. The battle wasn't over yet, but they had proven that they could face whatever came next. They had stood on the edge of survival, had stared into the depths of exhaustion and fear, and they had emerged unbroken.

Foster turned to him, his face set with a quiet resolve. "We're going to see this through, aren't we, Tom?"

Tom nodded, a faint smile on his face. "Yeah, we are. We didn't come this far just to turn back now."

They stood together, side by side, watching as the reinforcements moved into position, preparing to continue the fight. The snow still covered the ground, the air still held its icy bite, but for the first time in days, Tom felt warmth spreading through him—a warmth born not just from the coffee in his hands but from the knowledge that they were not alone, that they were part of something larger than themselves.

As the platoon prepared to move out, each man felt a renewed sense of purpose, a quiet but unbreakable determination. They had held the line, had proven their strength, and now, with the support of their allies, they would keep fighting until the end.

Tom looked out over the frozen landscape, the white fields dotted with the shapes of men moving forward, a line of soldiers pressing on despite the cold, the fear, the loss. They had been tested, and they had emerged stronger, their resolve as unyielding as the winter that surrounded them.

And as he moved forward, his breath mingling with the frosty air, Tom knew that they would see this through. They had faced the darkest moments of the war, had endured the harshest trials, and they would continue, side by side, until victory was theirs. The line had held, and so had they—soldiers, brothers, bound by the will to survive and the resolve to see this battle to the end.

Chapter 9: Entering Germany

The Rhine stretched out before them, a dark ribbon winding its way through the German landscape. It was wide, cold, and foreboding, the water moving with a steady, unyielding current. Crossing it would mean something monumental—the first real step into enemy territory, a shift from defending the line to invading Germany itself. For Tom and his platoon, it was a moment filled with both dread and resolve.

The Allied forces had been building up to this moment for months, pushing the Germans back, city by city, through France and Belgium, until now they were here, standing on the western banks of the Rhine, with Germany waiting just beyond. Captain Harris had assembled the platoon early that morning, his face reflecting the gravity of their task.

"This is it, boys," he said, his voice steady but solemn. "We've been through hell together to get to this point. We're crossing the Rhine, and once we're over that water, we're on German soil. From here on out, we're not just fighting to hold the line—we're fighting to end this war."

Tom felt a shiver run through him, one that had nothing to do with the cold. It was strange to think of crossing that invisible boundary, stepping into the land they had heard about but never seen. They were no longer just defenders; they were the invading force now, marching into Germany with the knowledge that every step would bring them closer to the heart of the enemy.

Foster stood beside him, his face pale but determined. "Feels different, doesn't it?" he murmured. "Being the ones going in, knowing this is their home."

Tom nodded. "Yeah. It's... it's strange. Like we're crossing into something we can't come back from."

Around them, the rest of the platoon was preparing for the crossing, checking their gear, sharing quiet words as they mentally steeled themselves. There was a weight in the air, a sense of purpose that had grown with each battle, each mile they had pushed through enemy lines. They had survived the Ardennes, held the line in the face of impossible odds, and now, they were here, ready to take the fight to the enemy.

The sound of engines rumbled in the background as transport boats pulled up along the bank, their steel hulls dull and gray against the dark water. The men began boarding in small groups, their movements tense, their faces set with a quiet resolve. Tom and Foster climbed into one of the boats, settling onto the cold metal benches, their rifles clutched tightly as they prepared for the crossing.

As the boat pushed off, the soldiers fell into a tense silence, each one lost in his own thoughts as the shoreline receded behind them. The current was strong, tugging at the boat as it made its way across the river, the water lapping against the sides in a slow, steady rhythm. The mist hung low over the water, creating an eerie, shrouded landscape that seemed to stretch endlessly into the distance.

Tom kept his gaze fixed on the opposite bank, his heart pounding with a mixture of fear and anticipation. Crossing the Rhine felt symbolic, a final line being crossed, a definitive statement that they were taking the war to the enemy, no matter the cost. They were no longer just soldiers defending their own land—they were invaders, marching into the heart of Germany.

As they neared the far shore, Captain Harris stood at the front of the boat, his gaze steady, his face set with a fierce determination. "Remember why we're here," he called out, his voice carrying over the water. "We're here to finish this. We've fought too hard, lost too much, to stop now. Every step we take is a step closer to ending this war, to seeing our homes and our families again."

The men nodded, their faces reflecting a shared resolve. They had come this far together, through battles that had tested their courage, their endurance, and their loyalty to one another. Now, on the verge of entering Germany, they felt the weight of that journey, the sacrifices they had made to get here.

The boat ground to a halt as it reached the opposite shore, the soldiers disembarking quickly, their boots sinking into the cold, muddy ground. Tom stepped onto German soil, feeling a strange mixture of pride and unease. They were here, at last, in the land of the enemy. Around him, his comrades shared the same sense of surreal awe, each one adjusting to the reality of where they stood.

They spread out, forming a defensive perimeter as they took in their surroundings. The landscape was quiet, eerily still, with rows of trees lining the riverbank, their branches bare against the winter sky. The village in the distance looked empty, its rooftops peeking out over the horizon, a reminder that this was someone's home, someone's land, now a battlefield.

Foster crouched beside him, his gaze fixed on the horizon. "I never thought I'd see this," he said softly. "Standing here, in Germany, after everything."

"Me neither," Tom replied, his voice equally quiet. "Feels like we're a long way from home."

They moved carefully, their rifles ready, each step filled with a sense of caution as they advanced into unfamiliar territory. Every shadow, every rustle of leaves, felt like a potential threat, a reminder that they were no longer on friendly soil. The Germans knew they were coming, knew that the Allies were pushing into their homeland, and Tom could feel the tension in the air, a sense of anticipation that hovered over them like a cloud.

Captain Harris directed them toward the village, their first objective as they established a foothold on German soil. The men moved in pairs, scanning the surroundings, each one aware that any moment could bring an ambush, an attack, a reminder that this was still enemy territory.

As they approached the village, Tom felt a chill run down his spine. The houses were quiet, their windows dark, the streets empty. It was a ghost town, abandoned by its residents, left to the soldiers who now moved through its quiet streets. The stillness was unnerving, a reminder of the lives that had once filled these homes, the families who had lived here, now gone.

They secured the village, clearing each house, moving through each room with a caution born from experience. The emptiness of the place felt heavy, a silent acknowledgment of the war that had come to this land, the devastation that had driven people from their homes. Tom felt a strange sense of reverence, a respect for the lives that had been disrupted, for the people whose homes they were now occupying.

Once the village was secured, Captain Harris gathered the men in the town square, his face set with determination. "This is just the beginning," he said, his voice steady. "We're on German soil now, and from here on out, every step we take brings us closer to ending this war. Remember why we're here, remember what we've fought for, and don't let anything stop you."

The men nodded, each one feeling the weight of his words settle over them. They had crossed the Rhine, had entered Germany, and now, there was no turning back. They were here to finish what they had started, to see this war to its end.

As they set up camp, Tom looked out over the empty village, the darkened houses, the quiet streets. They were invaders now, strangers in a foreign land, but they were here with a purpose, with a resolve that had been forged through months of hardship and sacrifice. They would carry that resolve with them, through every battle, through every challenge, until the war was over.

And as he looked out over the horizon, Tom felt a sense of calm settle over him, a quiet but unbreakable resolve. They had crossed the Rhine, had stepped onto enemy soil, and he knew that they would see this through. For their fallen friends, for the people back home, for the promise of peace—whatever it took, they would continue. They were here to end the war, to bring an end to the suffering, and they would not stop until that goal was within reach.

The first encounters with German civilians were tense, filled with uncertainty and a mixture of emotions that the platoon hadn't fully anticipated. After months of fighting an unseen enemy, the Germans had been little more than shadows, the people and the place itself almost abstract in their minds. But now, marching through small villages and towns, they were face-to-face with the reality of Germany and its people.

Tom noticed it the moment they entered the next village—a cluster of modest houses with smoke drifting from a few chimneys, the streets quiet and the windows shuttered. There was a sense of watchfulness, of eyes peering out from behind curtains, from darkened windows. The people hadn't fled, but they were clearly uneasy, their presence a reminder that the soldiers weren't just entering enemy territory—they were stepping into people's homes.

Captain Harris ordered the men to maintain a respectful distance, reminding them that these were civilians, not combatants. "We're here to end the war," he said, his voice low but firm. "We're not here to make enemies of the people. Treat them with respect, but be cautious. Not everyone here will welcome us."

As the men spread out, moving carefully through the village, Tom caught sight of a group of older men and women standing on a porch, watching the soldiers with hard, wary expressions. The civilians said nothing, their faces unreadable, but their eyes held a mixture of defiance and fear. It was strange to see Germans up close, people who were neither soldiers nor officers, just townsfolk caught in the chaos of war.

One of the older women called out something in German, her voice sharp. Tom didn't understand the words, but he recognized the tone—resentment, distrust. The woman's gaze was fixed on them, her body rigid with anger, her face drawn and lined. He could only imagine what she'd seen, what she had lost, how the war had changed her life.

Foster, who stood beside him, shifted uncomfortably. "Guess not everyone's glad to see us," he muttered.

Tom nodded. "Can't say I blame them. This is their home, and here we are, marching through it."

As they continued through the village, a few children appeared in doorways, their eyes wide with curiosity and fear. One boy stared at Tom, his expression serious beyond his years, clutching a toy soldier tightly in one hand. Tom felt a pang of guilt as he looked at the boy, wondering how much he understood of what was happening, what he thought of the soldiers who had arrived in his town.

They approached a small group of younger men standing near a shopfront, their faces hard, arms crossed over their chests. One of them, a tall man with a sharp jawline and piercing eyes, muttered something in German, his tone laced with bitterness. Tom didn't know the words, but the intent was clear.

"Let's keep moving," Captain Harris said, his voice calm but cautious. "We're not looking for trouble."

But as they passed, the young man spat on the ground, his gaze cold, defiant. A few of the soldiers tensed, one of them clenching his fists, his expression darkening. Tom could feel the tension rising, a clash of anger and frustration on both sides.

Harris stepped forward, his gaze steady as he met the young man's stare. "We're here to end this war," he said in a slow, measured tone, his words chosen carefully. "We don't want any trouble. But if you cross us, we'll defend ourselves."

The man held his gaze for a moment before looking away, muttering under his breath. The group dispersed, moving back into the shadows, their resentment palpable. The soldiers relaxed slightly, but the tension lingered, the unspoken animosity settling over the village like a heavy fog.

As they moved on, Tom couldn't shake the unease he felt. They were here as liberators, to put an end to the suffering, to bring peace. But he realized now that peace meant different things to different people. For the Germans, it was a bitter pill, a reminder of defeat, of lost loved ones, of a homeland that was now a battlefield.

Foster looked around, his expression thoughtful. "Guess it's easy to forget, isn't it?" he said quietly. "That these people... they're just people. Just like us."

Tom nodded. "Yeah. They didn't ask for this war either."

In another part of the village, an older man approached the soldiers, a cautious but hopeful look in his eyes. He held up his hands in a gesture of peace, speaking in halting English. "We... we are tired. Tired of war," he said, his voice heavy with weariness. "We want this... over."

Captain Harris nodded, extending a hand to the man, who shook it with a firm grip. "We're tired of it too," Harris said quietly. "Let's end it together."

The man nodded, his shoulders slumping with relief as he returned to his home. Tom felt a flicker of hope—a reminder that not everyone here saw them as enemies, that there were people who wanted peace as much as they did. But he knew that the tension would remain, that mistrust would linger on both sides.

As they continued through the village, a few women approached cautiously, offering bread and water. Tom accepted a small piece of bread, nodding his thanks, the gesture a fragile bridge between two sides who had lost so much. He could see the strain in their faces, the exhaustion that matched his own, the quiet desperation for an end to the suffering.

They moved through the village without incident, but the encounters left a mark, a reminder that this wasn't a simple battle of right versus wrong. They were fighting for peace, yes, but peace came at a cost, and that cost was written in the wary eyes of the people they passed.

As they left the village, Tom looked back at the quiet houses, at the faces that had watched them with such intensity. The German civilians were no longer just a faceless enemy; they were people caught in the same nightmare, people who had lost family, who had endured hardship and suffering. And while they would never be allies, there was a mutual understanding now—a shared burden of loss and longing for an end.

Foster walked beside him, his gaze thoughtful. "You think they'll ever forgive us?" he asked quietly.

Tom shrugged, his voice soft. "Maybe. Someday. But even if they don't, at least we can give them back some kind of peace."

Captain Harris gathered the platoon as they regrouped on the outskirts of the village, his face set with a quiet resolve. "Remember this feeling," he said, his voice steady. "Remember that we're not just here to fight—we're here to bring an end to all this. And that means respecting the people who are caught in the middle, no matter which side they're on."

The men nodded, each one feeling the weight of his words, the gravity of their mission settling over them. They had crossed into enemy territory, but they were not just soldiers anymore. They were ambassadors of peace, carrying the hope of an end to the violence, of a future free from the horrors they had endured.

As they moved on, Tom felt a renewed sense of purpose, a quiet determination to see this through. They were here to finish the war, to put an end to the suffering on both sides. And as he looked out over the German landscape, he knew that every step they took was a step closer to that goal—a step closer to peace.

The advance through Germany was anything but smooth. As the platoon moved deeper into enemy territory, German resistance intensified, each village, each stretch of road becoming a potential trap. The German forces, knowing that the Allies were closing in, had resorted to desperate tactics—ambushes, hidden mines, sniper nests. It was clear that the enemy was prepared to make a last stand, unwilling to give an inch without a fight.

Tom felt the tension in the air as they made their way along a narrow road flanked by dense forest. Every rustle, every snap of a branch made the soldiers flinch, their eyes darting from shadow to shadow, fingers tense around their triggers. The Germans were out there, watching, waiting for the right moment to strike.

Captain Harris signaled for them to halt, raising a fist as he surveyed the terrain. "Stay alert," he whispered. "We're in ambush country."

The platoon moved in silence, each man acutely aware of the danger surrounding them. They had encountered ambushes before, in the Ardennes, in France, but here, on German soil, the attacks were more frequent, more vicious. The German soldiers were fighting with a desperation born from defending their homeland, and they knew every inch of the terrain. They used it to their advantage, setting traps, attacking from hidden positions, then melting away before the Americans could retaliate.

As they advanced, a sharp crack shattered the silence—a gunshot from somewhere deep in the trees. The platoon dropped to the ground, rifles raised, scanning the forest for any sign of movement. Another shot rang out, then another, the bullets slicing through the air, sending chips of bark flying from the trees around them.

"Sniper!" Harris shouted. "Get down and find cover!"

Tom pressed himself against a tree, his heart pounding as he searched for the source of the shots. The forest was thick, the shadows deep, making it nearly impossible to pinpoint the sniper's location. The Germans were using guerrilla tactics now, fighting a war of attrition, wearing the Americans down with hit-and-run attacks that left them constantly on edge.

A scream echoed from further down the line as one of the men went down, clutching his shoulder. Foster scrambled to his side, dragging him behind cover as the rest of the platoon returned fire, aiming blindly into the trees. The sniper shots stopped briefly, only to be replaced by the staccato burst of machine-gun fire from the opposite side of the road.

"They've got us pinned!" Foster shouted, his voice barely audible over the gunfire.

Tom's mind raced, adrenaline coursing through him as he scanned the treeline. The Germans were entrenched, well-hidden, and they had the advantage. This wasn't a battle—it was an ambush, a calculated strike meant to disrupt and demoralize them. He could feel the frustration building, the helplessness of not being able to see their enemy, of fighting against an invisible force.

Captain Harris crawled over to Tom and Foster, his face set with grim determination. "We're going to flank them. Squad A, stay here and keep them distracted. Squad B, follow me—we're going around to the right."

Tom nodded, signaling to the others as they prepared to move. They crawled through the underbrush, their movements slow and cautious, each man acutely aware of the danger that lay in the shadows. The sounds of gunfire echoed around them, punctuated by the occasional scream, a reminder of the stakes of this desperate struggle.

As they reached the flank, Tom spotted the flash of a German soldier's helmet through the trees. He raised his rifle, taking a steady breath before squeezing the trigger. The soldier dropped, his body slumping to the ground. Around him, the other men fired, targeting the hidden German positions, breaking through the enemy's defensive line.

They pressed forward, using the cover of trees and rocks, their movements coordinated, precise. The Germans fought back with a fierce intensity, but they were outmatched, outflanked, and the Americans pushed through, securing the position with ruthless efficiency. One by one, the German soldiers fell, their last stand crumbling under the weight of the American assault.

But the victory was hollow, tempered by the knowledge that there would be more ambushes, more traps waiting for them further down the road. As they regrouped, Tom looked around at the exhausted faces of his comrades, each one marked by the strain of the relentless fighting. They were winning, yes, but at a cost that weighed heavily on them all.

Captain Harris moved among the men, his face etched with the same exhaustion that marked them all. "We're going to keep pushing," he said, his voice steady but weary. "The Germans are making their last stands, and they're desperate. Expect more of this. Stay sharp, stay together, and don't let them catch you off guard."

The platoon nodded, each man feeling the weight of his words settle over them. They knew that this was only the beginning, that the deeper they moved into Germany, the fiercer the resistance would become. The Germans had nothing left to lose, and they would fight with everything they had to defend their homeland.

As they moved out, the tension was palpable, a constant presence that gnawed at them with every step. They encountered more ambushes, more hidden snipers, each encounter a brutal reminder of the resolve of the German soldiers. The Americans retaliated with equal force, determined to push through, to break the enemy's will. But it was a battle that took its toll, each skirmish leaving them more weary, more wary.

In one village, the resistance was especially fierce. German soldiers had barricaded themselves in buildings, using the narrow streets as choke points, launching a desperate last stand that turned every corner, every alley, into a battleground. The platoon moved carefully, clearing each building, each room, their movements tense and calculated. The Germans fought with a ferocity that bordered on fanaticism, refusing to surrender even as the Americans closed in.

Tom kicked down a door, his rifle raised as he entered a dimly lit room. A German soldier lunged at him, his face twisted with desperation, his movements wild. Tom fired instinctively, the shot echoing through the room as the man fell. He felt a pang of something—guilt, maybe, or sorrow—as he looked at the fallen soldier, realizing that this was no longer a battle between armies, but between men who had everything to lose.

Outside, the fighting continued, the sounds of gunfire and explosions filling the air as the Americans pushed through the village, systematically dismantling the German defenses. The resistance was fierce, but it was clear that the Germans were outmatched, their desperation no match for the resolve of the American forces.

By nightfall, the village was theirs, but the victory felt hollow. The men gathered in silence, each one marked by the brutality of the day's fighting. They had won, but at a cost that felt increasingly heavy, the weight of each life taken, each ambush endured, settling over them like a shroud.

Captain Harris addressed them, his voice steady but somber. "We're here to end this war, but remember—we're fighting men just like us. They're defending their homes, their families. Show them respect, even in combat. We're here to bring peace, not to sow more hatred."

The men nodded, each one feeling the truth of his words settle within them. They were here to end the war, to bring peace, but the cost of that peace was one they felt deeply, each life lost a reminder of the brutal reality of war.

As they prepared to move out, Tom looked back at the village, the quiet streets, the darkened windows. They were pushing forward, but with every step, the weight of their mission grew heavier. They were bringing an end to the war, but at a cost that would linger, etched into their memories, a reminder of the sacrifices they had made.

They were soldiers, but they were also men, each one bound by the promise of peace, each one carrying the hope of a world free from the shadows of war. And as they moved forward, bracing for the next ambush, the next battle, Tom knew that they would see this through, whatever it took.

As the platoon pushed deeper into Germany, the horrors of war took on a new, more disturbing form. It was no longer just about battles and tactics; now, they were confronted with the reality of the atrocities that had unfolded in the enemy's homeland. News of concentration camps reached them, tales of unspeakable suffering filtering through whispers and rumors. With each town they liberated, each road they marched down, they began to see glimpses of the war's darker, hidden face—a face that left them questioning not only the enemy but their own role in this grim landscape.

The first real test of their resolve came when they encountered a small German village rumored to be harboring soldiers who had taken shelter among civilians. They were given orders to root out any resistance, to ensure that no one in the village posed a threat to the advancing Allied forces. But as they entered the village, a quiet place filled with scared families and wary eyes, Tom could feel the tension building within the ranks. These were civilians—women, children, the elderly—and yet they were living alongside German soldiers, some of whom were hiding in plain sight, wearing civilian clothes.

Captain Harris briefed the men, his face grave. "I know this isn't easy. We're not here to terrorize these people, but we have to be sure there's no threat. Keep your heads, stay calm, and remember that not everyone here is an enemy."

The platoon began the task of searching houses, moving through the village with a mixture of caution and apprehension. Tom entered a small farmhouse with Foster, their rifles raised as they checked each room. An elderly woman watched them from the doorway, her eyes filled with a mixture of fear and defiance, her hands clutched tightly around a rosary. Tom felt a pang of guilt as he scanned the modest belongings in her kitchen, feeling like an intruder in a place that had clearly seen enough suffering.

"We're sorry," Tom said quietly, lowering his rifle. "We don't mean any harm. We just... we have to be sure."

The woman said nothing, her gaze unwavering, and Tom moved on, leaving the farmhouse with a heaviness in his chest. It didn't feel right, this intrusion into people's lives, this suspicion that turned every villager into a potential enemy. They were here to liberate, to bring an end to the war, but it was becoming harder to tell who, exactly, they were liberating—and from whom.

The day took a darker turn when they reached the center of the village, where a group of German soldiers had been captured, dragged from hiding places in homes and cellars. Some were young, barely more than boys, their faces pale and frightened. Others were older, their eyes hard with defiance. A few of the American soldiers, hardened by months of combat and the recent ambushes, looked at these prisoners with undisguised contempt.

"Why do we even take them prisoner?" muttered one of the men in the platoon. "After what they've done? They'd kill us in a heartbeat if they could."

Tom felt a surge of anger and confusion. He understood the hatred, the desire for vengeance after all they'd endured. But he couldn't bring himself to see these men, these scared young soldiers and hardened veterans, as purely evil. They were human, like him, caught in the machinery of a war none of them had started.

Captain Harris stepped forward, his voice cold and firm. "They're prisoners. We treat them as such. We don't stoop to their level."

The soldier grumbled but fell silent, casting a glare at the prisoners. Tom could feel the tension simmering in the air, a mixture of anger and helplessness that was beginning to erode the lines between right and wrong. War had its own set of rules, its own brutal code of survival, but standing here, watching these men, Tom felt the weight of a different kind of battle—the battle within himself.

Later that night, as the platoon set up camp on the outskirts of the village, they received news that another unit had discovered a labor camp a few miles to the east. The soldiers listened in silence as a messenger relayed the conditions—starving prisoners, the sick and the dying, held captive in unimaginable circumstances. The stories of suffering filled the air, and Tom could see the horror and anger written on the faces of his comrades.

"How do you justify something like that?" Foster muttered, his voice trembling with a mix of disbelief and rage. "How do you look at another human being and treat them like... like animals?"

Tom had no answer. The news of the camps brought a grim clarity to their mission, a reminder of why they were here, of the evil they were fighting. But it also brought questions that lingered long after the fire had died down, questions that gnawed at their sense of justice, at their own humanity.

As they sat in the cold night, surrounded by the quiet of the German countryside, one of the soldiers spoke up, his voice heavy with sorrow. "So what do we do? Do we hold every German accountable? Do we treat them all like monsters, just because some of them committed atrocities?"

Captain Harris looked at him, his gaze thoughtful, troubled. "We don't get to make that choice," he said quietly. "We're here to end this war, to stop the suffering. That's all we can do. It's not our job to judge an entire people, only to ensure this never happens again."

The men nodded, though the words offered little comfort. They were soldiers, but they were also witnesses to the worst of humanity, grappling with the ethical lines that war had blurred. Every German they encountered now was a reminder of the suffering they had seen, the atrocities committed in the name of ideology. And yet, every civilian, every terrified child or wary mother, reminded them that people could be both victims and perpetrators in a war as brutal as this one.

As they moved out the next day, marching along a road lined with leafless trees, Tom felt the weight of the moral complexities they were facing. The war was a mess of gray areas, of blurred lines that made it hard to know who, if anyone, was innocent. They were here to fight an enemy, but they were also here to uphold a sense of justice, to hold themselves to a higher standard. It was a delicate balance, and each step forward felt like a step further into a moral abyss.

They encountered more villages, more civilians, and each encounter tested them, forced them to confront the uncomfortable truths of war. Some soldiers struggled with hatred, others with guilt, and all of them bore the weight of choices that would haunt them long after the war was over.

In one village, a German teenager was caught sabotaging a supply truck, his face defiant as he was brought before Captain Harris. The boy couldn't have been older than sixteen, his cheeks hollow, his eyes wide with fear but filled with a fierce determination.

"He's just a kid," Foster whispered, glancing at Tom. "But he'd kill us if he had the chance."

Harris looked at the boy, his face hard but his eyes troubled. He ordered that the boy be held as a prisoner, treating him with the same respect he would afford any soldier, but Tom could see the conflict in his expression—the tension between duty and compassion, between justice and vengeance.

As they continued their march, Tom knew that these questions would follow them, haunting each step they took deeper into Germany. They were here to end the war, to bring peace, but the cost of that peace was more than they had bargained for. They were soldiers, yes, but they were also witnesses, burdened with the responsibility of preserving their own humanity amid the horrors they encountered.

In the end, all they could do was press on, carrying with them the weight of their choices, the moral dilemmas that would remain long after the last shot had been fired. And as Tom looked out over the German countryside, he realized that peace would be harder won than any battle, that the scars of this war would linger in ways he was only beginning to understand.

The occupation of German territory brought a new set of challenges, a new layer of complexity that the men hadn't fully anticipated. They were no longer just soldiers advancing toward victory; now, they were enforcers of order in a land that had been both their battleground and their enemy's home. The initial sense of triumph had faded, replaced by the grim reality of what it meant to occupy a defeated, divided country.

Tom noticed the shift almost immediately. The towns they entered were marked by quiet hostility. Some Germans glared from doorways, resentment etched into their faces, while others looked on with hollow, defeated stares, their spirits broken by the endless war. The soldiers felt like intruders, a constant presence that was both resented and feared, a reminder of Germany's loss, of everything that had been taken from them.

Captain Harris briefed the men on their new duties, his tone somber. "This isn't like the fighting we've seen. We're here to keep order, to ensure that no one takes advantage of the chaos. It's a balancing act. We're liberators to some, but to many here, we're occupiers. Remember that."

The instructions were clear: keep the peace, respect the civilians, and avoid unnecessary conflicts. But it was easier said than done. Tensions simmered beneath the surface, and even the smallest incident could set off a confrontation. The soldiers, weary from months of battle, were constantly on edge, caught between their duty to uphold justice and the frustration of policing a place that still felt like enemy territory.

One day, as Tom and a few other soldiers patrolled a small town, they noticed a group of young German men gathered outside a shop, their expressions dark, their eyes tracking the soldiers' every movement. The soldiers exchanged wary glances, each one aware of the potential for trouble.

One of the Germans muttered something under his breath, his voice laced with bitterness. Tom didn't understand the words, but he recognized the tone—a mixture of resentment and defiance. The American soldiers slowed, unsure whether to intervene or keep walking. Tension crackled in the air, an unspoken challenge that felt like a spark waiting to catch.

Foster, standing beside Tom, shifted uneasily. "They're not exactly rolling out the welcome mat, are they?"

Tom shook his head. "Can you blame them? To them, we're just... invaders. I think we're here to bring peace, but they're seeing the end of everything they've known."

One of the German men spat on the ground, his glare defiant. The other soldiers tensed, and for a moment, Tom thought a fight might break out. But Captain Harris, who had joined them on the patrol, stepped forward, meeting the German's stare with a calm, steady gaze.

"We're not here to harm you," Harris said, his voice firm but measured. "We're here to end this war, to restore order. I know it's hard, but let's not make this any worse."

The German man's glare softened slightly, but the bitterness remained. He said nothing, turning away as the soldiers moved on, their presence a constant reminder of Germany's defeat.

That night, back at camp, the men gathered around a small fire, their faces illuminated by the flickering light. The conversations were quieter than usual, each man wrestling with the complexities of their new role as occupiers. They had expected hostility from German soldiers, but this quiet resentment from civilians left them questioning their purpose, their identity as liberators.

"How do you keep the peace in a place that doesn't want you?" Foster asked, his voice low. "We came here to end a war, but it feels like... like we're just stirring up new conflicts."

Tom nodded, staring into the fire. "It's hard to keep order when they see us as the enemy. We're here to do what's right, but that doesn't mean they'll see it that way."

The news of atrocities they had discovered, of concentration camps and suffering, weighed heavily on the men, adding another layer to their moral conflict. Some of the soldiers believed it justified their presence, a reminder of why they were here—to stop the horrors that had been hidden within Germany's borders. But for others, it only deepened the sense of unease, the awareness that not everyone was guilty, that they were occupying the homes of people who had been swept up in a war they hadn't chosen.

The next day, the platoon was ordered to oversee the distribution of food and supplies in another small town. It was a routine task, a gesture meant to show goodwill, to offer aid to the civilians who were struggling to survive. But the line between kindness and control was thin, and even this act of generosity felt strained, tainted by mistrust.

As they handed out rations, Tom noticed the expressions on the faces of the people who accepted the food. Some looked grateful, their eyes filled with quiet relief. Others accepted the rations with averted gazes, their faces tight with resentment, as though the food was a bitter reminder of everything they had lost. A few even refused, standing back with crossed arms, their defiance as clear as any words.

One older man approached the line, his gaze fixed on Tom. "You think this makes up for everything?" he asked in halting English, his voice filled with a quiet bitterness. "You come here, take our land, our people... and then you offer us scraps?"

Tom hesitated, the man's words hitting him with a force he hadn't expected. "We're... we're here to help. We're not trying to—"

"To help?" the man interrupted, his voice sharp. "Do you think this is help? Do you think you understand our suffering?"

Tom felt the sting of the man's words, the weight of a pain that went beyond the reach of rations or kind words. He wanted to say something, to explain, but he knew there was no explanation that would ease the man's suffering, no words that could bridge the gulf of grief and loss between them.

Later, back at camp, Captain Harris gathered the men, his face reflecting the same exhaustion and conflict that had settled over all of them. "I know this isn't what we signed up for," he said quietly. "I know it's hard to see ourselves as peacekeepers in a place where we're still seen as the enemy. But we're here to do what's right. We can't control how they see us, but we can control how we treat them. That's the only way we can live with ourselves after this is over."

The men nodded, each one feeling the weight of his words, the responsibility they bore to maintain their own humanity amid the bitterness and resentment that surrounded them. They were soldiers, yes, but they were also representatives of something larger, a promise of peace in a land scarred by war.

As they lay down that night, Tom reflected on the complexities of their mission, on the thin line they walked between liberators and occupiers. They had come to Germany to end the war, to bring peace, but he understood now that peace was not a gift they could simply hand over. It was something fragile, something that required patience, respect, a recognition of the wounds that war had left on both sides.

The days that followed brought more of the same—tensions with civilians, quiet resentment, moments of anger and defiance. They encountered families who had lost everything, young men who saw them as symbols of humiliation, children who looked at them with a mixture of awe and fear. Each encounter left a mark, a reminder that peace was not as simple as victory, that the road to healing was long and fraught with hardship.

In moments of quiet, when the camp was still and the sounds of war faded into the distance, Tom found himself thinking about the future, about what peace would look like after the last shots had been fired. He knew it wouldn't be easy, that the scars of this war would linger, that Germany would carry its losses as heavily as they did.

But he also knew that they had a duty—to show compassion, to offer respect, to be more than conquerors. They were here to lay the foundation for a world without war, to plant the seeds of understanding, even in the face of bitterness. And as he looked out over the quiet German landscape, he felt a grim resolve settle within him.

They were here not just to occupy but to rebuild, to help this fractured land find its way back from the brink. It was a daunting task, one that would test their patience, their humanity. But it was also a task worth fighting for—a chance to prove that even in the ruins of war, peace could be born.

Chapter 10: The Liberation of Concentration Camps

THE RUMORS HAD BEEN circulating for days—whispers from civilians, brief mentions from passing units, vague reports that trickled down through command. The platoon had heard about camps where people were held, starved, abused. But no one truly understood what that meant, what lay beyond the words. Tom and the others tried not to dwell on it; they had seen plenty of horror in this war, and the idea of yet another place of suffering felt almost abstract.

Captain Harris had mentioned that they were moving toward one of these sites, but he hadn't said much beyond that. There was an unspoken tension among the men, a sense of anticipation tempered by unease. Tom couldn't shake the feeling that they were on the verge of discovering something that would change them, that would make every horror they'd seen so far feel like a distant memory.

As they marched through the dense German countryside, the landscape was quiet, eerily so. The usual sounds of birds, of rustling leaves, seemed muted, as if the land itself was holding its breath. The villages they passed were empty, their residents either hiding or gone, leaving behind only silence and the occasional abandoned cart or torn piece of clothing fluttering in the wind.

Foster walked beside Tom, his face set, his eyes narrowed as he scanned the road ahead. "You think the rumors are true?" he asked quietly, his voice barely a murmur.

Tom shrugged, his gaze fixed on the path before them. "I don't know. I've heard stories... but it's hard to imagine anything worse than what we've already seen."

Foster nodded, but Tom could see the doubt in his eyes. They'd witnessed plenty of human cruelty in the war, acts that had shaken their faith in humanity. But there was a sense of dread hanging over them now, a feeling that they were about to confront a darkness beyond anything they'd encountered.

As they drew closer to the coordinates they'd been given, the air took on a sour, heavy quality, a strange staleness that felt out of place in the open countryside. The men exchanged glances, each one feeling a tightening in his chest, an instinctive recoil from something they couldn't yet see. Tom felt his pulse quicken, his senses heightened as they approached the tree line, where a faint shape began to materialize in the distance.

Captain Harris called a halt, signaling for them to proceed cautiously. "Keep your eyes open," he said quietly, his voice tense. "We don't know what we're walking into."

As they moved closer, the outlines of fences came into view—tall, barbed wire fences stretching across the landscape, enclosing low buildings and watchtowers. Tom felt a chill run through him, a sickening realization dawning as he took in the layout, the sheer scale of it. This wasn't just a camp—it was a compound, a place designed to confine, to control.

A strange, acrid smell wafted toward them, faint at first but growing stronger as they neared. It was a smell Tom couldn't place—something rotten, metallic, mingled with the unmistakable stench of decay. The soldiers wrinkled their noses, their faces pale, some covering their mouths and noses with their sleeves as they pushed forward.

As they approached the main gate, a figure stumbled out from one of the buildings, a thin, emaciated man wrapped in ragged cloth. His face was hollow, his eyes sunken, darkened by deep shadows. He moved slowly, his steps unsteady, his gaze fixed on the soldiers with a mixture of fear and disbelief, as if he couldn't quite believe they were real.

Tom felt his breath catch in his throat as he took in the man's appearance—the gaunt face, the skeletal frame, the haunted eyes. The man's skin was stretched tight over his bones, his cheeks sunken, his ribs visible even through the layers of dirty cloth. It was a sight that defied understanding, that felt almost unreal.

Captain Harris approached the man cautiously, his face a mixture of shock and sorrow. "We're... we're here to help," he said gently, his voice breaking slightly. "You're free now."

The man stared at him, uncomprehending, his lips trembling as he tried to form words. "Free?" he whispered, his voice barely audible. "You... you came."

The words hung in the air, heavy and raw, and Tom felt a wave of emotion rise within him—anger, sorrow, disbelief. This wasn't just a camp. It was a prison, a place where people had been reduced to shadows of themselves, stripped of their dignity, of their humanity.

As the men spread out, moving through the gates, they were met with scenes that would haunt them for the rest of their lives. Emaciated figures stumbled out of the buildings, their faces a mixture of fear and hope, their bodies weak, barely able to stand. Some clung to each other for support, their limbs thin and frail, their eyes hollow, as if life itself had been drained from them.

Foster looked around, his face pale, his voice a strained whisper. "How... how could anyone do this?"

Tom shook his head, feeling the weight of the scene settle over him like a suffocating blanket. "I don't know. I don't know how anyone could... could treat people like this."

They moved from building to building, each one revealing scenes of suffering that defied comprehension. There were bunkhouses filled with thin, filthy straw, where dozens of people had been crammed into small spaces. There were makeshift infirmaries with patients lying on bare wooden boards, their bodies riddled with sores, their eyes glazed with pain. In one corner, they found a pile of shoes, children's shoes, small and worn, a chilling reminder of the lives that had been lost here.

Captain Harris was visibly shaken, his hands trembling as he gestured for the medics to begin helping the survivors. "This... this isn't just war," he said, his voice thick with emotion. "This is... something else. Something evil."

Tom stood in silence, watching as his comrades moved among the survivors, offering food, water, words of comfort. But comfort felt hollow here, inadequate in the face of the suffering etched into the faces of these men and women. They were free now, but the scars of what they had endured would never fully heal.

One of the survivors, an older woman with hollow cheeks and sunken eyes, approached Tom, her gaze filled with a quiet strength that defied her frail body. She reached out, gripping his hand, her touch surprisingly strong. "Thank you," she whispered, her voice thick with emotion. "Thank you... for coming."

Tom swallowed hard, feeling tears prick at his eyes. "I'm... I'm so sorry," he managed, his voice breaking. "I'm sorry it took us so long."

She nodded, her gaze distant, as if she were looking beyond him, into a place he couldn't see. "It's over now," she said softly. "It's over."

The words echoed in his mind, a bittersweet reminder of both the victory they had achieved and the horror they had uncovered. They had come to end the war, to bring peace, but nothing had prepared them for this, for the depths of cruelty that humanity could reach.

As night fell over the camp, the soldiers set up a perimeter, guarding the survivors, providing whatever comfort they could. The men sat together in silence, each one lost in his own thoughts, grappling with the images that would be seared into their memories forever. They had seen the face of evil, had come face-to-face with suffering that went beyond anything they had imagined.

Captain Harris addressed the men, his voice low and steady, though his face was lined with sorrow. "We've seen something here that... that changes us.

But we can't look away. We can't forget what we've found, because this—this is why we're here. To put an end to this, to make sure it never happens again."

The men nodded, each one feeling the weight of his words settle within them, a silent vow to carry this memory forward, to bear witness to the suffering they had uncovered. They had come to end the war, but now they understood that their mission went beyond victory, beyond mere survival.

As Tom sat by the fire that night, he felt a quiet resolve settle within him—a promise to remember, to honor the lives of those who had suffered, to ensure that their voices would never be silenced. They were here not just as soldiers, but as witnesses, bearing testimony to the darkest chapters of humanity, carrying forward a message of hope and remembrance.

And as he looked out over the camp, at the survivors huddled together, at the men who had come to free them, he knew that they would carry this experience with them, that it would shape their lives, their understanding of the world. They had seen the face of suffering, and they would never be the same.

The platoon entered the camp in silence, their faces a mixture of disbelief and horror as they took in the sight before them. Rows of barbed wire stretched across the landscape, dividing the camp into sections, each one filled with grim, gray buildings that looked more like prison cells than shelters. The smell hit them immediately—a sickly, nauseating mix of decay, sweat, and something more sinister that clung to the air, refusing to dissipate. The men recoiled, covering their mouths, their eyes wide with shock.

Tom's stomach twisted as he stepped through the gates, his boots crunching over the gravel path. He had heard rumors, had listened to whispered stories from civilians, but nothing could have prepared him for this. The camp was a world unto itself, a place where light and life seemed to have withered away, leaving only the shadows of what had once been.

As they moved deeper into the camp, they began to see the people—the survivors. Thin, skeletal figures clad in torn, striped uniforms, their faces hollow, their eyes wide and empty. Some were slumped against the walls of the buildings, too weak to stand, while others wandered aimlessly, their movements slow, as though their bodies had forgotten how to function. Tom felt a wave of sickness wash over him as he took in their gaunt faces, their fragile limbs, the visible ribs beneath skin stretched taut over bones.

Captain Harris, visibly shaken, ordered the men to spread out, to check each building and provide what assistance they could. "Keep calm," he said, his voice steady but filled with emotion. "We're here to help. Remember that. No matter what we see, we're here to help."

Tom and Foster moved together, entering one of the large barracks. The inside was dark and cramped, filled with rows of wooden bunks stacked three high. The stench was overpowering, and as Tom's eyes adjusted to the dim light, he saw why. Dozens of people were crammed into the tiny space, huddled together on the narrow bunks, their eyes glazed with exhaustion and pain. Some looked up as the soldiers entered, their expressions a mixture of fear and disbelief, as though they were seeing ghosts.

A woman on the nearest bunk clutched her hands together, her lips moving in silent prayer as she watched them. Her face was pale and sunken, her cheeks hollow, and her eyes held a haunted, faraway look that Tom knew would stay with him for the rest of his life. She looked as though she had aged a hundred years, her body ravaged by hunger and suffering.

Tom approached her slowly, crouching down to her level. "We're here to help," he said softly, his voice catching in his throat. "You're free now. It's over."

The woman stared at him for a moment, as if trying to comprehend his words. Slowly, a tear slid down her cheek, and she covered her mouth with a shaking hand. "Is it... really over?" she whispered, her voice barely more than a breath.

Tom nodded, struggling to hold back his own tears. "Yes. You're safe now. We'll take care of you."

He looked around the barracks, his heart heavy as he took in the faces of the other prisoners—men, women, even children, all of them bearing the marks of unimaginable suffering. Some were so weak they couldn't lift their heads, their bodies reduced to fragile shells, their spirits nearly extinguished. He felt anger simmering beneath his sorrow, a burning rage at the people who had done this, who had turned human lives into mere shadows.

Foster, standing beside him, wiped a hand over his face, his expression one of utter disbelief. "I... I didn't know it could get this bad," he whispered. "How could anyone... how could anyone do this?"

Tom shook his head, unable to find an answer. Nothing in his experience, nothing in his understanding of war, had prepared him for this. It was as though they had stepped into another world, a place where humanity had been stripped away, leaving only suffering and despair.

Outside, Captain Harris called for medics, his voice shaking as he instructed them to bring food, water, anything they could to help the survivors. But the supplies they had brought with them felt inadequate, almost laughable in the face of such overwhelming need. How could a loaf of bread or a canteen of water begin to repair the damage done to these people?

As they moved through the camp, the soldiers encountered more scenes of horror—piles of discarded clothing, shoes scattered across the ground, and, in one corner, a mass grave partially covered with earth, a chilling reminder of the lives that had been taken here. The men stared at it in silence, each one feeling the weight of those lives settle over them like a heavy, suffocating blanket.

In another building, they found a makeshift infirmary filled with patients lying on bare wooden boards, their bodies riddled with sores, their breaths shallow and labored. A medic knelt beside one of them, his hands trembling as he tried to provide comfort, but his face was pale, his eyes filled with a kind of horror that words couldn't express.

One of the survivors, a young man with a shaved head and hollow cheeks, stumbled toward Tom, his eyes wide with desperation. "You... you came," he stammered, his voice hoarse. "We didn't think... we didn't think anyone would come."

Tom placed a hand on the man's shoulder, feeling the bones beneath his skin, the frailty of a body that had endured too much. "We're here now," he said, his voice thick with emotion. "We're here, and we're not leaving."

The young man's face crumpled, and he sank to his knees, sobbing quietly. Tom knelt beside him, his own heart breaking as he listened to the sound. This was more than liberation; it was an awakening to the reality of suffering on a scale he hadn't known was possible.

Captain Harris gathered the platoon together, his face lined with sorrow and rage. "We've seen a lot in this war," he said, his voice low but steady. "But this... this is beyond anything I could have imagined. We're going to help these people. We're going to do everything we can to make sure they're safe, that they get what they need. But we're also going to remember this. Every single one of us. Because the world needs to know what happened here. We need to make sure this never happens again."

The men nodded, each one feeling the weight of his words settle over him like a vow, a promise to carry this memory forward, to bear witness to the lives lost, the suffering endured. They were soldiers, but here, in this camp, they were also witnesses, their presence a testament to the horror that had unfolded in the shadow of war.

As night fell over the camp, the soldiers set up makeshift shelters, offering blankets and food, doing what they could to bring comfort to the survivors. But Tom knew that no amount of food or warmth could erase what these people had been through, could heal the scars etched into their bodies and souls.

He sat with a group of survivors by a small fire, listening as they shared their stories, each word a glimpse into a world of unimaginable pain. One man spoke of the day his family had been separated, his voice thick with grief as he described the last time he had seen his wife and children. A woman recounted the months she had spent in a dark cell, her only companion the hope that one day, someone would come.

As Tom listened, he felt a resolve settle within him—a promise to carry these stories, to remember these faces, to honor the lives that had been lost. They had come here as liberators, but they were leaving as witnesses, each one bearing the weight of what they had seen, a memory that would stay with them forever.

And as he looked out over the camp, at the figures huddled together for warmth, at the men and women who had survived the unthinkable, he knew that he would never forget this place. They had walked into a nightmare, but they had also brought a glimmer of hope, a reminder that humanity could endure, even in the darkest of places.

The camp was silent now, the fires flickering in the night, casting shadows over the faces of the soldiers and survivors alike. And as Tom sat there, the weight of his duty heavy on his shoulders, he made a vow—to carry this memory, to speak of what he had seen, to ensure that the world would remember the lives lost, the suffering endured. For in this place, in this camp, he had seen both the depths of human cruelty and the resilience of the human spirit. And he would carry that knowledge with him, always.

The work of rescue began at dawn, with the soldiers moving quickly to distribute food, water, and blankets to the survivors. The camp was a grim scene, each corner revealing new layers of suffering and desperation. The soldiers had seen battle, had faced horrors they thought would leave them numb, but nothing had prepared them for the sheer scale of pain within these barbed wire fences. Now, as they offered what little comfort they could, the reality of the place settled over them, sinking into their bones.

Tom handed a canteen of water to an older man whose trembling hands barely had the strength to hold it. The man's face was gaunt, his cheeks hollow, his eyes glazed with exhaustion. "Drink slowly," Tom said gently, watching as the man took a small, careful sip. The water seemed to renew him just slightly, bringing a faint spark of life back to his eyes.

"Thank you," the man whispered, his voice weak but filled with gratitude. He glanced at Tom, his expression both relieved and sorrowful. "We... we waited. We prayed someone would come."

Tom nodded, unable to find the words. The truth was, he didn't know what to say. All he could do was listen, to be there as the survivors shared pieces of their lives, fragments of the suffering they had endured.

One by one, the stories emerged, each more haunting than the last. An elderly woman spoke of the children who had been separated from their families, her voice breaking as she described the cries she had heard at night, children calling for mothers who would never come. She clutched Tom's hand as she spoke, as if holding onto him could somehow lessen the weight of her memories.

"Do they know?" she asked, her eyes searching his. "Do people outside know what happened to us?"

Tom felt a lump form in his throat. He wanted to promise her that the world would know, that people would understand the horror, the cruelty. But the words felt hollow, inadequate in the face of her suffering. "We'll make sure they know," he said finally, his voice thick with emotion. "We'll make sure no one forgets."

Nearby, Foster knelt beside a young woman who couldn't have been more than twenty. Her face was pale, her body thin and frail, but her eyes held a defiant strength. She spoke in broken English, recounting the months she had spent in the camp, how she had survived by clinging to the memory of her family, by refusing to let the cruelty break her spirit.

"They tried to take everything from us," she whispered, her voice low but steady. "But they couldn't take hope. They couldn't take the belief that someone... someone would come."

Foster listened in silence, his face drawn, his hands trembling as he offered her a small piece of bread. He could see the cost of survival etched into her face, the resilience that had kept her alive through unimaginable suffering.

Captain Harris moved among the survivors, his expression grave as he coordinated the aid efforts. He ordered medics to set up a triage area, where the most fragile survivors could be treated, given proper food and medical attention. But the supplies they had seemed pitifully small in the face of such overwhelming need. The medics worked tirelessly, each one grappling with the limits of what they could do, the reality that some of these people were too weak to survive much longer.

As they worked, a small boy appeared from behind one of the barracks, his thin frame barely able to support his weight. He looked at Tom and the other soldiers with wide, frightened eyes, clutching a small piece of cloth to his chest. Tom knelt down, reaching out gently. "Hey there," he said softly. "You're safe now. We're here to help."

The boy hesitated, his eyes darting between Tom and Foster, as if trying to decide if they were real. Slowly, he stepped forward, his grip on the cloth tightening. Tom noticed then that it was a piece of an old shirt, the fabric worn and frayed. He could see the remnants of a name embroidered on it, the only memory the boy had of a family he had lost.

"Are you hungry?" Tom asked, offering him a small piece of bread.

The boy nodded, his movements hesitant. He took the bread, biting into it with slow, careful bites, as if he didn't quite believe it was real. He chewed in silence, his eyes never leaving Tom's face, as though looking away might make everything disappear.

As the day wore on, the survivors shared more of their stories, each one a testament to the resilience of the human spirit, a glimpse into the depths of suffering they had endured. Some spoke of family members they had lost, of friends who had succumbed to illness and hunger. Others told of the kindnesses that had kept them going—the small acts of courage and compassion that had helped them survive one more day.

One man, his voice barely more than a whisper, recounted how he had been a musician before the war, how he had once played in a concert hall filled with people. "I played for them," he said, his gaze distant. "When things were bad here, when hope felt impossible, I would hum those songs, in my head. It reminded me that there was beauty somewhere, even if I couldn't see it."

Tom listened, his heart breaking as he realized how each survivor had found their own way to hold on, to survive in the face of unimaginable cruelty. They had lost everything—their homes, their families, their health—but they had clung to fragments of hope, to memories that kept them alive.

By nightfall, the soldiers had done what they could, distributing the last of their rations, setting up makeshift tents to provide shelter from the cold. But as Tom looked around the camp, he knew that what they had given was not enough, that it would take months, years even, for these people to recover from the horrors they had endured.

Captain Harris gathered the men, his face lined with exhaustion, his voice heavy with sorrow. "We've done everything we can here," he said quietly. "But we need to remember this. Every face, every story. We're their witnesses now. We carry this with us, and we make sure the world knows what happened here."

The men nodded, each one feeling the weight of his words, the responsibility they now bore. They were soldiers, but here, in this camp, they had become something more—witnesses to a crime that went beyond war, a darkness that had nearly swallowed humanity.

That night, Tom sat beside the survivors as they huddled around a small fire, sharing warmth and silence. The stars above were bright, indifferent to the suffering below, but Tom found comfort in their presence, a reminder that there was still beauty in the world, that there was still light to be found.

An older woman beside him, her face worn but filled with a quiet strength, reached out and took his hand. "You saved us," she whispered. "You brought us back from the darkness."

Tom looked at her, his throat tight. "I only wish we could have come sooner."

She nodded, her gaze filled with a depth of understanding that went beyond words. "You're here now. And that's enough."

As he sat there, surrounded by survivors who had endured the unthinkable, Tom made a silent promise—to remember, to carry their stories, to honor the lives that had been taken. They had come to liberate, to bring hope to a place that had forgotten it existed, and now they would carry that hope forward, a light in the darkness they had witnessed.

And as he looked around the camp, at the faces of the men and women who had been saved, he knew that they would never be the same. This place, these people, had changed them, had shown them the depths of both human cruelty and resilience. They had seen the worst of humanity, but they had also seen its strength, its capacity to endure.

They had come as soldiers, but they were leaving as witnesses, bearing testimony to the strength of the human spirit. And as they prepared to move on, each one carried with him a piece of that spirit, a reminder of the promise they had made—to remember, to honor, and to ensure that this would never happen again.

The soldiers camped outside the barbed wire that night, unable to bring themselves to rest within the walls of the camp. The horrors they had witnessed were too fresh, too raw. The images replayed in their minds: the hollow-eyed survivors, the emaciated bodies, the piles of shoes and discarded belongings that hinted at the countless lives lost. It was too much to bear, too much to understand. They had faced death before, had seen comrades fall in battle, but this—this was something beyond comprehension.

Tom lay in his tent, staring up at the canvas ceiling, his mind a swirl of emotions. He felt numb, hollow, as if some part of him had been stripped away in that camp. His hands shook, the tremors a reminder of the anger, the sorrow that had settled into his bones. He closed his eyes, but each time he did, the faces of the survivors filled his mind—gaunt, haunted faces, each one a testament to the suffering they had endured.

Foster was lying beside him, equally silent, staring blankly into the darkness. After a long silence, he finally spoke, his voice barely a whisper. "How... how do you wrap your mind around something like this?" He turned to look at

Tom, his eyes filled with a mixture of confusion and despair. "What kind of person does something like that? What kind of world allows it?"

Tom had no answers. He could feel the same questions gnawing at him, a sickening sense of disbelief mingling with a deep, festering anger. They had fought in battles, had taken lives, but there was a difference between fighting an enemy in war and systematically destroying innocent people. He felt as though he were trying to comprehend a darkness beyond anything he'd known, a cruelty that defied explanation.

Captain Harris walked past their tent, pausing when he saw the two men still awake. He crouched down, his face haggard, his eyes shadowed with the same anguish that marked them all. "You're not alone in how you're feeling," he said quietly, his voice steady but laced with sorrow. "None of us are prepared for something like this. It's not something we're meant to understand."

Foster shook his head, his voice trembling. "How can we move on, Captain? How do we walk away from this place knowing what happened here? Knowing that... that people did this to each other?"

Harris looked away, a pained expression crossing his face. "I don't know," he admitted. "I wish I had the answers. But we have a duty now—a duty to remember, to carry this with us so that the world can know what happened here. It's the only way to make sure it never happens again."

Tom sat up, his hands clenching into fists. "It's not enough," he said, his voice thick with anger. "It's not enough to just remember. Those people... they went through hell, and for what? So that we can just move on, keep marching as if... as if we haven't seen what we've seen?"

Harris placed a hand on Tom's shoulder, his grip firm but comforting. "I understand, Tom. I do. But we have to find a way to carry this without letting it destroy us. Those people, those survivors—they need us to be strong, to carry this memory so that their suffering isn't forgotten. They need us to be more than soldiers now."

Tom swallowed hard, feeling the weight of Harris's words settle over him. He knew the captain was right, but the anger, the grief, felt too large, too overwhelming to contain. He could feel it pressing against his chest, a suffocating weight that left him unable to breathe.

The next morning, as they resumed their work in the camp, the soldiers moved in silence, their faces marked by exhaustion and sorrow. They distributed food, provided blankets, offered what little comfort they could, but each act felt hollow, inadequate. They were haunted by the knowledge that no amount of kindness could erase what had been done here, could heal the scars etched into the survivors' bodies and souls.

Tom watched as one of the medics knelt beside a young girl, gently wrapping a bandage around her frail arm. She looked up at the medic with wide, untrusting eyes, flinching slightly with each movement. Tom felt a surge of sadness as he realized that even the smallest gesture of kindness was foreign to her, that she had learned to expect only cruelty.

The girl's gaze met his, and he forced a smile, a faint, shaky attempt to offer reassurance. But her expression remained wary, her eyes reflecting a fear that went beyond anything he could imagine. Tom looked away, his heart heavy. He didn't know how to help her, didn't know if there was any way to make this right.

That night, as the soldiers gathered around a small fire, the tension in the air was palpable. Each man was grappling with his own emotions, his own attempts to process what they had seen. Foster broke the silence, his voice bitter. "I thought I'd seen the worst of it, you know? The war, the fighting. But this... this is something else. It's like they were trying to erase these people, like they wanted to make them disappear from the world."

One of the other soldiers, his face shadowed by the firelight, nodded grimly. "It's evil. Plain and simple. There's no other word for it."

Captain Harris spoke up, his voice quiet but steady. "What we've seen here—this will stay with us. It'll haunt us. But we can't let it destroy us. We owe it to those people to carry on, to tell their stories, to make sure the world knows what happened here."

Tom looked into the flames, his mind filled with the images of the camp, of the suffering that had been inflicted within its walls. He felt torn between anger and helplessness, a desire for justice mingling with the sickening realization that there was no way to undo what had been done.

"They deserved better," he said softly, his voice almost lost in the crackle of the fire. "Those people, they deserved so much better than this."

Harris nodded, his gaze fixed on the fire. "Yes, they did. And we can't change what happened, but we can make sure their suffering isn't forgotten. We can carry this with us, honor their memory by being better, by refusing to let something like this happen again."

The soldiers fell silent, each one lost in his own thoughts, grappling with the weight of the responsibility they now carried. They had come to fight a war, but they were leaving as witnesses to something darker, something that had shaken their very sense of humanity.

Tom closed his eyes, feeling the grief, the anger, the sorrow settle deep within him. He knew he would carry this memory forever, that the images of the camp, the faces of the survivors, would remain etched in his mind. But he also knew that he had a duty, a responsibility to honor those lives, to bear witness to the suffering they had endured.

As the fire crackled and the night stretched on, Tom made a silent promise to himself and to the people they had saved. He would remember them, would carry their stories, their pain, so that the world would never forget. It was a burden, yes, but it was also a duty—a duty to ensure that the darkness they had seen would never be allowed to flourish again.

And as he looked around at his comrades, at the men who had shared this experience, he knew that they, too, would carry this burden, that they would be bound by this shared memory, this shared vow. Together, they would ensure that the world would know, that the suffering of those in the camp would not be in vain. They would be more than soldiers; they would be guardians of the memory, keepers of the promise that such horrors would never be allowed to happen again.

The morning after their discovery of the camp, the soldiers gathered just outside its gates, their faces hardened with determination, their expressions somber and resolute. They had spent the night wrestling with the images that haunted them—the skeletal figures, the silent screams of lives shattered beyond repair. They were soldiers, but the experience had transformed them, filled them with a new purpose, one that burned with an intensity they hadn't known before.

Captain Harris stood before them, his face marked by the same anguish that gripped them all. The usual formalities were forgotten; they were no longer just men in uniform. They were bearers of a burden that transcended ranks and orders. Harris's voice was low but fierce as he addressed them, the weight of his words resonating with the fury and sorrow they all felt.

"We've seen the truth of this war," he began, his gaze moving from one man to the next. "We've seen what we're up against—not just an enemy with guns, but a system that seeks to strip away humanity itself. This isn't just about territory or battles anymore. This is about stopping something far darker, something evil."

The soldiers nodded, each man feeling the fire of his words ignite a fierce resolve within them. They had come to Germany to end the war, but now they understood that their mission was about more than just victory. They were fighting to put an end to the atrocities, to stop the suffering that had been inflicted on innocent lives. They would not rest until every camp, every place of horror, was liberated.

Tom clenched his fists, his jaw tight as he listened. He felt the same anger simmering in his chest, a rage that he had never known before. The scenes from the camp were burned into his memory, and he knew that he could not leave this place unchanged. The people they had encountered, the survivors who had endured the unthinkable, deserved justice. He felt it as a duty, a vow he would carry until the last camp was liberated, until the last shred of cruelty had been torn from this land.

"We can't bring back those who've been lost," Harris continued, his voice steady. "But we can make damn sure that no one else suffers like this. We can bring down the ones responsible, end the system that allowed this to happen. We've got a job to do, and it's more important now than ever."

Foster stepped forward, his face pale but resolute. "Captain, I swear it—I'm not leaving this country until we've rooted out every last one of those camps. I don't care how long it takes. I don't care what it costs. We owe it to those people."

Tom nodded in agreement, his voice steady but filled with emotion. "We're with you, Captain. We've seen too much to turn back now. We'll see this mission through, for the survivors, for everyone who didn't make it. We owe them that much."

One by one, the men voiced their agreement, their words laced with determination and grief. They had been fighting a war of soldiers, of weapons and tactics, but now they were fighting for something deeper, something that went beyond the battlefield. They were fighting for justice, for humanity, for the countless lives that had been stolen by cruelty and hatred.

Captain Harris looked around at his men, pride and sorrow mingling in his gaze. "This is our promise," he said quietly, his voice filled with conviction. "We will find every camp, every place of suffering, and we will end it. We will make sure that those responsible answer for what they've done. And we will carry this memory with us, so that the world will never forget."

The men stood in silence, each one feeling the weight of the vow they had taken. They were no longer just soldiers in a foreign land; they were part of a mission to end the atrocities, to liberate the innocent and hold accountable those who had inflicted such horror. The memory of the camp, of the lives lost, of the suffering endured, was now a part of them, a fire that would drive them forward, that would guide them in the days and battles to come.

As they prepared to move out, to continue their march deeper into Germany, Tom felt a surge of purpose, a renewed sense of resolve. He knew that the path ahead would be long, that they would encounter more darkness, more cruelty. But he also knew that he was not alone, that he was part of a brotherhood bound by a shared promise, a collective vow to bring an end to the suffering.

The men walked forward, their steps heavy but purposeful, each one carrying with him the weight of what they had seen. They would fight not only to end the war, but to ensure that no one else would ever have to endure the horrors they had witnessed. They were bound by a promise to honor the lives of those they had liberated, and to avenge those who had not survived.

As they left the camp behind, the sky was tinged with the pale light of dawn, a reminder that even after the darkest of nights, morning would come. And as Tom looked back one last time, he knew that they would carry the memory of this place, this mission, with them forever.

They would not falter. They would not turn away. They would see it through, until every last camp was freed, every last survivor saved. This was their vow, their purpose, and they would honor it, no matter the cost.

Chapter 11: The Road to Berlin

The final push toward Berlin was a relentless march through towns and villages that bore the scars of war. The once orderly streets were now broken by shell craters, lined with rubble and burned-out buildings. The German army, battered and on the brink of collapse, was making its last stand. As the platoon neared the German capital, they encountered fierce resistance at every turn—a desperate attempt by the enemy to hold off the inevitable.

Tom and his comrades knew that Berlin was close. The intensity of the defenses told them as much; the closer they drew, the harder the Germans fought. The air was thick with smoke and the bitter scent of gunpowder, a constant reminder that the end of the war was near but not yet won.

Captain Harris crouched behind a wall of sandbags, studying a map as the sound of machine guns echoed in the distance. "Listen up, boys," he said, his voice steady but laced with urgency. "The Germans have fortified this area with artillery, sniper nests, and tank traps. They're throwing everything they have left at us. They know if we get through, Berlin falls. We're going to have to be smart, and we're going to have to be fast."

The men nodded, each one feeling the weight of the task before them. They had survived so much together, pushed through hellish terrain and brutal ambushes, but this was something else. This was the last stand, the final barrier between them and the end of the war. And the Germans were fighting with a desperation that could only come from defending one's homeland.

The platoon moved forward cautiously, keeping low as they crossed open fields and passed through bombed-out buildings. Every step brought the risk of hidden mines or sniper fire, each corner a potential ambush. Tom scanned the horizon, his rifle at the ready, his senses heightened by the knowledge that the enemy would stop at nothing to prevent them from reaching Berlin.

The first shots rang out from a machine-gun nest hidden in a crumbling building up ahead. Bullets ripped through the air, sending the men diving for cover behind piles of debris. Tom pressed himself against the ground, his heart pounding as he felt the sharp ping of bullets hitting the stones beside him.

"Get down!" Captain Harris shouted, signaling for the men to spread out. "Take that nest out—Tom, Foster, flank them from the left!"

Tom and Foster crawled through the rubble, keeping low as they made their way around the building, moving in silence. The machine gun rattled continuously, its bullets tearing through the air, pinning down the rest of the platoon. Tom's pulse quickened as they reached a narrow alley leading to the rear of the building. He could hear the German soldiers shouting orders, their voices tense, hurried.

They crept closer, weapons at the ready, until they reached the back door of the building. Tom signaled to Foster, who nodded, his expression tense but determined. With a swift motion, Tom kicked the door open, and the two of them stormed inside, catching the Germans by surprise. The soldiers manning the machine gun barely had time to react before Tom and Foster opened fire, taking down the crew with quick, precise shots.

"Machine gun down!" Tom called over the radio, relief flooding through him as he saw the rest of the platoon advance toward the building, moving quickly to secure the area. But there was little time to celebrate; they knew this was only one of many defenses they would face.

As they pushed forward, the resistance grew more intense. German soldiers emerged from foxholes and bunkers, firing with everything they had. Artillery shells rained down from nearby hills, sending up clouds of dirt and debris, creating a chaotic, nightmarish battlefield. The enemy was relentless, and the platoon was forced to fight for every inch of ground, moving forward yard by yard through the smoke and fire.

At one point, a German tank appeared, its turret swiveling toward them with deadly precision. Tom felt his stomach twist as he saw the massive machine bearing down on their position. They had no tanks of their own to counter it, only handheld explosives and their determination.

Captain Harris shouted for the men to spread out, to avoid bunching together as the tank's main cannon fired, sending a shockwave through the ground and scattering debris everywhere. Tom gritted his teeth, his mind racing as he tried to think of a way to disable the tank. They needed to stop it before it cut through their lines.

Foster crawled up beside him, clutching a satchel charge. "Tom, cover me," he whispered, his face pale but resolute. "I'm going to try to get close enough to plant this."

Tom nodded, raising his rifle and taking aim at the tank's machine-gun nest, firing to draw the gunner's attention away from Foster. His heart pounded as he watched his friend dash toward the tank, his movements quick and careful, darting from one piece of cover to the next. Every second felt like an eternity as he waited, his focus narrowed to Foster's path, praying he would make it.

Finally, Foster reached the tank, pressing himself against its side as he fixed the satchel charge to the tracks. He glanced back at Tom, giving him a quick thumbs-up before sprinting away. Tom held his breath as Foster dived behind cover, and seconds later, the charge detonated with a deafening explosion, the tank's track shredding, immobilizing it in a plume of smoke and flames.

"Nice work!" Captain Harris called out, rallying the men as they pressed forward. The path was clear, but only for a brief moment. The German soldiers, undeterred by the loss of their tank, regrouped, launching a fierce counterattack. The platoon was forced to dig in, taking cover as bullets and mortars filled the air.

The fighting was brutal, an unrelenting assault that pushed each man to his limits. Tom felt the sting of exhaustion, the weight of months of combat bearing down on him, but he forced himself to keep going, to keep pushing forward. They were close, so close to Berlin, and they couldn't afford to stop now.

As night began to fall, the platoon regrouped, hunkering down in a makeshift shelter within the ruins of a church. The once-beautiful structure was now a shell, its stained glass shattered, its walls scarred by bullets and fire. The men sat in silence, their faces drawn, their bodies weary, but their resolve unbroken.

Captain Harris looked at them, his expression a mixture of pride and sorrow. "We're nearly there," he said, his voice quiet but filled with determination. "We've made it this far. Berlin is within reach, and we're going to see this through. We're going to end this war. For everyone we've lost, for everyone we've seen suffer—we're not stopping until it's over."

The men nodded, each one feeling the weight of his words. They had been through hell together, had seen things that would haunt them for the rest of their lives. But they had a mission, a purpose, and they would see it through, no matter the cost.

As they prepared to move out again, Tom looked around at his comrades, at the men who had become his brothers, and felt a surge of pride. They had come so far, had survived against impossible odds, and now, standing on the brink of Berlin, they were ready to finish what they had started.

They would face whatever lay ahead with courage, with resilience, with the memory of everything they had endured driving them forward. The road to Berlin was littered with obstacles, with fierce defenses and desperate soldiers, but they would overcome them all. They would end this war.

With a final glance at his comrades, Tom took a deep breath and prepared to step forward, ready to face whatever awaited them in the heart of the enemy's capital. They were soldiers, yes, but they were also liberators, avengers, and the bearers of a promise—to bring peace, to end the suffering, to finish what they had come here to do.

As the platoon continued its advance toward Berlin, the remnants of the German army lay scattered in disorganized pockets across the countryside. The soldiers moved through towns and villages, encountering bombed-out buildings, abandoned artillery, and hastily discarded equipment—signs of a force that was retreating, unraveling. But while the German defenses had fractured, the resistance they encountered was still fierce, unpredictable, and deadly.

Tom and his comrades had grown accustomed to moving with caution. Every quiet street, every empty field could hide a small group of die-hard soldiers or a sniper intent on defending the Fatherland until the last breath. The German army was fighting a losing battle, but these scattered groups fought with a desperation that made them as dangerous as ever.

Captain Harris halted the platoon on the edge of a small village, scanning the landscape for signs of life. "Intel says there's a small detachment of German soldiers dug in somewhere around here," he murmured, his voice low. "They're isolated, but that doesn't make them any less of a threat. Keep your eyes sharp and stick close."

The soldiers fanned out, moving quietly through the empty streets. The silence was thick, broken only by the distant sounds of artillery and the occasional crack of gunfire from somewhere far off. Tom could feel the tension simmering beneath the quiet—a sense that something was waiting just beyond sight, ready to spring at any moment.

As they approached the town square, a sudden burst of gunfire erupted from one of the buildings. The platoon scattered, each man diving for cover as bullets tore through the air, ricocheting off stones and walls. Tom pressed himself against a low wall, gripping his rifle tightly, his heart pounding.

"Sniper!" someone shouted, and Tom scanned the upper windows, spotting a glint of metal just as another shot rang out, striking the wall inches from his head. He ducked lower, glancing toward Captain Harris, who was gesturing for the men to flank the sniper's position.

"Tom, Foster—circle around back and see if you can get an angle on him," Harris ordered.

Nodding, Tom signaled to Foster, and the two of them crept through the shadows, weaving their way around the side of the building. They moved silently, their footsteps careful, their breaths held as they slipped into the alley behind the sniper's location. Tom peered around the corner, spotting a narrow staircase that led up to the upper floors.

They climbed slowly, their rifles at the ready, each step deliberate. When they reached the top, Tom took a deep breath, steadying himself before pushing the door open. The sniper, a young German soldier, was crouched near the window, focused on his scope, unaware of their approach. Tom hesitated, a pang of something—pity, perhaps—passing through him as he looked at the boy who couldn't have been much older than him.

But there was no time for sympathy. Foster stepped forward, his rifle aimed squarely at the sniper's back. "Hands up!" he shouted.

The sniper froze, his hands twitching before he slowly raised them, his rifle slipping from his grasp. He turned, his face pale, his eyes wide with fear. He muttered something in German, his voice trembling, and Tom felt a flash of guilt as he took in the soldier's youth, the terror in his expression.

They escorted him downstairs, where Captain Harris was waiting. He glanced at the young soldier, his expression impassive but his eyes weary. "You're out of the fight now, son," he said quietly. "This war's over for you."

The sniper looked down, his shoulders slumping in defeat. Tom watched him for a moment, wondering how many other young men like him were still out there, clinging to orders, to an ideology that had long since crumbled. It was a sobering reminder that while the war might be nearing its end, the scars it left would linger.

The platoon moved on, but their progress was constantly interrupted by similar encounters—small groups of German soldiers hidden in farmhouses, sniper nests concealed in church steeples, isolated patrols lying in wait along rural roads. Each skirmish was brief but intense, a desperate clash that left them wary, jumpy, never sure when the next ambush would strike.

In one village, they came across a German squad holed up in a cellar, their weapons aimed at the entrance. The Americans called for them to surrender, their voices echoing down the narrow stone steps. After a tense silence, the Germans emerged, one by one, their faces lined with exhaustion and defeat. They handed over their weapons, their movements slow, each one casting wary glances at the soldiers who had once been their enemies.

As they marched the prisoners out of the village, Foster shook his head, his expression conflicted. "It's strange, isn't it?" he murmured to Tom. "They're fighting to the last, but you can see it in their eyes. They know it's over."

Tom nodded, his gaze fixed on the prisoners. "They're clinging to whatever they have left. Orders, pride... maybe even fear. But you're right. They know they've lost."

Captain Harris kept them moving, determined to press on despite the sporadic resistance. The soldiers were tired, their bodies worn down by the months of relentless combat, but their mission drove them forward. Each pocket of resistance they encountered served as a reminder of what they had come here to end—the ideology, the cruelty, the suffering. They were liberators, bringing with them the promise of peace, but that peace was only possible once Berlin was in Allied hands.

As they drew closer to the outskirts of Berlin, the skirmishes intensified. German forces, though disorganized, seemed to be rallying in greater numbers, a final, desperate attempt to defend their capital. The platoon found itself under near-constant fire, dodging mortar rounds, hunkering down in trenches and bombed-out buildings as they slowly inched their way forward.

One afternoon, they came across a group of German civilians who had been caught in the crossfire, their faces pale with fear as they huddled in the remains of a schoolhouse. Tom felt a pang of empathy as he looked at the frightened faces of children, the worn expressions of mothers clutching their sons and daughters.

"We're here to help," he assured them, gesturing for the civilians to stay low, to follow them to safety. Some of the villagers hesitated, their eyes filled with suspicion, but others took his hand, their relief palpable as they followed the soldiers through the chaotic streets.

As they moved, Tom noticed an older man who seemed lost, his eyes vacant, his steps unsteady. The man wore a worn jacket, his hand gripping a faded photograph. He clutched it tightly, as if it were a lifeline, his gaze distant. Tom approached him gently, guiding him along as he wondered who the man had lost, what memories he was clinging to in the final days of this war.

Each encounter, each skirmish, brought with it a deeper sense of urgency, a realization that Berlin was within reach but still defended by those who refused to surrender. The platoon fought with renewed determination, pushing back every pocket of resistance they encountered, knowing that every step brought them closer to ending the suffering they had seen.

By nightfall, they regrouped, taking cover in an abandoned farmhouse. The soldiers sat in silence, their faces marked by exhaustion, but their resolve unwavering. They knew that they were nearing the end, that Berlin was almost within their grasp. And as they prepared to press on, each man carried with him the memory of what they had seen—the suffering, the destruction, and the lives they had vowed to protect.

They would face whatever lay ahead, fight through whatever resistance remained, until Berlin was liberated, until the final symbol of the enemy's power had fallen. They were more than soldiers now; they were the instruments of justice, bearers of the promise they had made to end the atrocities, to bring peace to a world scarred by war.

And as Tom looked around at his comrades, he knew that they would see this mission through to the end. They had come too far, endured too much, to turn back now.

As the platoon moved closer to the heart of Berlin, the city unfolded before them in a mixture of devastation and resilience. Bombed-out buildings lined the streets, their windows shattered, their walls scarred by shrapnel and fire. Smoke billowed from various corners of the city, creating a haze that blurred the skyline, casting an eerie glow over the shattered remnants of Germany's once-proud capital.

Yet even in the midst of the ruins, Berlin's civilians persisted. Men, women, and children navigated the broken streets, their faces marked by exhaustion, fear, and a sense of desperation that seemed to hang over the entire city. The soldiers, hardened by months of combat, were surprised by the diverse reactions they encountered—some greeted them with hostility, others with weary resignation, and a few with cautious hope.

Captain Harris halted the platoon as they approached a group of civilians gathered near a bombed-out shop. They were mostly women and children, huddled together, their eyes wide as they watched the soldiers approach. A few older men stood protectively in front, their faces wary, their postures tense. The atmosphere was thick with suspicion, a silent question hanging in the air: Were these soldiers liberators, or had they come to conquer?

Tom stepped forward slowly, holding up his hands in a gesture of peace. "We're not here to hurt anyone," he said, his voice calm and reassuring. "We're here to end this war, to bring peace."

An older woman at the front of the group met his gaze, her expression a mixture of defiance and disbelief. "Peace?" she repeated bitterly, her voice laced with a deep sorrow. "You bring peace by bringing destruction to our city?"

Her words struck Tom, and he felt a pang of guilt as he looked around at the devastation surrounding them. He understood her anger, the bitterness of seeing one's home reduced to rubble. This war had cost them all dearly, but it was different to stand in the heart of someone else's suffering, to see the destruction through the eyes of those who called this place home.

"We've seen terrible things," he said softly, meeting her gaze. "And we're here to end those things. I know it's hard to believe, but we want this war over as much as you do."

The woman's expression softened slightly, but the pain remained in her eyes. She nodded, her gaze drifting to the ruins of her home. "I just want it to end," she whispered. "We've all lost so much."

One of the children clinging to her side, a boy no older than ten, looked up at Tom with wide, curious eyes. "Are you really here to make things better?" he asked, his voice small, hopeful.

Tom knelt down, offering the boy a gentle smile. "Yes," he said. "That's what we're here for."

As they moved on, the soldiers encountered more civilians, each one bearing the unique scars of the war. They passed a group of young men, who watched them with a mix of resentment and fear, their eyes hard, their postures defiant. One of them muttered something under his breath, a slur in German, but when Tom met his gaze, the young man looked away, his bravado faltering.

"They're just kids," Foster murmured, his voice laced with sadness. "They've grown up surrounded by this war. It's all they know."

"Yeah," Tom replied, glancing at the young men. "And now they're paying for it."

The soldiers continued through the city, and with each encounter, they gained a deeper understanding of the complexity of Berlin's civilians. Some of the people they met seemed resigned, defeated by the endless suffering and deprivation. They shuffled through the streets, eyes downcast, barely registering the soldiers' presence. Others were openly hostile, casting accusing glares, as if blaming the Americans for their plight.

In one neighborhood, they encountered a man who approached them cautiously, his hands raised in a gesture of surrender. His clothes were worn and tattered, his face lined with worry, but there was a spark of hope in his eyes.

"Thank you," he said in halting English, his voice filled with emotion. "Thank you for coming. My family... we were never with them. We never believed in this war."

Tom nodded, moved by the man's words. "You don't have to explain," he replied gently. "We're here to put an end to this, for everyone."

The man smiled, a faint, weary expression that spoke of years of fear and hardship. "I just want my children to grow up in a world without war," he said. "Without hate."

As they walked on, Tom and his fellow soldiers couldn't help but feel the weight of the city's suffering pressing down on them. They were liberators, yes, but to many of these people, they were also reminders of the war, of the destruction that had come to their doorsteps. For every grateful glance, there were two more filled with resentment, with suspicion, as the people of Berlin struggled to understand what this new presence meant for their future.

At a checkpoint near the center of the city, the platoon encountered a woman clutching a small bundle, her face drawn, her eyes hollow. She held her child close, shielding him from the noise and chaos around her. When she saw the soldiers, she froze, her gaze filled with fear.

"Please," she whispered in German, clutching her child tighter. "I have nothing left. Just let us go."

Captain Harris approached her, his voice calm and gentle. "Ma'am, we're not here to harm you. We're here to help."

The woman looked at him with tears in her eyes, her expression a mixture of disbelief and exhaustion. "Help?" she repeated, her voice a barely audible whisper. "Who can help us now?"

Tom watched her, feeling a sense of helplessness settle over him. They had come to bring an end to the war, to liberate the people oppressed by an unjust regime, but standing here, he realized that liberation was only one part of the story. These people would carry the scars of this war for years to come, their lives forever changed by the suffering they had endured.

As they made their way through the heart of Berlin, the soldiers saw glimpses of what had once been. Grand buildings, now reduced to rubble, hinted at the city's former glory. The people, though broken, bore themselves with a quiet resilience, a determination to survive even in the face of devastation. And amid the destruction, Tom caught glimpses of hope—a child's smile, a mother's protective embrace, a father's weary but grateful nod.

That night, as they set up camp on the outskirts of the city, the men gathered around a small fire, reflecting on what they had seen. The mood was heavy, each man weighed down by the complexity of their mission, the realization that ending the war was only the beginning of the road to healing.

Foster spoke up, his voice thoughtful. "I thought coming here would feel different, you know? Like we'd be heroes or something. But it just feels... complicated."

Captain Harris nodded, his face shadowed by the firelight. "War always leaves scars," he said quietly. "And sometimes those scars run deeper than we can see. We've brought an end to the fighting, but these people—they'll be picking up the pieces long after we're gone."

Tom looked around at his comrades, feeling a deep sense of unity with them. They had come to Berlin as soldiers, but they were leaving as something more—witnesses to a city's suffering, bearers of a promise to help rebuild a world fractured by violence and hate.

As he stared into the fire, Tom thought of the civilians they had encountered, each one carrying their own story, their own loss. They were no longer just Germans, no longer just the "enemy." They were people, caught in the storm of a war they hadn't asked for, just trying to survive.

And as they prepared to face the final days of the war, Tom made a silent vow—to remember these people, to carry their stories with him, to honor the strength and resilience he had seen in the heart of Berlin. They were here to end the fighting, but they were also here to help bring about a new beginning, a future where children could grow up in peace, where families could live without fear.

They would carry this memory, this understanding of the people they had encountered, with them forever. They would be more than soldiers; they would be guardians of a shared humanity, a reminder that even in the darkest times, there was still hope, still a spark of resilience that could light the way forward.

The push through Berlin was unlike anything the platoon had experienced. The city lay in ruins, a crumbling maze of twisted metal, shattered glass, and scorched stone. Every street, every alley, seemed to carry the remnants of fierce resistance. The sounds of sporadic gunfire echoed off the rubble, filling the air with a sense of tension that refused to fade.

Tom moved carefully through the debris-strewn streets, his rifle at the ready, his senses heightened. Berlin was a city under siege, and though the main German forces had fractured, small groups of soldiers continued to fight, determined to defend their capital to the bitter end. Every corner could hide an ambush, every abandoned building a sniper. The platoon had to stay sharp, ready for the fight that could come at any moment.

"Eyes open," Captain Harris whispered, signaling for the men to spread out as they approached a large intersection. "They know this city better than we do, and they're using every advantage they've got."

The platoon moved forward, ducking behind piles of rubble, slipping through the shadows cast by half-collapsed buildings. The destruction was staggering; entire blocks lay flattened, the remains of shops and homes scattered like broken toys. The people of Berlin had abandoned the streets, and it was as if the city itself had become a ghost, a husk of what it had once been.

Suddenly, gunfire erupted from a building ahead, shattering the quiet and sending the men diving for cover. Bullets ripped through the air, chipping away at the walls and ricocheting off metal beams. Tom pressed himself against a stone wall, peering over the edge to locate the source of the shots.

"Top floor, left side," he called out, spotting the glint of a rifle barrel sticking out from a shattered window.

"Foster, Tom—flank them," Captain Harris ordered. "The rest of you, lay down suppressive fire."

The platoon opened fire, sending a barrage of bullets toward the building as Tom and Foster slipped around to the side, moving quickly through the rubble. They found a narrow staircase at the back, the steps cracked and crumbling underfoot as they climbed toward the upper floors. Tom's pulse quickened as they neared the top, each step bringing them closer to the soldiers lying in wait.

When they reached the top floor, they could hear the Germans shouting to each other, reloading their weapons. Tom signaled to Foster, and the two of them burst into the room, catching the German soldiers by surprise. It was a quick, brutal fight, each man operating on instinct, their training taking over. Within moments, the gunfire ceased, and the room fell silent.

Tom stood there, breathing heavily as he looked at the fallen soldiers, young men whose determination to defend their city had driven them to fight to the last. He felt a pang of sadness, a sense of the futility of it all. This battle, this last stand—what would it accomplish for them?

"Let's go," Foster whispered, his face pale as he glanced around. "There's more ahead. I can feel it."

They rejoined the platoon, who had moved forward cautiously, clearing building after building, each encounter with German defenders a reminder of the city's defiant resistance. As they advanced through Berlin's war-torn streets, they encountered more civilians—people hiding in basements, families huddled together in makeshift shelters, their faces etched with fear and exhaustion. Some looked at the soldiers with guarded hope, while others glanced away, their expressions unreadable.

As they crossed a narrow street, an explosion rocked the ground nearby, sending up a cloud of dust and debris. Tom dropped to the ground, his ears ringing as he looked around, trying to make sense of the chaos. Mortar shells were raining down from a hidden German position, each impact sending shockwaves through the shattered landscape.

"Find cover!" Captain Harris shouted, his voice barely audible over the roar of the explosions.

Tom scrambled behind a pile of bricks, his heart pounding as he felt the ground tremble beneath him. He could hear the shouts of his comrades, the clatter of their equipment as they moved to safer positions. The mortar fire was relentless, each blast shaking the air, filling the streets with smoke and dust.

"Where's it coming from?" Foster shouted, ducking beside Tom as another shell exploded nearby.

Tom scanned the surrounding buildings, his gaze landing on a church steeple in the distance. He spotted the faint outline of a German mortar team, their figures barely visible against the skyline. "There, the church tower!" he pointed.

Captain Harris nodded, signaling for a group to advance while the others provided covering fire. They moved in bursts, darting from one piece of cover to the next, their steps measured, their breaths steady despite the danger. Tom felt the weight of each moment, the knowledge that every second counted, that their lives depended on speed and precision.

As they reached the church, Tom could see the mortar team repositioning, preparing to launch another shell. He raised his rifle, aiming carefully before squeezing the trigger. The first soldier dropped, and the others scrambled, their surprise evident as the American soldiers stormed the church grounds, securing the area and disabling the mortar.

The quiet that followed felt almost surreal, the sudden absence of explosions leaving a ringing in Tom's ears. He exhaled slowly, glancing around at the shattered church, the cracked stone walls, the stained-glass windows blown out by the blasts. It was a haunting sight—a place of worship reduced to a battlefield.

The platoon regrouped, pressing forward, weaving through Berlin's battered streets as they pushed toward the city center. Each step brought them closer to the heart of the German capital, to the final strongholds where the last remnants of resistance clung desperately to the idea of holding the line.

Along the way, they encountered more German defenders, each skirmish a grim reminder of the city's determination to fight until the very end. Some of the soldiers surrendered, their faces marked by exhaustion, their eyes hollow with the understanding that the war was lost. Others fought with a fierce resolve, refusing to give up, even as the Allies closed in around them.

One of the last skirmishes brought them face to face with a German officer, his uniform worn but meticulously kept, his expression defiant. He looked at the American soldiers with a mixture of hatred and resignation, his hands raised in surrender but his gaze unwavering.

"You think this victory will change anything?" he asked in heavily accented English, his voice cold. "You may win this battle, but the scars will remain."

Captain Harris met his gaze, his face impassive. "We're here to end this war. What comes after... that's up to all of us."

The officer's expression faltered, a flicker of something—doubt, perhaps—crossing his face before he looked away, his shoulders slumping in defeat.

As the platoon moved on, Tom felt the weight of the man's words settle over him. The scars of this war would indeed remain, etched into the lives of everyone who had been touched by its horrors. But they were here to ensure that the suffering, the cruelty, would end. They were here to liberate, to bring a final close to the nightmare that had consumed so many lives.

The soldiers pressed on, navigating through the ruins, each step bringing them closer to Berlin's heart. They were tired, battered, but their purpose was clear. They would finish what they had come here to do, no matter the resistance, no matter the cost.

The city lay under siege, its defenses crumbling, its people caught between fear and hope. And as the platoon advanced through the rubble-strewn streets, Tom knew that they were not just fighting to end a war—they were fighting to restore humanity to a place that had known only suffering and despair.

They would push through Berlin's ruins, face down the last defenders, and bring peace to a city that had been swallowed by darkness. This was their mission, their vow. They would see it through to the end.

The platoon advanced deeper into Berlin, and with each step, the signs of a crumbling defense grew more apparent. The German soldiers they encountered were weary, many too young or too old to fight effectively, clutching their weapons with trembling hands, their faces etched with exhaustion and defeat. Pockets of resistance still flared up, but they were sporadic, desperate, more a last gasp than a coordinated defense. The city itself was in ruins, its buildings reduced to hollow shells, its streets choked with debris and dust. But amid the devastation, Tom could feel it: victory was close.

Captain Harris led them with an unyielding focus, his gaze fixed on the route ahead. They were pushing toward the heart of Berlin, toward the government district, where the remnants of the German command were making their last stand. The soldiers could feel the shift in the air, a sense that the end was near. Months of grueling combat, of relentless fighting, were coming to a head, and the anticipation was a mixture of relief, exhaustion, and determination.

As they neared a large square flanked by buildings reduced to rubble, they halted, taking cover behind the remnants of a stone wall. Captain Harris scanned the area, his voice low but firm. "This is it, men. We're close to the Reichstag. This is where they're holed up, and they're going to fight hard to defend it. Stay sharp, stay focused, and let's finish this."

The men nodded, gripping their weapons tightly, the reality of their mission settling over them. They had fought across Europe, had survived the worst of the war's brutality, and now, standing in the heart of Berlin, they were poised to bring it all to an end. Tom could feel his heart pounding, his hands steady but his mind racing. This was the moment they had fought for, the moment that would bring peace, finally, within reach.

The platoon moved forward cautiously, advancing through the square as they watched for any sign of resistance. From somewhere ahead, the sound of gunfire echoed, a reminder that even now, in the final hours, Berlin's defenders were not ready to surrender. But the gunfire was weaker, sporadic, lacking the ferocity of the battles they'd fought just days earlier.

As they crossed the square, they encountered a small group of German soldiers, their uniforms tattered, their expressions hollow. One of the men raised his rifle, but after a tense moment, he lowered it, his shoulders slumping in surrender. His comrades followed suit, dropping their weapons with a sense of resignation, their eyes a mixture of fear and relief. The soldiers of the platoon kept their rifles trained on them, but the atmosphere was one of quiet understanding. The fight was over for these men, and they were ready to lay down their arms.

Tom felt a surge of sympathy as he looked at them, these young men who had been caught in the final throes of a war they hadn't started. They were defeated, but there was no triumph in their surrender, only a shared recognition of the end.

As the platoon moved deeper into the government district, the resistance faded further. They passed more soldiers, some fighting, some surrendering, each one a reminder of the toll the war had taken. The city's civilians, too, had begun to emerge from their hiding places, their faces pale, eyes wide with uncertainty as they watched the soldiers march past. Some offered cautious nods, others turned away, the weight of their losses evident in their hollow expressions.

Finally, they reached the last line of defense, a heavily fortified position near the Reichstag. The German soldiers there fired sporadically, their efforts more symbolic than strategic, a final act of defiance. Captain Harris gave the order, and the platoon returned fire, moving steadily toward the building as they neutralized the remaining defenders.

Tom could feel the tension ease as they moved through the final barriers, the once-imposing defenses now crumbling under the weight of their advance.

The gunfire slowed, then stopped, and a profound silence fell over the area as the last German soldiers surrendered, dropping their weapons, their faces marked by a mixture of relief and despair.

The platoon regrouped outside the Reichstag, the historic building now scarred and blackened, its once-grand architecture bearing the marks of war. They stood in silence, each man reflecting on the journey that had brought them here, on the countless battles, the comrades they had lost, the sacrifices they had made.

Captain Harris stepped forward, his voice carrying a quiet but powerful weight. "We did it, boys," he said, his voice thick with emotion. "We've brought it to an end."

The men exchanged glances, their expressions a mixture of exhaustion and pride. They had fought for this moment, had endured horrors and hardships beyond imagination, and now, standing here in the heart of Berlin, they had achieved what they had set out to do.

Foster placed a hand on Tom's shoulder, his voice soft but steady. "We're going home," he said, a faint smile tugging at the corners of his mouth. "After all this... we're finally going home."

Tom nodded, feeling a swell of relief and gratitude wash over him. The war was over, or as close to over as it could be. The end of the fighting, the promise of peace, felt almost surreal, a reality they had dreamed of but hardly dared to believe.

As the soldiers began to move out, Tom looked back at the city, at the ruins that surrounded them, at the faces of the civilians emerging from the shadows. Berlin had paid a heavy price, its people bearing the scars of a conflict that had torn their world apart. But amid the devastation, there was hope—a fragile, tentative hope that life could begin again, that the wounds of the past could one day heal.

For Tom and his comrades, the road to Berlin had been a journey of loss, resilience, and unwavering determination. They had come as soldiers, but they were leaving as witnesses to the strength of the human spirit, to the power of unity in the face of darkness. And as they walked away from the final battleground, each man carried with him the promise of a new beginning—a future defined not by war, but by peace.

Victory was in sight, but it was more than a military triumph. It was a victory of hope over hatred, of resilience over ruin. And as they left the city behind, Tom felt a quiet resolve settle within him, a vow to carry the memory of their journey forward, to honor the lives they had fought to save, and to ensure that the world would never forget the cost of peace.

Chapter 12: Germany's Surrender

The news came quietly, almost unexpectedly, as the soldiers rested in the heart of Berlin, regrouping after days of fierce, unrelenting combat. Word passed from soldier to soldier, a whisper at first, filled with a mixture of disbelief and cautious hope: Adolf Hitler was dead. The dictator who had led Germany into the darkest depths of war had taken his own life in his bunker beneath the city. For many, the news felt surreal, a moment they had envisioned for so long that the reality of it seemed distant, as though it were just another rumor in a city full of shattered dreams.

Tom and his comrades gathered around Captain Harris, their faces a mixture of exhaustion and wonder, as he relayed the confirmation: Hitler's reign was over, and the German government, now leaderless, was on the brink of surrender.

"Boys," Harris said, his voice steady but filled with emotion, "we're at the end. They're going to surrender. This war   it's almost over."

The men stood in stunned silence, the weight of the words settling over them like a wave. After years of bloodshed, sacrifice, and loss, they were hearing the end was finally within reach. It was a feeling they couldn't quite process, a strange blend of relief and disbelief. For so long, the war had been their reality, shaping every moment, every choice, and now, in what seemed like an instant, the world had shifted.

Foster leaned against a broken wall, rubbing a hand over his face as he took in the news. "Hitler's gone," he murmured, shaking his head. "After all this... he's finally gone."

Tom looked around at his fellow soldiers, at the men who had fought beside him, who had shared in the same struggles, the same nightmares. He saw the weariness in their eyes, the scars that marked not only their bodies but their spirits. For years, they had been driven by the need to survive, to end the violence, to bring peace. And now, as they stood here in the ruins of Berlin, they were beginning to realize that peace was not just a distant dream—it was something they had fought to the brink of exhaustion to achieve.

"It doesn't feel real, does it?" Tom said quietly, his voice almost a whisper. "After everything... it just doesn't feel like it could be over."

Captain Harris nodded, his gaze distant as he looked out over the wreckage of the city. "I know what you mean. We've all given so much... lost so much. It's hard to imagine life without this war."

For the next few hours, the soldiers moved with a sense of calm anticipation, the weight of their mission easing as they absorbed the news of Hitler's death. They began to hear rumors that German commanders were negotiating a ceasefire, that the war would soon be over not only in Europe but across the world. The thought was overwhelming—a world without war, a future defined not by bloodshed but by hope.

As the sun set over Berlin, casting a faint, warm glow over the battered city, Tom and his comrades sat together, reflecting on the journey that had brought them here. The faces of friends they had lost flickered in their memories, the battles they had fought, the lives they had saved and those they couldn't. Each man carried his own set of ghosts, a collection of memories that would stay with him long after he left the battlefield.

Foster broke the silence, his voice thoughtful. "Do you think... do you think it'll really be over? Or will there be something else, some other war waiting for us when we get home?"

Tom sighed, glancing at his friend. "I don't know," he admitted. "But I think... I think we've done what we came here to do. We've seen it through, and we've fought for something worth fighting for. Maybe that's enough."

Captain Harris nodded, his gaze fixed on the horizon. "We've done our part. We've seen the worst of humanity, but we've also seen what people are willing to sacrifice for each other. I think that's what matters. That's what's going to carry us through."

The men sat in silence, each one lost in thought, grappling with the enormity of what they had accomplished, of the lives they had touched and the lives they had lost. They knew that the end of the war would not erase the pain, that the scars they carried would remain. But for the first time in years, they could envision a world beyond the gunfire, beyond the devastation.

As night fell, they lay beneath the open sky, the stars shining brightly above the ruins. Tom felt a sense of peace settle over him, a quiet understanding that, while the path ahead would not be easy, they had made it this far together. They had survived, had fought for a world free from the horrors they had witnessed.

In the early hours of the morning, a messenger arrived, bringing official confirmation. The German High Command was preparing to surrender. The war, at last, was ending. The soldiers sat in stunned silence, absorbing the reality of what they had fought for, what they had lost, and what they had finally won.

The dawn broke over Berlin, casting the first rays of light on a new era. The city, battered and broken, held the promise of a future free from the shadow of tyranny. And as Tom stood there with his comrades, he knew that they had been part of something greater than themselves, a mission that would resonate for generations.

They had brought an end to the darkness, and now, as the sun rose over Berlin, they were ready to walk into the light of a world reborn.

As dawn broke over Berlin, the platoon found a quiet spot amid the rubble to rest, allowing themselves a rare moment of stillness. The city around them was silent, an exhausted calm settling over its scarred streets. The soldiers, too, were weary, their faces marked by the toll of the long journey that had brought them here. The war was nearly over, yet each man felt a strange reluctance to let go of the life that had consumed them for so long.

They sat together on broken pieces of stone and crumbled walls, some smoking cigarettes, others simply staring into the distance, lost in thought. The enormity of what they'd accomplished, of how far they'd come, was beginning to sink in, and with it came a flood of memories—both haunting and bittersweet.

Foster was the first to speak, breaking the silence with a quiet chuckle. "Remember Normandy?" he said, glancing around at his comrades. "Feels like a lifetime ago, doesn't it? I thought we were goners back then. I'd never seen so much chaos in my life."

Tom nodded, a faint smile playing at his lips as he remembered the beach—those first moments of sheer terror and adrenaline, the relentless roar of gunfire, the sight of his comrades fighting tooth and nail to make it to shore. It had been a baptism by fire, the beginning of a journey that had taken them through hell and back.

"It was chaos," Tom agreed. "But we pushed through. I remember thinking I wouldn't make it past the first wave, and yet... here we are."

Captain Harris looked around at his men, a proud but somber expression on his face. "You boys have come a long way," he said quietly. "When I saw you back then, I knew you were green, but there was something in all of you... something that made me believe you'd make it through. And you did."

Foster shook his head, his gaze distant. "Not all of us," he murmured, his voice heavy. "Remember Carter? He saved my life that day. Pulled me out of the line of fire without a second thought."

A quiet sadness settled over the group as they remembered their fallen comrades—Carter, who had been quick with a joke and even quicker to protect those he cared about; Lewis, who had dreamed of becoming a teacher after the war; and Daniels, who had always carried a worn photograph of his family, a reminder of the life he was fighting to return to. Each man carried the weight of these memories, a collection of ghosts that would stay with them long after the last battle had been fought.

Tom looked at Foster, his expression somber. "They didn't make it this far, but they're still with us," he said softly. "Every step we took, every battle we fought... we did it for them, too."

The men nodded, each one feeling the truth of Tom's words. They had been a unit, a brotherhood, bound by the shared experiences of battle and loss. Each step they took had been for each other, for the lives they had lost, and for the future they had hoped to build.

Captain Harris cleared his throat, his voice rough with emotion. "I think about them every day," he admitted, his gaze fixed on the ground. "I remember Carter's laugh, Daniels' stories about his kids... it's hard to believe they're gone. But I also know they'd be proud of us, of what we've accomplished."

They sat in silence for a while, each man lost in his own thoughts, remembering the journey they had shared, the battles that had defined them. The memories were a mix of pain and pride, a reminder of the strength they had found within themselves and in each other.

Foster took a deep breath, exhaling slowly as he looked around at the city. "You know, when we started this, I thought... I thought it was just about winning. About beating the enemy, proving ourselves. But now... now it feels like we've been fighting for something bigger."

Tom nodded, understanding the weight of Foster's words. "We were fighting for more than just victory," he said quietly. "We were fighting for the people we met along the way. For the villages we freed, the lives we touched... even the ones we lost."

Captain Harris looked at his men, his expression thoughtful. "War changes you," he said. "It strips you down to the core, makes you see the world for what it is—both the darkness and the light. But it also gives you a purpose, a reason to keep pushing forward. And I think that's what got us here."

The soldiers sat together, the memories of their journey washing over them. They thought of Normandy, of the push through France, the liberation of Paris, the fierce battles in the forests and fields of Germany. They remembered the faces of those they had helped, the gratitude in the eyes of civilians, the quiet resolve of the people who had endured so much.

"It's strange to think it's almost over," Tom murmured, a faint smile tugging at the corners of his mouth. "After everything we've seen, everything we've been through… I don't know if I even remember what it's like to live without war."

Foster chuckled softly, a hint of sadness in his eyes. "Me neither. But maybe that's the beauty of it. We've been through hell, and now… maybe we get to come back to life. To something normal."

Captain Harris looked at his men, a glimmer of pride in his eyes. "You've earned it, every single one of you. You've fought hard, and you've made sacrifices. And now, when this is all over, you'll carry those memories with you. But you'll also carry the knowledge that you made a difference."

As the sun rose higher over Berlin, casting a warm glow over the battered city, the soldiers sat together, united by the bond of shared experience, by the journey they had traveled side by side. They had seen the darkest depths of humanity, had endured loss and hardship, but they had also witnessed the strength of resilience, the power of hope.

And as they prepared to move forward, toward the final days of the war, they knew that no matter where life would take them, they would always carry this journey with them. They had come to Berlin as soldiers, but they would leave as something more—brothers, bound not just by the battles they had fought, but by the memories, the sacrifices, and the strength they had found within each other.

The war was ending, but their journey would remain a part of them forever. And as they looked toward the future, they felt a quiet resolve settle within them, a promise to honor the lives they had lost, to remember the lessons they had learned, and to live each day in tribute to the journey that had brought them to this moment.

The day of Germany's formal surrender arrived with a sense of calm anticipation. The platoon had been ordered to assemble in a large government building that, despite the damage to its exterior, had been hastily prepared for the signing ceremony. The soldiers gathered in silence, their faces marked by a mixture of relief, pride, and disbelief. This was the moment they had fought for, the one they had dreamed about but hadn't dared to believe would actually come.

Tom stood among his comrades, his uniform dusty and worn, his rifle resting at his side. The room was filled with Allied soldiers and officers, each one bearing the scars of a war that had cost them dearly. The air was heavy with the weight of history, the realization that they were about to witness a moment that would change the world forever.

Captain Harris approached the platoon, his expression solemn but calm. "Today marks the end, boys," he said quietly, his voice filled with emotion. "We've fought hard, lost friends, endured more than anyone should ever have to. But today, we see the fruits of that sacrifice. Today, we see peace."

The soldiers nodded, their eyes filled with a quiet resolve. They knew that this moment was not just for them, but for everyone who had given their lives in the name of freedom, for the families and friends they had left behind, and for the countless civilians who had suffered under the weight of tyranny.

The doors to the hall opened, and a hush fell over the room as a group of German officers entered. They were led by representatives of the German High Command, men whose faces bore the weariness of defeat, their uniforms immaculate but somber. They walked slowly, their expressions blank, their postures tense. There was no pride in their steps, only the acceptance of a reality they could no longer deny.

The Allied officers, including high-ranking generals from the United States, Britain, and the Soviet Union, stood at the front of the hall, their faces calm but unyielding. A large table had been set up, its surface covered in documents awaiting signatures. The German officers approached it in silence, their movements deliberate, each step heavy with the knowledge of what was about to transpire.

Tom felt his heart pound as he watched them, his mind racing with memories of everything he and his comrades had endured to reach this point.

He thought of Normandy, of the friends he had lost, of the civilians they had liberated. This was the culmination of all their sacrifices, the final act in a long, bloody play that had taken them across Europe and into the heart of the enemy's capital.

The German representatives stood before the table, their hands clasped behind their backs as they waited for the order to begin. An Allied officer stepped forward, his voice carrying through the hall with quiet authority.

"The world stands here today, unified in purpose, to bring an end to a war that has cost us all more than we could have imagined," he said. "The signing of this document marks the official surrender of Germany, the end of hostilities, and the dawn of a new era. We do this not in triumph, but in solemn remembrance of those we have lost and the price we have all paid."

The German officers nodded, their faces drawn, their gazes fixed on the table as the documents were handed to them. One by one, they signed, each stroke of the pen a quiet resignation, a final acknowledgment of their nation's defeat. The room was silent, the weight of the moment pressing down on everyone present as the signatures were completed, each line a step toward peace.

As the last signature was added, the Allied officer nodded, signaling the end of the ceremony. "It is done," he announced, his voice steady. "The war in Europe is over."

A wave of emotion swept through the room, a mixture of relief, sorrow, and pride. The soldiers exchanged glances, some offering quiet nods, others reaching out to clasp each other's shoulders in solidarity. The weight they had carried for so long, the burden of war, began to lift, replaced by a sense of calm, a fragile peace that felt almost unreal.

Tom looked at his comrades, a faint smile tugging at the corners of his mouth. He saw Foster wiping a tear from his eye, his expression one of quiet relief. Captain Harris stood beside them, his face unreadable, but his eyes shone with pride as he looked at the men he had led through the darkest days of the war.

As the German officers turned to leave, the silence in the hall broke, and the Allied soldiers stood straighter, their chins lifted, each one carrying the weight of victory with a quiet dignity. There was no cheering, no celebration—only a solemn acknowledgment of the sacrifices that had brought them here.

Outside the hall, as the soldiers filed out into the open air, the sounds of distant celebration began to echo through the streets. Civilians, hearing the news of surrender, had begun to gather, their faces alight with joy, with relief, with the hope of a future free from the shadow of war. Some cheered, others wept, and a few simply stood in silence, their hands clasped together as they took in the enormity of the moment.

Tom felt a lump in his throat as he watched them, a wave of gratitude and pride washing over him. They had fought for these people, for the hope and freedom that now filled the air around them. They had given everything, had endured the unendurable, and now, at last, they could see the dawn of a new world.

Foster clapped Tom on the shoulder, his voice choked with emotion. "We did it, Tom. We actually did it."

Tom nodded, swallowing hard as he looked at his friend. "Yeah, we did. We brought it to an end."

Captain Harris joined them, his face softened by a rare smile. "This victory belongs to all of us," he said. "We've seen things no one should ever have to see, but we've also proven that even in the darkest times, we can find the strength to fight for what's right. Remember this, boys. Remember what you fought for."

The soldiers nodded, each one feeling the weight of his words settle over them like a promise. They had been part of something larger than themselves, a force that had brought an end to one of the darkest chapters in history. And as they stood together, surrounded by the joy and relief of a liberated city, they knew that they would carry this memory with them forever.

As the day wore on, the sounds of celebration grew, filling the streets with laughter, with music, with the voices of people who had been freed from the grip of tyranny. For the soldiers, it was a bittersweet victory, a reminder of everything they had lost, but also of everything they had won.

They had fought for peace, and now, standing in the heart of Berlin, they could finally see it—a fragile, precious peace that they had earned with every step, every battle, every sacrifice. And as they walked away from the hall, from the signing that had changed the course of history, they did so with the quiet knowledge that they had been part of something that would live on, a legacy of courage and resilience that would endure for generations.

The war was over, but their journey was just beginning. They would return home, carry on with their lives, but they would always carry with them the memory of this day, of the victory they had won, and the peace they had fought to secure. And as they looked toward the future, they did so with hope, with pride, and with the knowledge that they had helped to shape a new world.

As night settled over Berlin, a quiet stillness enveloped the city. The celebrations had faded, replaced by a profound silence as soldiers and civilians alike began to process the reality of what had just happened. For the men of Tom's platoon, the realization that the war was truly over was both a relief and a weight. They had survived, but they had also lost so much along the way.

The platoon gathered around a small fire they'd built in the ruins of a nearby building, the flickering light casting shadows on their tired faces. They sat in silence, each man lost in his own thoughts, wrestling with the mixture of emotions that the end of the war had stirred within them. They were safe now, finally able to let their guards down, but with that safety came a flood of memories, of faces and voices that would remain with them forever.

Foster broke the silence, his voice low and filled with emotion. "I never thought I'd see this day," he murmured, staring into the fire. "All those nights, all those close calls... it just felt like there was no way out, like the war would go on forever."

Tom nodded, feeling the same sense of disbelief. He'd spent so long on the edge, constantly ready for the next battle, that the idea of peace felt foreign, almost unnatural. He looked at his hands, still calloused and scarred, as if they held the memory of every rifle, every trench, every loss.

Captain Harris spoke up, his voice steady but laced with sadness. "It's strange, isn't it? We spent all these years fighting to make it here, to survive... and now that we have, I can't stop thinking about the ones who didn't make it."

The men fell silent again, each one haunted by the faces of friends who had fallen along the way. Carter, Daniels, Lewis... the list was long, each name carrying its own story, its own memories. These were the men who had shared their hopes, their fears, their laughter. They had been brothers, bound not just by the war, but by the sacrifices they had made for each other.

"It doesn't feel right, does it?" Foster whispered, his gaze fixed on the flames. "Celebrating while they're... they're gone. They deserved to be here as much as any of us."

Tom felt a lump form in his throat as he remembered the night in Normandy when Carter had saved him, pulling him out of the line of fire without hesitation. Carter's laugh, his easy smile, the way he'd lifted everyone's spirits during the darkest times—those memories were now all they had left.

"They're with us," Tom said softly, his voice breaking. "Every step we took, every battle we fought, we did it for them. We carried them with us, and I think... I think we'll carry them for the rest of our lives."

The men nodded, their expressions solemn, each one feeling the weight of his words. They had survived, but their survival carried a responsibility—to honor the lives of those who had not made it, to remember their sacrifices and carry forward the legacy they had left behind.

Captain Harris took a deep breath, his eyes reflecting the firelight. "We owe it to them to live, to go back and find peace. That's what they fought for, too.

They'd want us to carry on, to live in a world they helped create. We don't forget them, but we also don't let the weight of it pull us under."

Tom looked around at his comrades, feeling a profound sense of unity. They had all lost pieces of themselves in this war—pieces they would never fully regain—but they had also forged bonds that would endure. The grief was heavy, yes, but it was shared, spread among them like a burden they would carry together.

Foster sighed, his face etched with both sorrow and a flicker of hope. "So what now?" he asked, his voice barely above a whisper. "How do we... go back to normal after all of this?"

Captain Harris gave him a reassuring nod. "I don't think there is a 'normal' to go back to. We're different men now. This war... it's changed us. But maybe that's not such a bad thing. Maybe we take what we've learned here, what we've been through, and we build something better."

They sat in silence, reflecting on his words. The idea of "normal" felt impossible, an illusion that had shattered with each battle, each loss. But perhaps there was a different kind of life waiting for them—a life shaped by everything they had endured, by the strength they had found in each other, by the memories of those they had lost.

Tom gazed up at the night sky, the stars shining brightly above the ruined city. In that moment, he felt a strange peace settle over him, a sense of connection to the friends who had fallen. It was as though they were watching over him, reminding him that he was here, that he had survived, that he had a duty to honor their sacrifices by living fully, by cherishing the peace they had all fought to achieve.

"We go on," Tom said quietly, his voice steady. "For them. For the ones we lost. We live, and we remember."

The men exchanged quiet nods, each one feeling the weight of his words settle over them like a promise. They had made it through the war, had seen its horrors, had lost more than they could ever put into words. But now, standing on the other side, they carried with them a strength, a resilience, a vow to live in a way that honored the friends who would never return.

As the fire crackled and the night deepened, they shared memories, stories of the men they had lost, laughter and tears blending together in a tribute to those who had fought beside them. They spoke of Carter's jokes, of Lewis's dreams of teaching, of Daniels' stories about his kids. They let themselves feel the grief, the loss, but they also let themselves feel the gratitude for having known such men, for having shared in a journey that had forever changed them.

When the fire finally died down, they sat in silence, each man carrying a quiet resolve. The war had ended, but its impact would linger, shaping their lives, their choices, their memories. They would return home with scars, but they would also return with a deeper understanding of life, of sacrifice, of brotherhood.

And as they rose, ready to face the dawn of a new day, they knew that they would carry this night with them forever—a night of remembrance, of grief, of resilience. They had survived, but they had also found a purpose beyond survival. They had fought for peace, and now they would live in honor of those who had given everything to achieve it.

The world had changed, and so had they. But as they walked away from the fire, from the ruins of Berlin, they did so with a promise in their hearts—a promise to live, to remember, and to never forget the journey that had brought them here.

The morning sun broke over Berlin, casting a soft, golden light over the ruined city. For the first time in years, the soldiers could feel a sense of peace settle around them. The war was over, and now, as they prepared to leave this place and return to the lives they had left behind, a cautious hope took root. They had survived, and with survival came the promise of something new, something that had once felt distant and unreachable: the chance to live without war.

Tom stood with his platoon, his bag slung over his shoulder, his gaze fixed on the horizon. He could hardly believe it was real—that he was heading home, that he would see his family again, that he would step back into a world where the sounds of gunfire and the fear of battle no longer dictated his every move. The thought was both exhilarating and terrifying, a leap into an unknown that felt almost as daunting as the war itself.

Foster walked up beside him, adjusting his gear and offering a faint smile. "Hard to believe, isn't it?" he said, his voice laced with wonder. "We're actually going home. I feel like I don't even know what home is anymore."

Tom nodded, understanding exactly what he meant. "It's strange to think about going back to... normal. I mean, how do you even start again after everything we've seen?"

Captain Harris joined them, his face softened by a rare, genuine smile. "You start by taking it one day at a time," he said. "We've all been through hell, but we've also survived it. That's not something you forget, but it's also not something that has to define you forever. You carry it with you, yes, but you let it make you stronger."

The men gathered around, sharing quiet smiles and hopeful glances, each one processing the reality of the journey that lay ahead. They had faced so much together, had endured losses that would forever change them, but now they had the chance to rebuild, to find out who they were beyond the war.

Foster scratched his head, a wistful look on his face. "You know, before all of this, I never thought much about the future. But now... I'm thinking about things I want to do. I want to see my family, maybe settle down somewhere quiet, maybe even start a family of my own. I don't know... I feel like I owe it to myself, to all of us, to live a life that matters."

Tom felt a warmth spread through him at Foster's words. The idea of a life beyond the battlefield, filled with family, with love, with purpose, was something he had clung to during the darkest nights. He could picture it now—sitting around a dinner table, laughing with loved ones, watching the seasons change in a world at peace. It was a future he had fought for, and now it felt within reach.

"I think you're right," Tom said, his voice soft but steady. "We've been given a second chance. We owe it to ourselves—and to the ones we lost—to make the most of it."

Captain Harris looked at his men, his eyes filled with pride and a quiet, unspoken understanding. "Each one of you has shown a strength I didn't know existed. You've faced things no one should have to, and you've come through it with courage, with loyalty, with honor. When you go home, remember that strength. Remember what you're capable of, and don't let the world's darkness take that away."

The soldiers nodded, absorbing his words, each one feeling the weight of the promise they carried. They had survived a war that had changed them, but they were determined to use that change as a foundation for something good, something hopeful.

As they prepared to leave, civilians began to gather, cautiously emerging from the rubble-strewn streets to watch the soldiers who had liberated them, who had brought peace to their shattered city. Some of the Berliners offered grateful nods, others approached to shake hands, their expressions a mixture of relief and gratitude. For the first time in years, they could see a future without fear, without oppression.

A young German boy approached Tom, clutching a small flower he had found amid the ruins. He held it out, his eyes wide with admiration. "Thank you," he said softly, his voice barely a whisper.

Tom took the flower, his heart swelling with emotion. "You're welcome," he replied, smiling as he tucked the flower carefully into his pocket. It was a small gesture, but it felt symbolic—a fragile bloom of life and hope, surviving despite the destruction all around them.

Foster patted Tom on the shoulder, a smile tugging at his lips. "Maybe there's hope for all of us after all," he murmured.

They began their march out of Berlin, each step taking them further from the war, closer to home. The road ahead was uncertain, filled with challenges they could only begin to imagine. But for the first time, the uncertainty felt exciting, a chance to discover who they were beyond the uniforms, beyond the battles.

As they walked, Tom felt a sense of peace settle over him, a quiet resolve that he carried like a shield. The war had taken so much, but it had also given him something precious: a profound respect for life, a bond with the men who had stood by him, and a renewed sense of purpose. He knew he would never forget his fallen comrades, that he would carry their memories with him for the rest of his life. But he also knew that he had a duty to live fully, to embrace the world they had fought to protect.

The sounds of Berlin faded behind them as they moved further away, replaced by the quiet rhythm of their footsteps, the gentle rustling of the wind, and the promise of new beginnings. Each man held his own vision of the future—Foster with his dream of a family, Captain Harris with his wisdom and strength, Tom with the simple, powerful hope of peace.

As the sun rose higher, casting its warm light over the landscape, they looked ahead with renewed purpose, ready to build a world free from the shadows they had left behind. It wouldn't be easy, and the scars of war would always be there, reminders of everything they had endured. But together, they would face whatever came next, with hope, resilience, and a promise to honor the past by creating a future worth living for.

They had come through darkness, but now they walked toward the light, toward a hopeful future that was theirs to shape. And as Tom looked around at his comrades, at the brothers who had fought beside him, he knew that no matter where life would take them, they would carry this journey with them forever.

Chapter 13: Homecoming

The long journey back home was marked by both anticipation and an unspoken sadness, for the soldiers knew that they were nearing the end not only of the war but of their time together. They had been brothers in arms, had survived battles that had claimed so many lives, and now, after all they had shared, they were preparing to part ways. The bond between them was unbreakable, forged in the fires of war, but they knew that each man's path would take him in a different direction.

The train pulled into a small station, its whistle piercing the morning air as it came to a halt. The soldiers gathered their belongings, each of them carrying only a small bag, but the weight of their experiences filled the air between them. They had arrived at the place where they would say goodbye, where each man would leave to begin the journey back to his own life, his own family, his own dreams.

Tom looked around at his comrades, his heart heavy with both gratitude and sorrow. These men had become his family, a part of himself he couldn't imagine letting go. He saw Foster, standing nearby with a faint smile, his eyes filled with the same bittersweet feeling.

Foster walked over, extending a hand. "Well, this is it, Tom," he said, his voice steady but laced with emotion. "Never thought we'd make it, but here we are."

Tom shook his hand, his grip firm, and looked him in the eye. "You kept me going, Foster. I don't know what I would have done without you."

Foster laughed softly, the sound warm and genuine. "Same here, brother. You saved me more times than I can count."

They stood in silence for a moment, each man acknowledging the unspoken depth of their friendship. They had been through so much together, had faced death and loss, but they had also found strength in each other, a strength that had kept them alive.

Captain Harris approached, his expression softening as he looked at the men who had followed him through hell and back. He placed a hand on Tom's shoulder, then Foster's, his gaze filled with pride and respect.

"You boys have done me proud," he said quietly. "Each one of you has shown a courage and resilience I'll never forget. I know you'll go on to do great things, and I want you to know that if you ever need anything, I'm here. We may be going our separate ways, but this bond—it's not something that ever fades."

Tom felt his throat tighten, the weight of the moment pressing down on him. "Thank you, Captain," he said, his voice thick with emotion. "For everything. You led us through the worst of it. We wouldn't be here without you."

Harris gave a small nod, his face betraying the depth of his own feelings. "You're a good man, Tom. All of you are. Remember that. No matter where life takes you, remember who you are and what you've accomplished."

The men gathered in a loose circle, taking a moment to exchange handshakes, claps on the back, and quiet words of encouragement. Each farewell felt final, yet laced with the knowledge that they were bound by something deeper than distance. They were brothers, united not just by war but by a shared promise to honor the lives they had lost, to live fully in tribute to those who had not made it home.

Foster grinned, his usual humor breaking through the sadness. "You all better write. I'll track you down if I don't hear from you, mark my words."

The men laughed, the sound lightening the mood. Tom couldn't help but smile, knowing that Foster's words were genuine. They would stay in touch, they would hold onto these friendships, because they had been through too much together to let go.

As the train whistle blew again, signaling that it was time for each man to board his separate route, they lingered for one last moment, sharing silent nods and glances. No words could capture the gratitude, the loyalty, the love they felt for each other, but in that final look, they understood.

One by one, they stepped onto their trains, glancing back with quiet smiles, lifting hands in farewell. Tom stood there as the last train pulled away, watching as the faces of his brothers disappeared from sight, feeling the weight of their journey settle in his chest.

The station grew quiet, the rumble of the trains fading into the distance, and Tom felt a strange mixture of peace and sadness. He was going home, but he was leaving behind a part of himself—a part that would forever belong to these men, to the shared memories of a time and place that had changed them all.

He took a deep breath, lifting his bag over his shoulder, and turned toward the path that would lead him back to his own family, his own life. The future was uncertain, but he felt a flicker of hope in his heart, a quiet promise to live fully, to honor the past and embrace the future.

As he walked away from the station, he knew that no matter where life would take them, he and his brothers would carry this journey with them forever. And in that knowledge, he found the strength to take his first steps toward home, toward a hopeful future shaped by courage, by love, and by the unbreakable bonds of friendship.

The train ride home felt surreal. Tom watched the familiar landscapes roll by, each passing field and town bringing him closer to the life he had left behind. He could hardly believe it was real—that he would soon see his family, walk the streets of his hometown, and sleep under a peaceful sky. Yet, woven into the excitement was a quiet unease, a lingering shadow that whispered reminders of all he had seen and done. He knew he was coming home changed, that the man stepping off this train was not the same one who had boarded it years ago.

As the train finally pulled into the station, Tom's heart raced. He could see the small crowd gathered on the platform, people waving, cheering, their faces bright with joy and relief. His gaze swept over them, searching for the familiar faces of his family, his chest tightening as he spotted his mother and father standing at the edge of the platform, waiting with open arms and tear-filled eyes.

Tom stepped off the train, and in an instant, he was swept into his mother's embrace, her arms wrapped tightly around him as though she would never let go. He felt her tears on his shoulder, her soft murmurs of gratitude and love, words she had likely repeated in countless prayers, hoping for this very moment. His father stood nearby, his own eyes misty as he clapped a hand on Tom's shoulder, a gesture that conveyed pride, relief, and all the words he couldn't bring himself to say.

"Welcome home, son," his father said, his voice rough with emotion.

Tom managed a smile, feeling the warmth of his family wash over him, filling him with a sense of belonging he hadn't realized how much he missed. But beneath that warmth was a heaviness, a feeling he couldn't quite shake, as though part of him was still on the battlefield, still standing alongside his brothers, feeling the weight of their shared struggles.

They led him to their car, the conversation flowing easily as his mother filled him in on the news of their town, on the changes that had taken place while he was away. His father listened, occasionally glancing at Tom with a look of quiet pride, as if seeing him here, safe and whole, was enough to fill every unspoken hope he'd held onto for so long.

Back at the house, Tom's siblings greeted him with wide smiles and laughter, their excitement palpable as they welcomed him back. They treated him like a hero, asking about his journey, hanging on his every word, and he found himself answering with a mixture of pride and reluctance. He told them about the places he had seen, the people he had met, but he left out the harder truths—the battles, the friends he had lost, the memories that haunted his nights.

At dinner that evening, as his family gathered around the table, Tom felt the weight of their love and joy, their relief that he was finally home. But as they laughed and reminisced, he found himself feeling distant, as though part of him was watching from a place they couldn't reach. He felt the scars left by the war, the invisible marks that set him apart, and he wondered if he would ever fully feel like he belonged here again.

His mother noticed, her gaze softening as she reached across the table to take his hand. "You've been through a lot, haven't you, Tom?" she asked gently, her voice laced with understanding.

He nodded, his throat tight as he struggled to find the words. "Yeah... I guess I have," he replied, his voice barely more than a whisper.

His father leaned forward, his eyes filled with quiet compassion. "It's all right, son. You don't have to talk about it if you don't want to. Just know... we're here for you. We're just glad you're home."

Tom felt a rush of gratitude, his family's love grounding him in a way he hadn't expected. He realized then that he didn't have to carry the weight of his experiences alone—that they were willing to support him, to understand the parts of him that had been shaped by the war. It was a comfort he hadn't realized he needed, a reminder that he was not as alone as he sometimes felt.

That night, as he lay in his childhood bed, Tom stared at the ceiling, feeling the quiet of the house settle around him. It was a strange feeling, this silence. After years of constant noise, of gunfire and explosions, the stillness felt almost overwhelming. He could hear his own breathing, his own heartbeat, and it brought with it memories of nights spent under starlit skies with his platoon, of whispered conversations and shared fears, of the friends he had left behind.

Sleep didn't come easily. When he finally drifted off, his dreams were filled with fragmented memories—images of his friends, of the places they had fought, of faces he would never see again. He woke in the early hours, his heart pounding, his skin clammy. For a moment, he felt the familiar urge to reach for his rifle, to stand at attention, but then he remembered where he was. Home. He was safe.

In the days that followed, Tom found himself adjusting slowly, relearning the rhythms of home life. He took long walks through the town, reconnecting with old friends, meeting neighbors who welcomed him back with warm smiles and firm handshakes. Yet, despite the familiarity, he felt different, as though he were seeing everything through new eyes. The world was the same, but he was not.

One afternoon, he visited the local cemetery, making his way to a quiet spot beneath a large oak tree. He sat there for a long time, thinking of his fallen brothers, of Carter and Daniels and all the others who had fought beside him. He spoke to them softly, sharing the thoughts he hadn't been able to express since leaving the battlefield, telling them that he would never forget them, that he would carry their memory forward as a part of himself.

The return to civilian life was not without its struggles, but each day he found himself growing stronger, the love and support of his family helping to fill the emptiness left by the war. There were moments when he still felt like a stranger in his own skin, but there were also moments of peace, of joy, when he could laugh with his family, share a meal, or walk in the quiet woods without fear.

Over time, he began to see the possibility of a future—a life beyond the battlefield, one where he could live fully, carrying the lessons of the past without letting them overshadow his happiness. He knew he would always be changed, that the scars of war would remain, but he also knew that he had the strength to carry on, to honor the lives of those he had lost by living his own to the fullest.

And as he looked toward that future, Tom felt a cautious but genuine hope, a quiet resolve to embrace life with all the courage and resilience that the war had instilled in him. He was home, and while the journey had changed him, it had also given him a profound appreciation for the simple beauty of peace, for the love of family, and for the strength of the human spirit.

He knew now that he was ready to begin again—to forge a path forward, to find joy and purpose, and to live in a way that honored both the sacrifices of his brothers and the hope of a new beginning.

As the weeks passed, the euphoria of homecoming began to fade, replaced by the quieter, harder reality of returning to civilian life. For Tom, and for the other veterans he saw around town, the memories of war lingered, haunting them like shadows that refused to fade. The familiar streets and faces should have brought comfort, but instead, they often triggered memories that pulled him back to the chaos and darkness he had fought so hard to leave behind.

One evening, Tom found himself at the local diner, sitting across from Foster. They had stayed in touch since returning home, finding solace in each other's company when the weight of their shared experiences became too heavy to bear alone. Foster looked tired, his eyes shadowed, as though sleep had eluded him for days. They spoke in fragments, words coming and going, but both knew they didn't have to explain the struggle. It was etched in their expressions, in the way their voices faltered when they mentioned the past.

"Do you... do you ever get a break from it?" Foster asked quietly, stirring his coffee absently. "I mean, even when I close my eyes, it's all there. Normandy, Berlin, Carter..." His voice trailed off, and he shook his head, as if trying to shake off the images that haunted him.

Tom nodded, feeling a pang of empathy. "Every night, Foster. Every single night. Sometimes it's like I'm back there, like I can hear the gunfire, feel the weight of my gear." He paused, his voice dropping to a whisper. "I think... I think part of me never left."

They sat in silence for a moment, each man lost in his memories. Tom knew that Foster understood in a way no one else could. They had both survived, but survival came with its own cost. The dreams, the flashbacks—they weren't things that could be left behind on a battlefield. They had come home with them, woven into the fabric of their minds.

As they walked home together, Foster broke the silence. "You ever wonder if we'll be able to live normal lives again? I mean, I look around at everyone, the way they laugh, the way they talk about the future... and I feel like I'm on the outside looking in. Like I don't belong."

Tom's heart ached as he listened, knowing exactly what Foster meant. Every time he walked through town, he felt a strange disconnect, as though he were watching life unfold through a glass wall. He saw families laughing, children playing, couples talking about their plans, but he felt removed from it all, as though the war had left him adrift in a world he no longer understood.

"I don't know if we'll ever be the same," Tom admitted. "But maybe that's okay. Maybe we're meant to carry this with us, to remember... so that others don't have to."

Foster looked at him, his gaze softened. "Yeah, maybe. Doesn't make it any easier, though, does it?"

Tom shook his head, his expression weary. "No. It doesn't."

The nights were the hardest. Tom would lie awake, staring at the ceiling, his mind a battlefield of memories. The sounds of gunfire, the cries of his fallen friends, the endless marches through bombed-out villages—they played in his mind like a film he couldn't turn off. He felt guilty for surviving, for being here while others were not, and he struggled to reconcile the two parts of himself: the man who had come home and the soldier who was still fighting, still watching, still haunted.

One evening, as he sat alone in his room, Tom pulled out a small box he had kept since returning home. Inside were letters, photos, and mementos—reminders of his friends, of Carter, of Lewis, of Daniels. He ran his fingers over the faded photographs, his chest tightening as he looked at their smiling faces. They were frozen in time, forever young, while he was here, growing older, trying to build a life.

"I miss you guys," he whispered, his voice breaking. "I don't know how to do this without you."

The following day, Tom decided to visit a support group for veterans in the nearby city. He had heard about it from another veteran and, though hesitant at first, realized he needed to try something—anything—to help him understand what he was feeling. The group was small, made up of men and women who had served in different theaters of the war. They sat in a circle, sharing stories, voicing the fears and guilt they couldn't admit anywhere else.

As Tom listened to their stories, he felt a sense of kinship he hadn't realized he was missing. These people understood him in a way others couldn't. They spoke of the sleepless nights, of the memories that played on a loop, of the difficulty in connecting with family and friends. For the first time, he felt a glimmer of hope, a reminder that he wasn't alone.

One of the older veterans, a man named Walter, looked around at the group, his voice steady and filled with quiet wisdom. "We may never forget what we've seen," he said. "But we have a choice about how we carry it. We can let it pull us under, or we can use it to find strength, to help others who are struggling. It's a hard road, but it's not one we have to walk alone."

Tom let the words sink in, feeling a spark of something he hadn't felt in a long time—purpose. He knew that he would never fully escape the memories, that they would always be a part of him, but perhaps he could find a way to live with them, to use them as a source of resilience, of compassion.

As the days passed, Tom began to share more with his family, letting them into the parts of himself he had tried to keep hidden. He told them about his friends, about the moments of courage and fear, about the things he still didn't understand. Slowly, he found that sharing his experiences lightened the burden, that by speaking the memories aloud, they became easier to bear.

His mother would listen quietly, her hand resting on his arm, her eyes filled with a mixture of love and sadness. His father offered quiet nods and words of support, a steady presence that grounded him. His siblings, once in awe of his service, now saw the human side, the vulnerability he had hidden beneath his uniform.

One night, as Tom sat with his family around the fire, his mother reached over and took his hand. "We're so proud of you, Tom," she said softly. "Not just for what you did over there, but for who you are now. You're still our son. You're still here, with us, and that's all that matters."

Her words brought a sense of peace, a reminder that he wasn't defined solely by the war, that he was more than his memories. He was part of a family, of a community, and though the shadows of battle lingered, he had the support he needed to face them.

Each day was a struggle, but each day also brought a small victory—a moment of laughter, a quiet evening, a chance to share in the simple joys of life. Tom knew that the journey would be long, that the memories would never fully fade, but he was learning to live with them, to accept them as part of his story.

And in those moments of acceptance, he found strength, resilience, and a glimpse of a life beyond the war—a life shaped by love, by courage, and by the unwavering support of those who had waited for him to come home.

As time passed, Tom and his fellow veterans began to search for meaning in their lives beyond the battlefield. The memories of war were ever-present, but slowly, they realized they could transform those memories into something that might help others. They began to understand that their experiences, though painful, could be a source of strength—not only for themselves but for those around them.

For Tom, it started when he was invited to speak at a small local event honoring veterans. At first, he hesitated, uncertain about opening up to strangers about the experiences he had kept guarded. But then he thought of Carter, of Lewis, of all the friends he had lost. He realized that sharing their stories might keep their memory alive, might help others understand the sacrifices made by so many.

Standing in front of the audience, he felt the weight of his words. He spoke about the camaraderie, about the friendships that had sustained him, about the resilience he had witnessed in his platoon. But he also spoke of the loss, of the fear and uncertainty, of the nights spent wondering if he'd ever make it home. He didn't shy away from the difficult truths, and as he shared his story, he felt a sense of release, as if a part of the weight he had carried was finally lifting.

After the event, a young man approached him, his eyes wide with admiration. "Thank you for sharing that, sir," he said. "My grandfather fought in the war, too. He never talks about it, but... hearing you speak, I feel like I understand him a little better."

Tom smiled, a warmth filling his chest. "Thank you for listening. Sometimes it's not easy to talk about, but I think it's important. Your grandfather... he's a hero, just like so many others."

That evening, Tom realized he had found something he hadn't expected: a sense of purpose. Sharing his story allowed him to honor his fallen friends, to give voice to the experiences they could no longer share. It was a way to remember them, to ensure that their sacrifices would not be forgotten.

He began volunteering at the veterans' support group he had visited earlier, becoming a familiar face to other men and women who, like him, were grappling with memories they couldn't leave behind. In that space, he found comfort in helping others who felt lost, offering his story as a bridge between the past and the future. He listened, provided a shoulder to lean on, and, in turn, received strength from the resilience he saw in others.

One evening, he was joined at the group by Foster, who had been struggling with his own path since returning home. Tom had encouraged him to come, and to his relief, Foster agreed, recognizing that he, too, needed a sense of direction, a way to cope with the past.

"Didn't think I'd end up here," Foster admitted as they sat together in the circle, a half-smile on his face. "Guess I was too stubborn to admit I needed this."

Tom chuckled, clapping him on the shoulder. "We all need something, Foster. And sometimes... sometimes the best way to heal is to help each other."

Foster nodded, his gaze thoughtful. Over time, he began sharing his own experiences, finding that talking about them helped lessen the burden. He became an active member of the group, offering his support to others, finding purpose in connecting with people who understood the journey he had been on. For both Tom and Foster, the group became a lifeline, a place where they could turn the pain of their past into a source of healing.

Outside the group, Tom began visiting local schools, talking to students about the importance of peace, resilience, and understanding. He felt a sense of pride as he watched young faces listen intently, their curiosity and compassion a reminder of the future he had fought to protect. He shared stories of courage and friendship, emphasizing that while war was brutal, there was a strength in humanity that could endure even the darkest times.

In one classroom, a girl raised her hand after his talk, her eyes bright with curiosity. "Mr. Tom, does being a soldier make you brave?"

He paused, considering her question. "I think being brave means facing things that scare you," he replied. "Sometimes that's going into battle. Sometimes it's learning to live after the battle is over. Being brave isn't just about being a soldier. It's about finding strength in hard times, no matter who you are."

The students listened quietly, their expressions thoughtful, and Tom felt a sense of fulfillment. In sharing his experiences, he was helping the next generation understand the cost of war, but also the power of resilience, the importance of compassion.

Through these conversations, Tom began to find a way forward. He still carried the memories, the ghosts of his friends and the scars of battle, but he was no longer defined by them. Instead, he was learning to use those memories as a source of strength, a way to honor the past while building a better future.

Foster, too, found his own path. Inspired by their shared experiences, he decided to work with veterans in need, helping them navigate the often difficult transition back to civilian life. Together, he and Tom began organizing small gatherings for local veterans, creating a space where men and women could come together to share stories, to laugh, to cry, and to support each other.

One evening, after one of their gatherings, Foster looked at Tom, his expression filled with a quiet satisfaction. "You know, I never thought I'd find purpose in all of this," he said. "But being here, helping others... it feels like it's giving my life meaning again."

Tom nodded, understanding completely. "Me too. I think... I think we're exactly where we're supposed to be."

As they looked around at the room full of veterans, each one bearing their own stories and scars, they felt a sense of peace, a recognition that they had found a way to carry the weight of the past while moving forward. They had turned their experiences into a source of hope, a way to help others navigate the difficult journey of coming home.

In finding purpose, they had found healing—not by forgetting, but by transforming their memories into a testament to resilience, to courage, and to the unbreakable bonds of friendship. And as they continued to share their stories, to support their fellow veterans, they knew they were honoring the lives they had lost, creating a legacy of strength, compassion, and hope for those who would come after them.

As the years went on, Tom, Foster, and the other veterans found ways to build new lives, yet they knew that the bonds forged in war would remain with them forever. Though time softened some of the memories, their brotherhood endured, woven into the fabric of who they were. They gathered together each year, a reunion of friends and comrades, bound by a connection that went beyond words. They were family—not by blood, but by experience, by loyalty, by the shared promise to honor those who had fallen.

On the first anniversary of the end of the war, Tom and Foster organized a small gathering at a local memorial where the names of their fallen friends were etched in stone. They invited the other members of their platoon who had made it home, and together, they stood before the monument in silence, each man lost in his own memories. Some brought flowers, others simply placed their hands on the cold granite, tracing the names of the friends who had given everything.

Captain Harris was there, standing beside them, his face lined with age and memory. He looked at his men, the pride in his eyes unmistakable, and spoke with a voice that was steady yet filled with emotion.

"We were more than soldiers out there," he said quietly. "We were brothers. We shared our hopes, our fears, and our dreams. And while we lost many along the way, we carry them with us every day. Their legacy lives on in us, in how we live, in how we remember."

The men nodded, each one feeling the truth of his words. The memories of their fallen friends, of Carter's laughter, of Daniels' unwavering courage, of Lewis's dreams of a future that had been cut short, were alive within them. They were stories they would pass down, memories they would carry forward, reminders of the courage and resilience that had sustained them through the darkest times.

Foster stepped forward, his hand resting on the monument as he spoke. "We may have come home, but they're still with us. I feel them every day, guiding me, reminding me to live in a way that honors them. We were lucky to have known them, to have fought beside them."

Tom took a deep breath, his voice steady as he looked around at his friends. "We made it through because we had each other. That's something no one can take away. We fought together, we survived together, and we carry on together. No matter where life takes us, this bond—it's forever."

The men spent the rest of the day sharing stories, laughter, and tears, each one cherishing the rare connection they shared. They spoke of their friends who were no longer there, recalling their bravery, their quirks, the moments that had brought them closer. Each memory was a thread in the tapestry of their brotherhood, a reminder that while the war had ended, their friendship was timeless, unbreakable.

As the years went by, their gatherings grew, sometimes including family members who came to hear the stories, to understand the bond that had kept their loved ones close to these men. Tom watched as children and grandchildren listened, wide-eyed, to the tales of courage and sacrifice, of humor and kindness, and he felt a deep sense of fulfillment. They were keeping the legacy alive, passing it down to a new generation who would remember the men who had given so much.

Each reunion was a reminder of the journey they had taken, of the lives they had saved and the lives they had lost. They were growing older, the lines of age appearing on their faces, but the bond they shared remained as strong as ever. And as they looked around at each other, they knew that the brotherhood forged in war had become something timeless, a legacy that would endure long after they were gone.

On the fiftieth anniversary of the war's end, Tom, now an old man, stood with Foster and Captain Harris before a new generation of veterans, sharing the lessons he had learned, the strength he had found in his friends, the love and loyalty that had seen him through. His voice was soft but clear as he spoke of the power of friendship, of the importance of remembering those who had sacrificed everything.

"We were lucky," he said, his gaze drifting to his friends, now aged but still standing strong. "We came home, and we had each other. We carried those who didn't make it back with us, and in doing so, we built something that can never be broken. That's the legacy of brotherhood—knowing that no matter what happens, you're never alone."

As they left the gathering that evening, Tom looked at Foster, who gave him a knowing nod. They had come full circle, had lived lives marked by both joy and sorrow, but through it all, they had found purpose, hope, and a bond that had carried them through the years.

And as they walked away, side by side, they knew that their brotherhood was more than a memory. It was a promise, a legacy that would live on, a testament to the strength of friendship, to the resilience of the human spirit, and to the love that had bound them together through war, peace, and everything in between.

Chapter 14: In Gratitude

To the brave men and women who served in World War II, we owe a debt that can never be fully repaid. They were ordinary people who answered an extraordinary call, who left their homes and families, their towns and cities, to stand against forces of darkness, tyranny, and unimaginable cruelty. They did not know what the future held or if they would even return, but they went willingly, armed with courage, resilience, and an unwavering sense of duty.

These veterans carried more than weapons and gear; they carried the hopes and dreams of entire nations. They fought not only for their own freedoms but for the freedom of future generations, for the right to live in a world where peace could flourish. From the beaches of Normandy to the dense jungles of the Pacific, from the deserts of North Africa to the cities and villages of Europe, they pushed forward through fear and pain, driven by a mission that went beyond themselves.

In the face of overwhelming odds, they found strength in each other. Brothers and sisters in arms, they forged bonds that transcended the chaos of battle, bonds that would last a lifetime. They laughed together in quiet moments, shared stories of home, and leaned on one another when the weight of war grew too heavy to bear alone. They endured hardships that we can barely imagine, facing sleepless nights, hunger, and the constant threat of danger. Many of them witnessed loss on a scale that would haunt them for the rest of their lives, but they pressed on, knowing that their sacrifices were not in vain.

Each of them had their own reasons for serving. Some were driven by a fierce sense of patriotism, others by a need to protect their loved ones, and still others by a moral duty to stand against injustice. Whatever their reasons, they each brought a piece of themselves to the fight, each one a thread in the tapestry of courage and resilience that would come to define a generation.

They were not perfect—they were human, filled with doubts and fears—but their bravery lay not in a lack of fear, but in the decision to keep going despite it.

To the families of those who served, we extend our deepest gratitude. For every soldier on the front lines, there were loved ones waiting at home, carrying the heavy burden of uncertainty and worry. They, too, were part of the fight, waiting with bated breath for letters, clinging to hope in the face of fear. They supported the war effort in countless ways, filling the roles left vacant, rationing their food and supplies, and volunteering their time and energy. They, too, sacrificed, and their strength, patience, and resilience deserve our utmost respect.

For those who did not return, who gave the ultimate sacrifice, we honor their memory and recognize the price they paid. They laid down their lives in the pursuit of a world free from oppression, a world where future generations could live without fear. Their names are etched into memorials around the world, but more importantly, they are etched into our hearts. We remember them not as mere soldiers, but as sons and daughters, brothers and sisters, friends and loved ones. They are the true heroes, whose legacies live on in the freedoms we enjoy today.

The veterans who returned home carried the scars of war, both visible and unseen. They returned to their families, to their communities, forever changed by what they had endured. Many of them did not speak of their experiences, choosing instead to bury their memories, to carry their burdens in silence. But through their actions, through the quiet strength they displayed in rebuilding their lives, they showed us what true resilience looks like. They taught us that even in the face of unimaginable hardship, it is possible to move forward, to build, to heal.

These men and women were not just warriors; they were builders of peace. After the war, they worked tirelessly to ensure that the horrors they had witnessed would never be repeated. They helped to rebuild the very places they had fought to free, extending a hand of friendship and unity to former enemies. They established organizations, institutions, and alliances dedicated to peace, security, and human rights. Their legacy is not only one of victory in battle but of enduring commitment to a world where people of all nations might live in harmony.

For all of this, we thank them. We thank them for their bravery, for their sacrifices, for their unwavering dedication to a cause greater than themselves. We thank them for the lessons they left us, lessons in courage, unity, and compassion. Because of them, we know that even in the darkest times, there is hope. Because of them, we understand the true meaning of freedom and the responsibility that comes with it.

As the years pass, as the faces of our veterans grow older, we hold their stories close, ensuring that future generations remember. We tell our children of their bravery, we teach them the history of their sacrifice, and we instill in them the respect and gratitude these veterans deserve. The legacy of their service is a part of all of us, woven into the very fabric of our society.

To the veterans of World War II: thank you. Your courage, your sacrifices, and your enduring legacy will never be forgotten. You stood on the precipice of history and, through your actions, shaped a future where freedom could prevail. We are humbled by your strength, inspired by your dedication, and forever indebted to the gift of peace you have given us.

May we honor your memory not only with words but with actions, by striving every day to create a world worthy of your sacrifices. May we remember you not just on special days or in solemn moments, but in the way we live our lives, in the respect we show each other, and in the commitment we make to protect the freedoms for which you fought. You have left us a legacy of hope, courage, and unity, and we are better for it.

Thank you, heroes. You are forever remembered, forever honored, and forever loved.

Don't miss out!

Visit the website below and you can sign up to receive emails whenever kirsten Dickson publishes a new book. There's no charge and no obligation.

https://books2read.com/r/B-A-AOQAD-EPWTF

BOOKS 2 READ

Connecting independent readers to independent writers.

Did you love *Into the Heart of the Reich*? Then you should read *Shadows In The Pacific*[1] by kirsten Dickson!

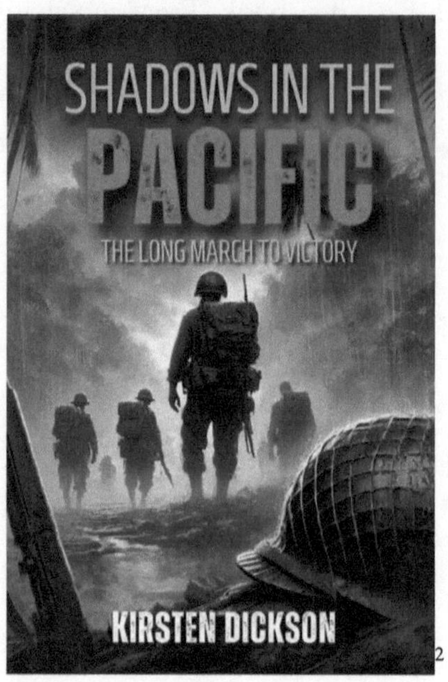

Shadows in the Pacific is a gripping World War II novel that immerses readers in the harrowing experiences of a U.S. platoon navigating the brutal Pacific Theater. Through the eyes of Jack Miller, a young soldier thrust into the chaos of battle, the story delves into the raw realities of war—unwavering brotherhood, profound loss, and the relentless fight for survival.

From the perilous beach landings to the intense jungle skirmishes, each chapter vividly portrays the physical and emotional toll on the soldiers. As they confront the enemy and the unforgiving environment, they grapple with their own fears and the haunting memories of fallen comrades.

Drawing inspiration from true accounts, *Shadows in the Pacific* offers an unflinching look at the sacrifices made by those who served. It's a testament to the resilience of the human spirit and the enduring bonds forged in the crucible of war.

---

1. https://books2read.com/u/3kVMEL

2. https://books2read.com/u/3kVMEL

For readers of historical fiction and military narratives, this novel provides a poignant and authentic portrayal of World War II's Pacific front, honoring the legacy of the brave men who fought there.**Get your copy now!!!**

Also by kirsten Dickson

Shadows In The Pacific
Into the Heart of the Reich
Eagles in the Mist. The 101st Airborne's journey through hell.